In the sinister world of 1938 New Orleans, grizzled private detective Jack Callahan navigates through a labyrinth of corruption, vengeance, and dark secrets, unraveling a web that ties the cruelly murdered jazzman to the city's most powerful, while battling his own demons and pondering the elusive nature of morality and redemption in a world where every truth hides a deeper deceit.

THE JAZZMAN'S REQUIEM

A Delta Private Investigations Book

WILLIAM ALAN WEBB

And

KEVIN STEVERSON

THE JAZZMAN'S REQUIEM
Copyright © 2023 by William Alan Webb and Kevin Steverson

Primary print ISBN 9798866463046

All rights reserved. No part of this book may be reproduced in any form or by any means without written consent, excepting brief quotes used in reviews.

This book is licensed to the original purchaser only. Duplication or distribution via any means is illegal and a violation of International Copyright Law, subject to criminal prosecution and upon conviction, fines and/or imprisonment. No part of this book can be reproduced or sold by any person or business without the express permission of the publisher.

Thank you for respecting the hard work of these authors.

This is a work of fiction. Names, places, characters, and events are entirely the produce of the author's imagination or are used fictitiously, and any resemblance to persons living or dead, actual locations, events, or organizations is coincidental

1

New Orleans at dusk was always a sight to behold. The sky, a bruised canvas of purples and reds, bled onto the horizon as the sun dipped low towards its nightly slumber. Shadows crept through the streets like tendrils seeking their next victim, while the city's neon lights flickered to life, casting an eerie glow across the rain-slicked pavement in a never ending attempt to hold back the night. In reality, the lights only advertised it. New Orleans was a city that thrived in darkness, where secrets were currency and danger lurked around every corner.

Jack Callahan found solace in the dark corners of The Blue Parrot, his favorite bar. The joint was nestled deep within the heart of Bourbon Street, a haven for those who sought refuge from the unforgiving world outside. Faint echoes of Leon Prima's band playing at the Shim-Sham Club down the street followed leery-eyed men into the dimly lit interior. Draped in velvet and smoke, the atmosphere inside The Blue Parrot hung thick with tension as patrons huddled close, whispering furtive secrets over glasses of amber liquor.

Leaning against the bar, Jack nursed his whiskey, the ice clinking softly as he swirled the glass in his hand. His eyes, heavy with the weight of too many sleepless nights, scanned the room, taking in the familiar chaos of desperate souls and lost dreams. He couldn't help but feel a kinship with these people, all of them trying to do right in a city that always seemed to choose wrong.

Jack took a long sip of his drink, the burn in his throat temporarily distracting him from the gnawing sense of failure that had been clawing at him since his last case went sideways. A missing girl, a trail gone cold, and a grieving family left without answers... it was a bitter pill to swallow, even for a man as hardened as Jack. But in this line of work, the wins were few and far between, and he knew it all too well. Lane Walsh, his best friend and partner in Delta Private Investigations, told him to forget it, but Jack wasn't made that way.

"Another one, Jack?" Riley the bartender asked, wiping down the counter with a rag that had seen better days.

"Make it a double," Jack replied, his voice roughened first in the World War and after by years of chain-smoking and late-night shouting matches. "I've earned it. Where's that new sax player?"

"You know how those guys are, he might be drunk, he might be dead."

"This place needs some juke."

"Feel free to get up there and blow your own horn."

Jack grunted. "I'd have to be a lot drunker than this."

Riley nodded and filled his glass as he stared into its depths, the liquid shimmering like fool's gold. He'd become a PI to level the playing field for the average joe trying to get justice in a city where corruption was part of the fabric. But some days Jack couldn't help but wonder if he was really making a difference in this godforsaken city, or if he was just another cog in the machine, doomed to spin his wheels until he broke down completely.

"Chin up, Callahan," said the man on the stool beside him, slapping a hand on Jack's shoulder. "You'll get 'em next time."

"Easy for you to say," Jack said, taking another swig of his whiskey. "You're not the one picking up the pieces."

"Maybe not," the man conceded, "but I've seen you work, and I know you won't let this one go. You never do."

"Sometimes I wish I could," Jack said, "except I can't." His resolve steeled as he drained the last drop from his glass. Jack couldn't remember the man's name, but that didn't matter; The Blue Parrot was where everybody knew everybody, even if they'd never met before. "New Orleans may be a cesspool, but someone's got to keep their head above water."

The man raised his glass in a toast.

"Damn straight. And it's *our* cesspool."

Just as Jack was about to signal for another round, a folded piece of paper slid across the counter and came to rest beside his empty glass. Riley shook his head, denying any involvement. Jack picked up the note, unfolded it carefully, and read. He couldn't help but notice the elegant handwriting.

"*Meet me in the booth at the back. There's something you should know.*"

Jack searched the crowded bar for any sign of the note's sender. His gaze came to rest on a veiled figure seated in a shadowy corner booth. It had to be her. He knew many of the others in the place. Half of them couldn't spell every word in a sentence right, forget having a steady hand when they wrote it.

As he approached, the woman looked up, her eyes wide and imploring.

"Jack Callahan?" she asked hesitantly, her voice barely audible above the low hum of conversation and clinking glasses.

"Who's asking?" Jack replied, cautious but intrigued by the urgency in her tone.

"Evelyn Marsden," she answered, removing her veil to reveal a face marred by grief and desperation. "I need your help."

"Seems like a lot of people do these days," Jack remarked, taking a seat opposite her. "What's your story, Miss Marsden?"

"Please hear me out," she said, hands trembling as she tried to hold herself together. "My brother... he's gone, and I think someone wanted him dead."

"Murder, huh?" Jack mused, gauging her sincerity. Pretty women in low-rent bars didn't usually come so well put together. "Why come to me? Why not go to the police?"

"Because," Evelyn whispered. She leaned in closer, "I think they're involved, too. And I can't trust anyone else."

"Alright," Jack said, his curiosity piqued. "You've got my attention. Let's hear it."

Evelyn hesitated for a moment, then reached into her purse and produced a crumpled photograph. Jack was impressed. Not everyone could afford to have photographs taken. She handed it to Jack, who studied the image of a young man with dark hair and a crooked smile. Nothing stood out.

"That's my brother, Thomas," she said, her voice cracking. "He was found dead last week, but nobody can explain what happened."

"Looks like a decent enough guy," Jack said, handing the photo back to her. "What makes you think he didn't have an unfortunate accident?"

"Because," Evelyn replied, as she wiped away a tear, "the last time I saw him, he told me he had stumbled onto something big. Something that could bring down some very powerful people in this city. He wouldn't tell me any more than that, but he made me promise to find someone who could help if anything happened to him."

She stared off a moment, her beautiful green eyes unfocused...distant, remembering... telling.

"Tommy, please," Evelyn begged, gripping her brother's arm as they stood in the alley behind their apartment building. "Tell me what's going on. I'm worried about you!"

"Evie, I can't," Thomas whispered, glancing around nervously. "It's too dangerous. But if anything happens to me, you need to find someone who can help. Don't go to the police. Trust no one."

"Who do I go to, then?" she demanded, tears streaming down her face.

"Find Jack Callahan," he instructed, his eyes pleading with her to understand. "He's the only one who can help us now." With that, he disappeared into the night, leaving Evelyn standing there, heart pounding with fear and confusion.

"That's quite a story."

"Every word is true, I swear it."

"I don't remember any Tommy Marsden," Jack said, fishing in his coat for a cigarette.

"I can only tell you what my brother told me."

"Okay," Jack said, considering the information she had presented. "Any idea what your brother stumbled across? Any leads at all?"

"Nothing," she admitted, frustration evident in her voice.

"He wouldn't tell me a thing. He just said that there were people in this city who would do anything to keep their secrets, and he had made himself a target."

"Sounds like he was playing with fire," Jack observed, taking a sip of his drink. "And he wasn't wrong. Alright. I'll consider looking into it. No promises, though."

"Thank you," Evelyn whispered, her eyes shining with gratitude and hope. They seemed greener, if that was even possible. Could she possibly be telling the truth?

"But first, if I do...there's the matter of my fee. A man can't work for free. A guy has to eat and pay for things in this city. You know, half the office rent and light bill, a new shirt or pair of shoes on occasion."

He sat back.

"A new hat, I got." He admitted and reached up to straighten it. Well, not really straight but tilted slightly like he always wore it. He shrugged. "These days it cost two bucks to fill up the tank in my coupe."

"I understand." She reached into her clasp. "I hope this is enough to get you started."

She handed him a fistful of fivers. He counted them but didn't bother to check if they were Silver Certificates or Federal Reserve Notes. It didn't matter now. They all spent the same.

"Thirty bucks gets you three full days honest work."

"Thank you for helping me."

"I said it *would* pay for three day's work. I didn't say it *will.*"

"Oh."

Thirty bucks wasn't chump change, and she'd paid awfully fast. He couldn't shake the feeling that he was stepping into something much bigger than he could have anticipated. If he pocketed the money and the photograph of Thomas Marsden, he knew there was no turning back.

The air remained thick with the scent of stale liquor and cigarette smoke, a constant reminder of the underbelly that thrived within New Orleans. Jack smoked and thought, his latest drink untouched as he weighed the choice before him. His instincts told him to walk away, to leave Evelyn Marsden and her problems behind. But there was something about her story that gnawed at him, an itch he couldn't quite scratch.

"Jack," came a voice from the table across the narrow aisle. "You gonna sit there all night or you gonna do somethin' about it?"

Sometimes knowing everybody could be a problem.

"Mind your own damn business, Mickey," Jack said. By instinct his eyes scanned the place for any sign of trouble. 'Restless Eyes' Lane called it, the reflex that made you inspect everything, all the time, one more scar from the war. Every shadow seemed to hold a secret, every corner a potential threat. He knew that getting involved in this case could be dangerous, but something compelled him onwards, a desire for justice in a city so often devoid of it. He knew firsthand what it was like to deal with New Orleans cops.

As Jack mulled over his decision, he noticed a shadowy figure standing by the entrance, watching him and Evelyn with unnerving intent. The figure was clad in a long coat and fedora, their face obscured by shadows and smoke. A cold shiver ran down Jack's spine, a sense of foreboding settling on his shoulders like the heavy fog outside.

"Something wrong, Jack?" Mickey asked, his brow furrowed in concern.

"Maybe," Jack replied, his gaze locked on the mysterious stranger. "Keep an eye on things, will ya Mickey?"

"Sure thing."

Jack slid out of his seat and stood, but the stranger was gone. He sat back down.

Evelyn's eyes glistened with unshed tears, her pleading gaze boring into Jack. "Please, Mr. Callahan," she implored, her voice trembling with fear. She put her hand on his forearm. "I don't know who else to turn to."

Jack still hesitated, and looked at himself and the woman seated across from him in the mirror behind the bar, weighing his options. Like his image at a distance in this light, the shadows of New Orleans seemed to be closing in around him, whispering for caution and distrust. But as he studied the desperation in Evelyn's face, he couldn't help but remember the ghosts that haunted his own past.

Jack turned back to Evelyn, desperation etched into the lines of her face. As he considered the consequences of his actions, he realized that his need for redemption outweighed the risks. He failed to find the girl, but maybe finding out what happened to Tommy Marsden would help balance the scales.

"Alright, Evelyn," he said, finally making his decision. "I'll help you find out what happened to your brother." He tucked the money and picture into an inside pocket of his suit jacket.

"Thank you," she breathed, relief flooding her features.

"Meet me at my office tomorrow morning," Jack instructed, his tone firm as he withdrew from her touch. "Come alone."

As he watched her leave, Jack wondered how much of Evelyn Marsden's story was true.

Shadows danced and twisted as if in tune with the wail of the saxophone from the lone musician in the corner of the room. The man had finally showed up, only now Jack slumped back in his seat, fingers drumming on the table as he mulled over his decision, wondering if the whiskey affected his decision either for good or bad. The Blue Parrot hummed around him like a chorus of lost souls, but there was something about Evelyn Marsden's distress that struck a chord within him. He could sense the darkness lurking beneath the surface of her story, a festering wound waiting to be revealed.

"Damn it," he muttered under his breath, taking a swig from his glass. The whiskey burned his throat, a reminder of the fire he'd chosen to walk through to help Evelyn. Images of hopeless faces and broken dreams haunted him, faces of refugees he'd seen in France, and of those he'd failed to save as a PI. But this time... this time, maybe he could make a difference.

"Hey, Callahan," a gravelly voice called out, dragging him back to the present. A beefy guy in his 50s stood next to Riley behind the bar. "Quit sulking, will ya? You're bringing down the mood."

"Buzz off, O'Malley," Jack snapped, his eyes flicking towards the club's second bartender who had dared to disturb his thoughts. Riley he liked, O'Malley he didn't. "I've got more important things to worry about than your precious atmosphere."

"Suit yourself," O'Malley shrugged, turning away to polish

another glass. Jack's gaze drifted back to the table, where a single tear-stained napkin lay crumpled beside his whiskey glass. He frowned, realizing that it must have belonged to Evelyn.

"Can't get her out of your head, huh?" O'Malley said, smirking as he caught sight of Jack's furrowed brow. "She's a real piece of work, that one. Watch your step, Callahan."

"Why does everybody around here think they're my partner all of a sudden?" Jack growled, snatching up the napkin and unfolding it. His eyes widened as he caught sight of what was scrawled across the delicate paper; a hastily scribbled address, accompanied by a series of numbers that looked like some sort of code. The ink had smeared, evidence of Evelyn's tears, but the message was clear enough.

"Looks like I've got a lead," Jack said to himself, pocketing the napkin as he stood up and tossed a few coins onto the table. "Time to find out what you're hiding, Miss Marsden."

"Careful out there, Callahan," Riley warned as Jack headed for the door, "this city's a dangerous place, especially for those who go digging up trouble."

"Tell me something I don't know," Jack replied, his hand on the handle. He pointed at O'Malley. "And tell your boyfriend over there the same is true of sticking your nose where it don't belong."

The night air whispered around him as he stepped out into the darkened streets, the scent of danger and mystery hanging heavy on the breeze. He could feel the weight of the impending storm and the secrets that lay hidden in the shadows of New Orleans. Somewhere on those streets was a murderer, a murderer he'd pledged to find, and no matter the risk, he couldn't turn back now.

"Here goes nothing." He pulled down his hat and disappeared into the night. The shadows enveloped him as he walked away from the desperate reach of the nearest flickering streetlamp.

2

Rain lashed against the precinct windows, giving the world outside a blurred, murky appearance. Jack took a drag from his cigarette and tried to shake off the chill that had settled in his bones since he stepped foot in the godforsaken building. The new-style fluorescent lights flickered overhead, casting unflattering shadows on the faces of the cops shuffling through the room, washing out their complexions and leaving their faces looking like death masks.

Jack laid his open wallet on the counter.

"Callahan," snapped Sgt. Malone, a heavyset man with a ruddy face and hands like hams. He didn't bother checking Jack's P.I. credentials. He had seen them plenty of times before. "What the hell do you want?"

"Official details," Jack replied, tapping ash into a nearby tray. Malone glared at him, but Jack just stared back, eyes hard as granite. "The Marsden case."

"Out of your league, Callahan," Malone growled. "That's NOPD business."

"Last I checked, I still had friends in this place." Jack's gaze never wavered, and something in his tone hinted that he wasn't asking for a favor – it was a warning.

"Fine," Malone spat, tossing a file onto the desk between them. "Take a look, but don't let it leave the room."

"Thanks, Malone. You're a real pal," Jack said, sarcasm dripping from every word.

As he flipped through the thin file, Jack heard the click of heels on linoleum behind him. He didn't need to look up to know who it was, her scent alone stirred memories better left buried. Lt. Rebecca Davis crossed the room, her tailored uniform hugging her curves. She stood out among the sea of rumpled suits and stained ties – a woman who had fought her way to the top in a man's world.

"Didn't expect to see you here, Callahan," she said, her voice cool and detached.

"Didn't expect to be here, Davis," he responded, his eyes still scanning the file.

"Looking into the Marsden case?" she asked, a hint of curiosity in her tone.

"Something like that," Jack said, not giving away any more than he needed to. He closed the file with a snap and met her gaze. "Where's the rest and what's it to you?"

"Nothing," she replied, her eyes narrowing. "Just don't get in our way."

"Wouldn't dream of it." Jack smirked, his mind already racing with questions.

She turned to go, looked back, and stopped in the doorway. "The rest is back here."

He gathered his things and followed her.

The walls in the room were stained from decades of cigarette smoke. The stale air was heavy with unspoken resentment that settled over everyone like a suffocating blanket. Jack leaned against a dusty filing cabinet, his fingers drumming an impatient rhythm on the cold metal as he looked at few pieces of paper she let him see. It wasn't much more than he had read in the lobby.

"Is this how you spend your days now, Callahan? Loitering in precincts?" Rebecca's voice cut through the fog of tension, her words sharp as a barber's razor.

"Only when I'm looking for a good time," he replied, his tone dripping with sarcasm.

"Good luck with that. This place is about as fun as a funeral," she said, crossing her arms defensively.

"Speaking of which," Jack began, the corner of his mouth lifting into a wry smile, "I heard the Marsden case has some people around here rattled."

"Maybe they should be. We've got a killer on the loose and no clear leads."

"Yet." Jack's eyes flicked to the file in her hand, the complete one he had been itching to get his hands on since he walked through the door.

"Are you offering to help, Callahan?" Her gaze narrowed, suspicion written all over her face.

"Me? No, just making conversation." He held up his hands innocently. "But, if you wanted to give me a peek at the rest of that file..."

"Absolutely not." She clutched the file tighter, as if it were a precious gem. "This is official police business."

"Fine, fine." He took a step back, feigning defeat. "I'll find my own answers."

"Try not to break any laws while you're at it," she warned, her voice stern but masking something softer beneath.

"Wouldn't dream of it." As she turned to leave, he took advantage of her brief distraction, snatching the file from her grasp and flipping it open.

"Callahan!" she hissed, but he was already scanning the pages, his mind racing to keep up with the inconsistencies that jumped out at him.

"Interesting," he murmured, his fingers tracing a name that shouldn't be there. "Very interesting."

"Give it back," Rebecca demanded, her hand outstretched, but Jack had seen enough. He put the loose pages in it and tossed the file back to her, his smirk widening as he caught the flicker of uncertainty in her eyes.

"Thanks for the chat, Davis. It's been... enlightening." And with that, he stepped past her and strode out of the file room, the lobby, and the precinct, the ghosts of their history left to haunt the stale air behind him.

The sun dipped low in the New Orleans sky, casting long shadows across the cracked pavement as Jack walked out of the precinct. The air was thick with the scent of beignets and gasoline, the sounds of jazz and laughter drifting from a nearby bar. The music was enticing, but Jack had no time for any of that.

"Callahan!" a voice called out. It was Slim, one of his street informants, leaning against a lamppost, cap pulled low over his eyes. "Heard you been sniffin' 'round this murder case."

"Word travels fast," Jack drawled, stopping in front of the wiry man. "You got something for me?"

Slim grinned, revealing a gold tooth. "Maybe I do, maybe I don't. Depends on your pockets."

"Always the capitalist." Jack's hand slipped into his coat, pulling out a couple of crumpled bills. Slim snatched them up eagerly, his grin widening.

"Alright. Word is there's a fella named Benny hangin' around the murder scene. Seen him there a few times. Might be worth talkin' to."

"Where can I find him?"

"Last I saw, he was headin' toward Lafitte's." Slim tipped his cap. "Good luck."

"Thanks." Jack turned away, heading in the direction of the old blacksmith shop now turned into a bar, his thoughts were racing. Benny, the name he'd seen in the report. *What was he doing at the scene of the crime?* He needed answers, and it seemed Benny might have some of them.

As Jack approached Lafitte's, the thumping sound of a stand up bass along with a piano and saxophone, along with the raucous laughter of its patrons spilled onto the street. Just outside, he spotted his quarry – a man with a slicked-back hair and a shifty gaze, just like Slim had described, was lighting a cigarette in the dim glow of the neon sign.

Jack hung back and watched from the shadows as Benny smoked, casting furtive glances up and down the street. When he stubbed out his cigarette and began to walk away, Jack followed, staying a few paces behind. The sound of his footsteps were muffled by the distant wail of a trumpet.

They wound through narrow alleys and crowded streets, the city's vibrant energy pulsing around them. Jack kept his eyes fixed on Benny's retreating figure, the hair on the back of his neck prickling with anticipation.

"Hey there, handsome." A woman in a tight red dress stepped out from a doorway, her sultry smile aimed at Jack.

The dress stood out. She did not. There were many like her in New Orleans. They worked in one of the the world's oldest professions. He ignored her, his focus never wavering from Benny. She frowned and disappeared back into the shadows with a huff.

Benny led Jack to a rundown apartment building, its windows dark and its door hanging half off its hinges. They climbed rickety stairs, a chorus of creaks and groans accompanying their ascent. Jack did his best to step when Benny did.

On the third floor, Benny stopped outside a door marked 3B. As he reached for the doorknob, something shifted in the darkness behind him – a figure emerging from the blackness, a gun gleaming coldly in its hand.

"Hello, Benny," the figure whispered softly.

The smoky air in the cramped apartment stung Jack's eyes, but he barely noticed as he studied the gun aimed at Benny. The figure holding it was shrouded in shadow, a silhouette with malicious intent. Jacked unbuttoned his jacket and stepped fully around the corner.

"Who are you?" Jack growled, shifting his weight to prepare for action.

"Wrong question, Callahan," the figure replied, voice low and menacing. "You should be asking who's paying me."

"Cut the crap," Jack snapped back. "What do you want?"

"Consider this a friendly warning," the figure said, the gun never wavering. "Back off this case, or your days of snooping around in this dirty city are over."

"Is that right?" Jack asked, a cold smile spreading across his face. He eased his hand towards his chest, slipped it into his jacket, and gripped his 45. He wanted to be ready if the man decided to move the pistol in his direction.

Jack didn't quite draw his weapon. "Well, I got news for you – it'll take more than an empty threat to scare me off."

"Empty?" The figure chuckled darkly. "Remember those words when you're lying in a gutter, gasping for your last breath." With that, the shadowy figure slipped away into the darkness, leaving Jack and Benny alone.

"Damn it," Jack muttered, pushed his gun solidly back into it's holster, and rubbed the stubble on his chin. Inside, he was seething. *Who would go to these lengths to keep him off the case? And why?*

Benny took advantage of the moment and slipped into the apartment. Jack heard at least two bolts slide into locked positions. He knew Benny wouldn't talk to him tonight. Especially, through a closed door.

Pushing the questions aside for now, Jack decided to visit the scene of the brother's death. He needed to uncover any remaining clues before anyone else tried to force his hand again. He turned back to the stairwell.

As he stepped out onto the damp street, Jack felt the oppressive humidity cling to his skin, though his suit, the weight of the air echoing the weight of his thoughts. Even in winter it was present. He started walking. It wasn't far enough to warrant the need of his car.

Even the normally vibrant jazz music seemed muted and somber as he approached the alley where the murder had taken place. Despite the weather, crimson splotches still stained the cracked pavement, a grisly reminder of the life that had been snuffed out. Jack crouched down, running his fingers over the rough surface, feeling the grooves of a desperate struggle.

"Brother didn't go down easy," he murmured to himself, lost in thought. "But who wanted him dead? And why?"

The air hung heavy with the stench of decay, a putrid reminder of the recent violence. Jack's eyes darted around the scene, searching for anything out of place. He knew he had to tread carefully; New Orleans was a city full of secrets, and he couldn't afford to let himself get swallowed up in its murky depths.

His heart hammered against his ribs as he spied something glinting in the shadows. Pushing aside a pile of debris, Jack uncovered a gold cufflink, bearing the unmistakable logo of a prominent political figure. The discovery sent a jolt down his spine - this was bigger than he'd anticipated.

"Looks like we're playing with the big boys now," he muttered under his breath. His mind raced, trying to piece together how this seemingly insignificant trinket could blow the case wide open.

"Jack," came a voice from behind him. He turned sharply and his hand moved instinctively inside his jacket before he recognized the familiar silhouette of Lt. Rebecca Davis. Her eyes were filled with wariness, her lips pressed into a thin line.

"Rebecca," he acknowledged gruffly, shoving the cufflink deep into his pocket. "What brings you here?"

"I should ask the same of you." she shot back, crossing her arms defensively. "This is an active crime scene, Jack. You know better."

"Active? More like buried," he retorted, watching as her jaw clenched. "I found something, Rebecca. Something that tells me there's more to this case than meets the eye."

"Show me," she demanded, her voice barely above a whisper. Jack hesitated, his trust in her wavering. But if anyone could help him dig deeper, it was Rebecca.

"Alright," he relented, pulling the cufflink from his pocket and placing it in her outstretched hand. Her eyes widened in recognition, her grip on the piece of evidence tightened as she scanned the area for any sign of prying eyes or ears.

"Where did you find this?" she asked urgently. Jack could feel the tension radiating off her, a stark contrast to the cool facade she typically maintained.

"Right here," he replied, pointing to the spot where he'd uncovered it. "What do you think it means?"

"Trouble," Rebecca murmured, her voice laced with concern. "Big trouble. This isn't just some two-bit gangster, Jack. We're dealing with someone who has connections. Power. If we want to get to the bottom of this, we'll need to be careful. Watch our backs."

"Agreed," Jack said, his mind already racing ahead to plan their next move.

The stakes were higher now, and they couldn't afford to make any mistakes. The shadows of New Orleans seemed to close in around them, threatening to swallow them whole as they stood in the dimly lit alleyway.

"Meet me at Louie's Bar tonight," Rebecca instructed, her gaze never leaving his. "We'll talk more then. And Jack...be careful." With that, she slipped away into the darkness, leaving Jack alone with his thoughts and the oppressive weight of what they'd just discovered.

Jack glanced back to where he found the cufflink as the wind caused a small piece of paper to flutter. On a whim bent over and picked it up even though it looked like so much of the other trash in the alley. He read what was on it and looked in the direction she had gone.

"Careful?" he mused bitterly. "In this city? Not likely."

The neon lights of Louie's Bar flickered and buzzed, casting shadows to dance across Jack's face as he sat hunched over at the bar. The whiskey burned a trail down his throat, but it did nothing to dispel the gnawing uncertainty that twisted in his gut.

"Another?" the bartender asked, eyeing him with a mix of pity and wariness.

"Sure," Jack muttered, swirling the remnants of his drink before downing it. "Why not?"

He'd spent the better part of the day grappling with whether or not to share another clue with Rebecca. She was a good cop, hell, maybe the only good one left in this godforsaken city. But there was something about her that made him hesitate, something he couldn't quite pin down. He thought back to their conversation earlier, replaying her words in his head like a broken record.

"Trouble," she'd said. "Big trouble." He could still hear the urgency, the fear in her voice.

"Jack!" The sharp sound of his name brought him back to reality, and he looked up to see Rebecca sliding onto the barstool next to him. Her eyes were hard, her jaw set, but there was a vulnerability behind it all that she couldn't quite hide.

"Rebecca," he acknowledged, taking a sip of his fresh drink. "You look like you've been chewed up and spit out."

"Feeling's mutual," she shot back. She nodded at the bartender for her own glass of liquid courage. "So, what do we have?"

Jack hesitated, weighing his options. The trust between them was tenuous at best, but if they had any chance of getting to the bottom of this mess, they needed each other. With a sigh, he pulled the piece of paper from his pocket and slid it across the bar towards her.

"Found this at the scene, too," he said, watching as her eyes scanned the information. "Someone's pulling strings, and they ain't small ones."

"Damn it," she muttered. "This is worse than I thought."

"Tell me about it." Jack took another swig of whiskey and tried to ignore the sinking feeling in his stomach.

As they talked, the evening settled over New Orleans like a shroud, darkness creeping into every corner of the city. The ever oppressive humidity clung to everything, making the air heavy and stifling even in February.

The bar was warm and every now and then, a bead of sweat would make its way down Jack's temple, but he barely noticed. All his attention was focused on the woman next to him, and the dangerous game they were about to play.

"Alright," Rebecca said finally. She drained her drink and stood up. "We'll need to be careful, but we can do this. Together."

"Agreed." Jack followed her lead, throwing a few bills onto the bar before heading for the door. She was quickly through and gone into the night.

He waited a few moments to give her time to go in a different direction than he planned, but as he stepped out into the thick New Orleans evening, a prickling sensation crawled up his spine, and he couldn't shake the feeling that he was being followed. As always, the city was alive with the sounds of jazz and laughter, but beneath it all lurked something darker, more sinister. And it was closing in on them, one step at a time.

3

The first thing that hit Jack as he entered the hidden jazz club was the smoke, thick and heavy like a blanket, followed by the wail of a lone saxophone. A musician of sorts, himself, it was his own preferred instrument.

It wasn't as if he had a singing voice, not with the damage done to it long ago. Damned military issued gas masks didn't always completely seal and hints of Mustard Gas in the trenches sometimes made its way in. For some, it did more than a little damage. Jack considered himself lucky. He'd seen what it did in some of the trenches in the Great war. It was a bad way to go.

It was a wonder he had the breath to play a wind instrument. He knew as the years passed it would become difficult. He shook off the thought. It wasn't as if he could change the future...In that, anyway.

The joint was crowded. He moved through bodies pressed together so tight that it was hard to tell where one person ended and another began. It was the perfect place for secrets to be whispered in the dark.

"Jack, over here!" Evelyn Marsden's voice cut through the noise, drawing him to a dimly lit booth at the back of the room. She looked right at home, her eyes smoky and mysterious, lips the color of blood.

"Didn't think I'd find you in a place like this," Jack said, sliding into the booth beside her.

"Everyone has their vices, Jack." She smirked, taking a sip from her glass. "Some of us are just better at hiding them."

"Speaking of hiding..." Jack glanced over the crowd, searching for any sign of the man they were after. Frankie "Fingers" Malone. He wasn't one for subtlety, but even a notorious gangster needed to lay low now and then.

"Jack, do you trust me?" Evelyn asked suddenly, her gaze locked on his.

"Trust is a luxury we can't afford, sweetheart," he replied, though a part of him wanted nothing more than to believe in her. She had her secrets, but so did he. "You did stand me up on meeting me at my office the first time."

"Fair enough. I did come later, though." She countered and then nodded, seeming to accept his answer. "But I need you to trust me tonight."

Before Jack could respond, a shadow fell over their booth, accompanied by a gravelly voice that made the hairs on the back of his neck stand up. "Well, if it ain't little Miss Marsden and Mr. Detective himself."

"Frankie," Jack muttered, peering up at the man who had somehow managed to sneak up on them.

"Sit down, Frankie," Evelyn said, her voice steady despite the tension in the air. "We have business to discuss."

"Business, huh?" Frankie laughed, sliding into the booth across from them. "Now why would I want to talk business with you two? Last I checked, we weren't exactly on the same side."

"Times change," Evelyn replied coolly. "And so do alliances."

"Is that so?" Frankie leaned back in the booth, studying them both. "Well then, what's this about?"

"Your connection to me," Evelyn said, and Jack could hear the steel in her voice. "It's time to stop hiding the truth, Frankie."

Frankie raised an eyebrow, a smirk playing at the corner of his mouth. "Alright, doll. You want the truth? Fine. You and I go way back, farther than you'd like to admit. We were thick as thieves once, partners in crime, until you decided to play the grieving sister out for justice." He paused, glancing over at Jack. "Guess you didn't tell your detective friend here everything, did you?"

Jack felt a chill run down his spine, though he fought to keep his face impassive. He knew there was more to Evelyn than met the eye when she hired him, but this...this was something else entirely. The game had just become infinitely more complicated.

"Let me guess," Jack drawled, trying to mask his surprise. "You're gonna tell me you two were lovers too?"

"Jack, don't—" Evelyn began, a warning in her eyes.

"Wouldn't you like to know?" Frankie chuckled darkly. "But that's not important right now. What matters is I've got something you want, Detective. Information. And maybe, just maybe, I'm willing to make a deal. But first, you've got some decisions to make about who you trust and who you don't."

With that, Frankie pushed back from the table, leaving Jack and Evelyn in a tense silence. The saxophone wailed once more, a mournful cry that seemed to echo the turmoil in Jack's mind.

The smoke in the room swirled around Jack like a shroud, threatening to choke him as he watched Frankie disappear into the shadows. He could practically taste the deceit that hung in the air, thick as tar. Evelyn's eyes burned into him, but he couldn't bring himself to look at her just yet.

"Jack." Her voice was cold steel, a sharp edge against his throat. "What the hell were you thinking?"

He finally turned to face her, feeling the weight of the lies she'd been hiding behind. "I'd ask you the same question," he shot back, his mouth curling into a bitter sneer. "You and Frankie? Partners in crime? What else haven't you told me?"

"Jack, you don't understand—" she began, but he cut her off with a snarl.

"Damn right I don't understand! I thought you wanted to know what happened to your brother and we were on the same side, and then..." He gestured vaguely toward where Frankie had vanished. "Now I find out you've been playing me for a fool."

"Please, Jack, let me explain." There was desperation in her eyes, a plea for understanding. But Jack couldn't bring himself to trust her now. How much of what she'd told him had been a lie?

"Save it," he growled. "We've got bigger fish to fry right now."

He opened his hand and revealed a crumpled piece of paper, the words scribbled across it suddenly taking on a new level of importance. "Frankie gave me this before he left. Said there's a secret transaction going down tonight at the old warehouse on Bayou Road. Seems our mutual friend has some kind of deal set up with someone in City Hall."

"No, You need to know more about me...this."

Jack sat back and listened. When she was finished, she remembered what was in her hand.

Evelyn studied the paper, her face a mask of carefully controlled emotions. "So, what are you going to do?"

"Find out who's behind it, of course." He pocketed the paper, stood up, and hardened his gaze. "And then I'm going to take them down."

"Jack, wait!" Evelyn reached out, her hand gripping his arm like a vice. "You can't go in there alone. It could be a trap. Let me help you."

"Help me?" Jack laughed without humor; the sound grated against his own ears.

"I think you've helped enough, sweetheart." He shook off her grip and strode toward the door, leaving her standing alone amidst the haze of cigarette smoke and broken trust.

Jack stepped out into the night. He couldn't shake the feeling that he was caught in a spider's web, with unseen forces pulling him every which way. As he walked the dimly lit streets, his thoughts drifted back to Evelyn, her past, and her connection to Frankie.

It had been a different time, a different world. The city had been vibrant, alive with music and laughter. But beneath that shimmering surface lay a dark underbelly, where men like Frankie Malone thrived.

Evelyn had been young then, barely more than a girl when she had first crossed paths with Frankie. They had met in a smoke-filled jazz club, their eyes locking across the room with an intensity that could melt steel. It hadn't taken long for them to become entangled in more ways than one, their lives interwoven like strands of a rope.

But as the years passed, their bond became strained.

Frankie's criminal empire grew, while Evelyn found herself sinking deeper and deeper into the shadows. She began to realize the truth about Frankie - that beneath his charming exterior lay a ruthless man who would stop at nothing to achieve his goals.

"Damn it," Jack muttered, the memory of Evelyn's confession echoing in his ears. She had told him everything, laid her soul bare before him. And now, as he stood on the precipice of another dangerous encounter, he couldn't help but feel the weight of her past bearing down on them both.

"Callahan!" a voice called out, shattering the silence. Jack looked up to see a figure standing in the alleyway ahead, the shadows obscuring a face. "We need to talk."

"About what?" Jack asked, his hand instinctively reaching for the gun under his jacket. He didn't like surprises, especially not in this part of town.

"Frankie sent me," the figure said, stepping forward into the dim light. Jack's eyes narrowed as he tried to make out their features. "He said you might be in over your head."

"Frankie also told me not to trust anyone," Jack replied, his voice edged with suspicion. "And right now, I'm not inclined to believe a word that comes out of your mouth."

"Suit yourself," the figure shrugged, turning to leave. "But if you go into that warehouse tonight, you're signing your own death warrant."

Jack hesitated for a moment, torn between his determination to solve the case and the nagging doubt in the back of his mind. Was this just another trap? Or was there something more to Frankie's warning?

"Wait," he called out, the word catching in his throat like smoke.

Rain pelted the grimy streets of New Orleans, each drop washing away another layer of the city's filth. There would never be enough rain to complete the job, though it was a welcome attempt.

Jack stood in the doorway of another seedy bar; his trench coat pulled tight around him to ward off the chill. He could feel the weight of the city bearing down on him like an oppressive fog, but he wasn't about to let it break him.

"Hey, Callahan," a voice called out from behind him, as gruff and worn as the cobblestone beneath their feet. Jack turned to see a disheveled man sidle up next to him, a tattered fedora shielding his eyes from the rain. "I got somethin' for ya."

"Spit it out, Mickey," Jack replied, his voice dripping with impatience. The informant was notorious for dragging things out, always trying to squeeze every last penny from those desperate enough to rely on him.

"Got a message here," Mickey said, producing a crumpled envelope from within his ragged coat. "Came through the grapevine. Figured you might be interested."

Jack snatched the envelope from Mickey's trembling hand and tore it open to reveal a scrap of paper covered in symbols and numbers. He scanned it quickly, feeling his brow furrow in confusion. It was different than the scraps he had accumulated in this case.

"Looks like some kind of code," he muttered, mostly to himself. "Who sent this?"

"Couldn't say," Mickey shrugged nonchalantly, shoving his hands deep into the pockets of his coat. "Just thought you should know."

"Fine," Jack sighed, reaching into his own pocket to pull out a handful of crumpled bills, tossing them to Mickey. "Now get lost."

"Thanks, Callahan," Mickey grinned, greedily pocketing the money before slinking back into the shadows, leaving Jack to make sense of the message.

As the rain continued to fall, Jack retreated to his office. The dimly lit room provided a welcome refuge from the storm outside. Before sitting at one of the two battered desks he poured himself a stiff drink from the office emergency supply and slid a folded dollar bill under the bottle of Bacardi. His partner, Lane, knew a guy and always got the real stuff for them to drink. It was never the rotgut in the fake-label bottles sold to those unsuspecting.

He chipped in to help pay for the bottles now and then and Lane put change in a cracked cup to help with the coffee fund. Not that they brewed it in their office, but to slip down the street to one of a handful of places to grab a quick cup and retreat back to the office.

He sat down, leaned forward as the chair squeaked loudly, and began to decipher the mysterious code.

"Damn it," he muttered, frustration seeping into his voice as the minutes ticked by. If there was one thing Jack hated more than anything else, it was codes. They were like a tangled knot, and he wasn't always sure he had the patience to unravel them.

His thoughts were interrupted by a knock on the door. "It's open," he called out, not bothering to look up from the paper.

"Looks like you could use some help," a familiar voice drawled, stepping into the room with an air of nonchalance. Evelyn, her fiery red hair contrasting sharply against her pale skin, moved toward Jack's desk, eyes narrowed in curiosity.

"Got a lead," Jack explained, gesturing to the coded message. "But I can't make heads or tails of it."

"Let me take a look," Evelyn offered, reaching for the scrap of paper. Her nimble fingers traced the symbols and numbers, a sly smile playing at her lips. "I think I've got it."

"Already?" Jack asked, impressed despite himself. He knew she was sharp, but this was another level entirely.

"Seems like a rendezvous," she murmured, still studying the message. "Tonight, at the old warehouse on Bourbon Street."

"Of course, it's Bourbon Street," Jack grumbled, downing the last of his drink before standing up and shrugging on his coat. "Well, let's go see what we can find."

"Are you sure about this, Jack?" Evelyn asked quietly, concern etched in her features. "You know how dangerous these things can be."

"Never stopped me before," he replied, a wry smile tugging at the corner of his mouth. "Besides, I've got you watching my back tonight, don't I?"

"Yes," she confirmed, her voice unwavering.

As they walked through the rain-slicked streets, Jack couldn't help but feel the tension in the air, as though an unseen danger lurked just around the corner. He kept a hand inside his jacket and gripped his gun tightly, a silent vow to make it out of this alive.

"Jack," Evelyn whispered, suddenly stopping in her tracks. "Do you hear that? Someone is talking."

The old warehouse loomed before Jack and Evelyn, its shadowy silhouette a stark contrast against the hazy glow of the streetlights. The rain had let up earlier and left behind the damp smell of wet pavement and the distant murmur of the city's nightlife.

"Stay close," Jack warned as he pushed open the creaky door, his Colt 1911 in hand. World War veterans, he and Lane both kept contacts to supply them with military grade rounds.

Moonlight seeped through the broken windows, casting eerie shadows across the cavernous space. Stacks of abandoned crates, remnants of a forgotten business venture, lay scattered about, providing just the right amount of cover for anyone who might be lurking.

"Over there." Evelyn pointed to a dimly lit corner where two figures stood, their voices low and hushed.

"Keep your eyes peeled, doll," Jack muttered as they cautiously approached the clandestine meeting. He strained to pick up their conversation, his every sense heightened with anticipation.

"...shipment arrives tomorrow night," one figure said, his voice barely a whisper. "Be ready."

"Got it," the other replied, his voice deeper, more menacing. "I'll take care of it."

"Alright, I'm going in," Jack decided, his heart pounding in his chest. He knew this was their chance to get answers – but it also meant walking into danger. He didn't think twice.

"Wait, Jack–" Evelyn began, but he was already moving.

"Evening, gentlemen," Jack interrupted, stepping into the dim light. The two figures reacted instantly; one pulled out a switchblade while the other reached for a hidden gun.

"Who the hell are you?" the first man snarled, his eyes narrowed dangerously.

"Name's Callahan," he replied, leveling his gun at them. "I've got some questions about a certain transaction."

"Looks like we've got ourselves a snoop," the second man

growled, his fingers tightening around the grip of his revolver. "What say we teach him a lesson, Danny?"

"Wait!" Evelyn shouted, her own weapon trained on the pair. "Drop your weapons or I'll shoot."

"Alright, alright," Danny smirked, lowering his knife. "What do you want to know?"

"Who's behind this?" Jack demanded; his voice steady even as adrenaline coursed through his veins.

"Can't help you there," Danny shrugged, feigning innocence. "We're just the middlemen."

"Try again," Evelyn snapped, her hand rock-steady on her small pistol.

"Look, lady–" the second man started, but Jack cut him off.

"Enough games," he growled, taking a step closer. "One last chance to talk, or we do things the hard way."

"Alright, fine," the second man relented, raising his hands in surrender. "The boss is–"

But before he could finish, the sharp crack of gunfire echoed through the warehouse. A bullet whizzed past Jack's ear, narrowly missing its mark.

"Get down!" Evelyn yelled, grabbing Jack by the arm and pulling him behind the nearest stack of crates. The two figures took advantage of the chaos and disappeared into the darkness.

"Stay here," Jack ordered, his eyes scanning the gloom for any sign of the shooter. Whoever it was...They were gone. He knew they were running out of time – and their lives were hanging in the balance.

New Orleans was a city that breathed secrets, and tonight, the air hung heavy with them. Jack stood in the shadows of an alleyway, smoking a cigarette as he pieced together the fragments of his investigation. He listened to the music from an opened back door of a club and debated going around the front and entering.

He didn't think he would be able to enjoy the atmosphere tonight. The mystery he had been chasing was far bigger than he could have ever imagined – a twisted conspiracy that seemed to snake through every corner of the city.

"Callahan," a voice called out from the darkness. He recognized it. Frankie Malone. He stepped out of the shadows, his fedora casting a sinister shadow over his face.

"Malone," Jack replied, taking another drag from his cigarette. "Fancy seeing you here."

"Cut the small talk," Frankie said, leaning against a brick wall. "We both know what's at stake. You've uncovered something big, haven't you?"

"Maybe I have," Jack said, blowing smoke into the night air. "What's it to you?"

"Turns out we got ourselves a common enemy," Frankie admitted, his eyes narrowing. "I never thought I'd say this, but I think we need to work together on this one. I mean actually work, not just give hints of information."

"An alliance?" Jack mused, flicking the ash from his cigarette. "You must be desperate."

"Desperate times, Callahan," Frankie responded, a wry smile playing on his lips. "Besides, there are things I know that you don't. And vice versa."

"Alright, Frankie," Jack said slowly, weighing his options. He didn't trust Malone as far as he could throw him, but if they had a shared enemy, maybe it was worth the risk. "Let's hear what you've got."

"Good," Frankie nodded, pulling another crumpled piece of paper from his pocket. "I've been keeping tabs on some of the higher-ups in this town. They've been meeting in secret, making plans that ain't good for either of us."

"Like what?" Jack asked, his eyes scanning the paper Frankie handed him.

"Smuggling, bribery, murder," Frankie listed off casually. "You name it, they're in on it. And from what I can gather, they're planning something big. Something that's gonna shake this city to its core."

"Who's running the show?" Jack questioned, his mind racing with the implications.

"Can't say for sure," Frankie admitted, a hint of frustration in his voice. "But I do know there's a meeting tonight. And if we're gonna expose this conspiracy and bring them down, we need to be there."

"Alright," Jack agreed reluctantly. "We'll do it your way. For now."

"Trust me, Callahan," Frankie said, grinning. "We're about to blow this whole thing wide open."

As they walked together towards their uncertain fate, Jack couldn't shake the feeling that he was stepping into a lion's den – one where the line between friend and foe was blurred beyond recognition.

4

With the front that had moved in, the rain came down in sheets, a cold, merciless deluge that soaked Jack to the bone as he stood outside Evelyn Marsden's apartment. He'd been tailing her for days, despite an uneasy alliance formed in the search for justice. But when he raised his hand to knock on the door, it swung open a few inches, revealing a room in disarray.

"Damn," he muttered under his breath, pushing the door wide and stepping into the chaos. "Evelyn!"

Furniture was overturned, papers scattered like leaves in an autumn storm. Someone had been looking for something, and they hadn't been too concerned with keeping things neat. Jack's heart raced as he searched for any sign of Evelyn, that mysterious femme fatale who'd dragged him back into the shadows of New Orleans.

"Where are you, doll?" he said, half to himself, as his eyes darted around the room.

A shattered vase lay near the door – its jagged edges glinting menacingly. In the dim light, Jack spotted a piece of paper, partially hidden beneath an upturned chair. He unfolded it, revealing an address scrawled in haste *2356 Rue d'Espoir*. Jack's gut clenched; hope seemed to be in short supply these days.

"Rue d'Espoir, huh?" Jack pocketed the note, determination settling in like a heavy fog. "If that's where you are, Evelyn, that's where I'm headed."

He ventured out into the rain once more, his coat collar turned up against the biting wind. The city loomed over him as he walked, the streets grew narrower, the buildings more rundown. It wasn't long before he found himself standing outside a seedy underground club, the faint thud of a bass line vibrating through the cracked concrete.

"2356 Rue d'Espoir," he thought, looking at the crumbling brickwork and flickering neon sign. "Well, here's to hoping it's not another dead end."

Taking a deep breath, Jack pushed open the club's grimy door and stepped into the dimly lit interior. Smoke hung thick in the air, tendrils curling around the low-hanging lamps like grasping fingers. None of the new neon fixtures graced the place. The patrons were an unsavory mix of shadows and whispers, their eyes sliding away from his as he scanned the room for any trace of Evelyn.

"Desperate times call for desperate measures," Jack mused as he wove through the crowd, each step taking him deeper into the heart of New Orleans's hidden underworld. But there was no turning back now – not when Evelyn's life could be hanging in the balance.

The stale stench of spilled beer and cheap perfume assaulted Jack's senses as he made his way to the bar, stepping over discarded cigarette butts and a couple too lost in each other's lustful embrace to notice him. He caught the bartender's eye, a man with a face like a clenched fist.

"Whiskey," Jack rasped, his voice barely audible above the pulsating cacophony of music and laughter. He threw a few crumpled bills on the counter and waited.

"New face, huh?" The bartender said, sliding the glass across the worn wood. He looked Jack up and down. "You sure you're in the right place?"

"Depends on who you ask," Jack replied, taking a swallow of the fiery liquid. He coughed, shaking his head. "Say, I'm looking for someone. Name's Evelyn Marsden. You seen her around?"

"Can't say I have," the bartender answered, his eyes narrowing. "But ask Charlie. He owns this joint. Maybe he knows something."

"Charlie, huh? Where can I find him?"

"Office in the back," he jerked his thumb toward a grimy

THE JAZZMAN'S REQUIEM

door partially hidden from view by a row of slot machines. "But watch yourself. Charlie don't like strangers pokin' their noses where they don't belong."

"Good thing I've got a talent for making friends," Jack thought as he downed the rest of the whiskey and stalked toward the office. He rapped on the door, twice, sharply.

"Come in," a voice called from within. Jack pushed the door open, revealing a balding man in a rumpled suit, idly flicking a switchblade between his fingers.

"Charlie, I presume?" Jack said, leaning against the doorframe. "I need your help."

"Help ain't free," Charlie snarled, his eyes darting between the knife and Jack's face. "What's it worth to you?"

"Depends on what you know." Jack tossed a photo onto Charlie's desk, watching as his eyes widened in recognition. "Evelyn Marsden. I need to find her."

"Sure, I've seen her," Charlie replied, pocketing the photo. "But information like that'll cost ya."

"Name your price," Jack said, gritting his teeth.

"Two hundred." Charlie smirked, clearly enjoying the power he held over Jack.

Jack hated to part with that much money, even though his partner had given him a grand earlier, but the urgency gnawed at Jack's insides, and he reluctantly pulled out a wad of cash, tossing it onto the desk.

"Last I saw her, she was with a couple of guys from the East Side Syndicate," Charlie said, counting the money. "They've got a place down by the docks. Abandoned warehouse. You can't miss it."

"Thanks," Jack said, the word tasting like ash in his mouth. As he turned to leave, Charlie called after him.

"Hey, Callahan! Good luck. You're gonna need it."

The continuing rain drummed a sullen rhythm as Jack made his way through the labyrinth of dark alleyways. He could smell more of the rot and decay that pervaded New Orleans, mixing with the acrid tang of smoke from nearby factories. His heart beat like a ticking clock, each thud reminding him that time was running out for Evelyn.

"Stick to the shadows," he muttered under his breath, eyes scanning his surroundings for any sign of danger. As if on cue, a flicker of movement caught his eye. Three men stepped into the dim light of a streetlamp, their silhouettes revealing the unmistakable bulge of concealed weapons.

"Looking for someone, pal?" one of them sneered, blocking Jack's path. The others flanked him, cornering him against the cold brick wall.

"Maybe," Jack replied coolly, his mind racing. He needed a way out, but brute force wouldn't cut it against these odds. "But I don't think you boys can help me."

"Think you're smart, huh?" The thug spat on the ground, his eyes narrowing with contempt. "We don't like snoops 'round here. Especially ones asking about East Side business."

"East Side Syndicate, huh?" Jack allowed himself a grim smile, feeling the pieces fall into place. "You know, I've heard your boss isn't too happy with you lately."

The men exchanged glances, their bravado faltering. Jack pressed on, seizing the opportunity.

"Word on the street is that there's a traitor in your ranks," he said. He let his voice drop to a conspiratorial whisper. "Someone's been feeding info to the Coppers. And I hear your boss would pay handsomely for whoever rats him out first."

"Whaddaya mean?" one thug asked, as suspicion clouded his face. "You tryin' to turn us against each other?"

"Consider it friendly advice," Jack replied, his eyes never leaving the first one's face.

He shrugged. "But if you want to pass up the opportunity to save your own skin, that's your choice."

The seeds of doubt had been sown, and as the tension grew, the thugs began eyeing each other warily. Jack could practically see the wheels turning in their heads, as they tried to calculate the odds of betrayal. He knew he only had moments before the fragile truce shattered.

"Think about it," he urged them, inching towards an exit from the situation. "What's more important? Loyalty to a bunch of criminals, or saving your own neck?"

As fists clenched and tempers flared, Jack made his move. He ducked under a wild swing and slipped out of the alley, leaving the thugs to their infighting. He didn't have time to look back, his thoughts already focused on finding Evelyn.

Jack pushed open the door to a dimly lit room. His eyes scanned the shadows and landed on Evelyn Marsden, tied to a chair in the center of the room. Her makeup was smeared, her dress was torn, but her fierce spirit still blazed behind those frightened eyes.

"Jack..." she whispered, relief washing over her face.

"Save your breath, doll. I'll get you out of here," he muttered, his fingers working quickly at the knots binding her wrists.

"Behind you!" Evelyn shouted, her voice strained and desperate.

Jack didn't need to be told twice. He spun around, fists raised, just in time to block a punch from one of her captors. The thug's knuckles grazed his jaw, the force of the swing sending him staggering back a step.

"Nice try, pal," Jack sneered, lunged forward and drove his left fist into the man's gut. "But you're gonna have to do better than that."

"Callahan, you should've stayed out of this," another voice growled from the darkness. A man stepped forward with a smug grin on his weasel-like face. "You really think you can save her? You're out of your depth."

"Depth? Buddy, I've been swimming in this cesspool of a city for years," Jack shot back, his eyes never leaving the weasel-faced man. "You're just another piece of scum I'm about to wash down the drain."

"Brave words, detective," the weasel sneered. "But can you back them up?"

"Try me," Jack dared him, shifting his weight onto the balls of his feet, ready for whatever was coming next.

"JACK!" Evelyn cried out as a third thug emerged from the shadows, wielding a knife.

Jack's instincts kicked into overdrive as the blade arced through the air, its gleam a deadly promise. He sidestepped, grabbed the man's wrist, and twisted, forcing him to drop the weapon. With a swift kick to the knee, Jack sent him crashing to the floor, groaning in pain.

"Three on one? You guys really need to work on your odds," Jack taunted, his adrenaline surging through his veins like a freight train. But he knew he couldn't keep this up forever. One slip, one misstep, and it'd be curtains for both him and Evelyn.

"Enough!" the weasel shouted. He pulled a gun from his coat pocket and leveled it at Jack. "You've had your fun, Callahan, but it's time to face the music."

Jack had not pulled his own weapon for fear of a stray round hitting Evelyn. "Put the gun down, or I swear I'll—"

"Or what?" the weasel interrupted. His grin widened. "You'll what, detective?"

Jack's mind raced, searching for an escape route, a way out of this deadly game of cat and mouse. He could feel Evelyn's eyes on him, her fear and hope mingling in the smoky haze.

"Fine," Jack spat, lowering his fists. "You win. Just let her go."

"Sorry, Callahan. You know I can't do that."

"Then what do you want from me?" Jack demanded, trying to buy time, to come up with a plan. The room seemed to close in around him, the shadows pressing down like a vise.

"Simple." Your life for hers."

"Jack," Evelyn whispered, her voice trembling. "Don't do it. It's not worth it."

"Quiet!" the weasel snapped, his finger tightening on the trigger. "What's it gonna be, Callahan?"

"Alright," Jack replied, his voice steady despite the turmoil churning within him. "You win. Let her go, and you can have me."

"Jack, no!" Evelyn begged, but he silenced her with a look.

"Swear it," he demanded of the weasel.

"Fine, I swear."

"Good." Jack took a deep breath, preparing for the worst. But as the gun swung in his direction, he spotted an opportunity. The man had glanced toward the others with a grin on his face. He lunged forward, catching Weasel off guard, and pulled the weapon from his grip.

"Surprise," he growled, driving his knee into the man's

stomach before delivering an uppercut that sent him sprawling to the floor. The man was out like empty milk bottles on a doorstep.

"Thanks," Evelyn whispered as Jack untied her bonds. "I knew I could count on you."

"Always, doll," Jack replied, a hint of a smile tugging at the corners of his mouth. "Now let's get out of here before they wake up."

"Agreed," she said, her voice still shaky but filled with resolve. Together, they stepped over the bodies of their would-be captors and slipped out of the room.

Jack and Evelyn slipped through a narrow, dimly lit corridor. The sound of their footsteps echoed ominously off the damp, moldy walls. It was a labyrinth down here – a rat's nest of twisting passageways that seemed designed to trap them, to lead them deeper into this hellish underworld.

"Any idea where we're headed?" Evelyn whispered, her voice hoarse from disuse and fear.

"Would it matter if I did?" Jack replied with a sardonic grin. "We're making this up as we go along, doll."

"Delightful," she muttered and rolled her eyes. They continued on in silence for a moment, the tension between them palpable.

"Wait," Jack said suddenly. He pressed himself against the wall as he heard footsteps approaching. He motioned for Evelyn to do the same. Her breaths came shallow and quick. The footsteps grew louder, then stopped just around the corner.

"Boss said they got away. We gotta find 'em before they spill our secrets," came a gruff voice, muffled by distance and the fetid air.

"Keep your eyes peeled, then," another replied, its sinister edge sliced through the gloom.

"Damn," Jack cursed under his breath. He glanced at Evelyn, who looked more frightened than ever. "We're gonna have to be real quiet-like, now. Stick close."

"Wasn't planning on doing anything else," she murmured, her face pale but determined.

As the thugs moved past their hiding place, Jack caught sight of a door, partially hidden behind a stack of crates. "There," he mouthed, pointing at it. She nodded. They crept towards the exit, praying that it would lead them to safety.

"Jack," Evelyn whispered once they'd slipped through the door and found themselves in a dank stairwell. "If we don't make it out of here..."

"Hey now, none of that," Jack interrupted, his rough voice was surprisingly gentle. "We're getting out of this place, remember? Together."

"Right," she said, offering him a tremulous smile. "Together."

"Besides," he added with a wry grin, "you really think I'd let you off the hook that easy? After all the trouble you've gotten me into? You still owe me some bread. I got bills to pay."

"Perish the thought," Evelyn replied, her eyes flashing with a hint of their usual fire.

"Exactly. Now come on, let's find our way out of this godforsaken maze."

They continued up the stairs, their steps echoing in the darkness like the footsteps of ghosts. The oppressive atmosphere weighed heavily upon them, but the newfound determination burning within their hearts lent them strength.

The faint odor of stale cigars and empty broken liquor bottles permeated the air as Jack and Evelyn emerged from the dank stairwell. They found themselves in a narrow alleyway behind a club. The moon, shrouded by clouds, cast an eerie glow over the dingy brick walls and overflowing dumpsters.

"God, this place stinks worse than a slaughterhouse," Evelyn muttered, covering her nose with the back of her gloved hand.

"Speaking of which, I think we might've just stumbled upon something," Jack said, his eyes narrowing at a piece of paper lying near a puddle. He picked it up and unfolded it, revealing a list of names – some crossed out, others circled. Among them was Evelyn's brother.

"You'd think that anyone who writes notes to themselves

would be sure to keep up with them. Or tear them up or something before tossing them." He shook his head.

"Any idea what this means?" he asked, handing the paper to her.

"Maybe... someone was keeping tabs on potential targets."

"Or witnesses," Jack countered, scanning the names again. "Either way, it's a solid lead into whatever the hell's going on in this city. We need to find out who made this list and why."

"Agreed," she said, tucking the paper into her purse for safekeeping.

"Let's get moving before those goons catch up to us." Jack's voice was low and urgent as the continued through the darkened maze of trash-strewn alleys, the shadows swallowing them up like hungry predators.

"Jack," whispered Evelyn, slowing her pace as they approached a dead-end. "This whole thing...it feels like we're being played. Like someone's pulling the strings, setting us up."

"Welcome to New Orleans, sweetheart," Jack replied bitterly. "Where everyone's got an angle, and nobody plays fair."

"Is there really no one we can trust?"

"Trust's a luxury we can't afford, not here. We can trust my partner but he's been scarce of late...But we've got each other, and that's something." Jack's hand found hers in the darkness, gripping it tightly.

"Right," she said, her voice wavering slightly. "Together."

"Damn straight." He smiled grimly, a lone wolf bearing his teeth at the world. "Now, let's see if we can find our way back to civilization before this place swallows us whole."

As they retraced their steps through the labyrinth of alleys, an unseen figure watched from the shadows. Eyes gleamed with malice in the moonlight. The game was just beginning, and Jack Callahan had no idea what he'd stumbled into.

5

The night was a relief over the past few days. Clear, the moon hung low in the sky, casting its cold light over the derelict warehouse. Its crumbling walls and rusted gates whispered stories of better days, now long gone. Jack leaned against a nearby lamppost, scowling as he lit a cigarette. Evelyn stood beside him. Her emerald eyes scanned their surroundings with a quiet intensity.

"Rumor has it," she said, her voice low and sultry, "this is where the Mayor's goons have been meeting up. The place reeks of conspiracy."

Jack took a drag from his cigarette. "Doesn't everything?" he muttered, more to himself than to her. He had seen too many betrayals, too many lies, to put his faith in anything anymore.

"Are you sure about these rumors, doll?" Jack asked, eyeing the darkened windows of the warehouse skeptically.

"Positive," she replied, her tone betraying no doubt. "My brother was killed because he got too close to whatever's going on in there."

"Then let's get closer," Jack said grimly. He tossed his cigarette aside and walked towards the warehouse.

As they approached the building, memories of Jack's past flooded back. He had fought in the trenches during the Great War, struggling to survive amid the mud, blood, and chaos. And after the war, he had spent years in Chicago working as a Private Detective for Pinkerton with his friend Lane Walsh. After they both decided they couldn't stand another winter up north, they came back to New Orleans to work for themselves, determined to make the city a little less corrupt, a little less rotten. But the shadows seemed to grow longer and darker with each passing year. The city he loved was slipping away from him like smoke through his fingers.

"Jack," Evelyn whispered, snapping him out of his reverie. "There's an open window here."

"Good find," he murmured, helping her through the narrow opening before climbing in after her.

Inside, the warehouse was a tomb of forgotten industry. The air was thick with dust, and the only sound was the distant dripping of water. Jack scanned the space and let his eyes adjust to the darkness. He could make out crates piled haphazardly in the corners and ancient machinery abandoned like the carcasses of some great prehistoric beast.

"Any idea where we should start?" Evelyn asked, her voice echoing through the cavernous room.

"Let's split up," Jack suggested, nodding towards a rickety staircase that led to a second level. "I'll check up there. You take a look around down here."

"Be careful," Evelyn warned, her concern genuine but tempered by the urgency of their mission.

"Always am," he lied, starting up the steps.

As he climbed, the stairs groaned under his weight, threatening to give way at any moment. Jack knew that every step took him deeper into danger, but he couldn't turn back now. Not when the truth was so close.

The creaking of the stairs beneath Jack's feet seemed to echo through the very bones of the warehouse as he ascended. A chill breeze snaked its way around him, carrying with it the familiar scent of damp and decay. He reached the top, his eyes scanning the dimly lit space for any sign of life. But the only movement came from the shadows themselves, dancing as if taunting him with their secrets.

"Find anything?" Evelyn called out from below.

"Nothing yet," Jack replied, his voice low and tense. "Keep looking."

He stepped into a room filled with old filing cabinets, their once-pristine surfaces now marred by rust and disuse. It was here, buried among the forgotten records of a city that didn't want to remember, where he hoped to find the key to unlocking the dark heart of this conspiracy.

Jack's fingers brushed against the cold metal, opening drawer after drawer in search of something - anything - that would prove Mayor Hale was not the man the public believed. In the back of one cabinet, hidden behind layers of dust and grime, he found what he'd been searching for.

"Got something!" he called out, his pulse quickening as he held a stack of documents that would shake New Orleans to its core.

Moments later, Evelyn appeared at his side, her eyes wide with anticipation. "What is it?"

"Proof," Jack said, flipping through the pages. "Mayor Hale's tied up with some secret society, pulling strings from the shadows."

"Let me see," she demanded, snatching the papers from him.

As Evelyn scrutinized the documents, Jack felt a weight settle on his chest, heavier than any pair of muddy boots he'd worn in the trenches during the Great War. The truth was coming to light, but it brought back memories he'd rather forget.

"Jack?" Evelyn asked, noticing the change in his demeanor. "You alright?"

"Fine," he muttered, but the strain in his voice betrayed him.

"Been a while since I've seen that look on a man," she said, her eyes softening. "Talk to me."

Jack hesitated, then let out a heavy sigh. "It just reminds me of something from my past. A case, years ago, involving another secret society."

"Go on," she urged, her curiosity piqued.

"Back then, I was still new to the New Orleans detective game," Jack began, his voice thick with emotion. "I got involved in a case concerning a kidnapped girl. The deeper I dug, the more I realized it wasn't a simple abduction. It was all connected to this secret society – twisted rituals, dark desires."

"Sounds familiar," Evelyn murmured, glancing at the documents in her hand.

"Only difference is, back then, I didn't make it in time,"

Jack confessed, his throat tight. "The girl died, and I never forgave myself."

"Jack, you can't blame yourself for that," Evelyn said softly, placing a reassuring hand on his arm.

"Maybe not, but I won't let it happen again." His face hardened with determination. "We're going to take Mayor Hale down and expose this whole rotten conspiracy."

"Damn right we are," she agreed, her own resolve mirrored in her gaze.

"Let's go," Jack said, pocketing the incriminating documents. "These people need to know what kind of monster their mayor really is."

The moon hung low and heavy in the sky, casting a sickly yellow light on the derelict warehouse. Jack and Evelyn stood in its hollow center, their breaths hanging ghost-like in the chilly air. The place reeked of decay and desperation – a perfect hideout for the mayor's twisted secret society.

"Before we move forward," she replied, her eyes darting around the gloomy space, "there's something you need to know." She hesitated, then met his gaze, her expression resolute. "I'm not just in this for my brother's sake... I have my own score to settle with Hale."

"Spill it," Jack urged, his curiosity piqued.

"Mayor Hale..." She swallowed hard, as if the words were painful to utter. "He was my father's partner until he betrayed him, left him for dead."

"Damn," Jack muttered, his jaw clenched. "I'm sorry, Evelyn."

"Save your pity," she snapped, her eyes flashing with anger. "I don't want it. All I want is to see that man pay for what he's done."

"Fine by me," Jack agreed, his own hatred for the corrupt politician simmering beneath the surface. "Let's get moving. We've got a lot of ground to cover before dawn."

As they stepped cautiously through the darkened warehouse, the sound of footsteps echoed from above. Shadows flitted across the walls like specters, and Jack tensed, ready for whatever danger lay ahead.

"Looks like we've got company," he whispered, body coiled to strike.

"Mayor's guards, no doubt," Evelyn murmured, her eyes

narrowed as she assessed their surroundings. "They must've followed us."

"Stay close," Jack instructed, his hand on the butt of his gun. "We'll have to fight our way out of this one."

The guards descended upon them like a pack of wolves, their faces masked by darkness and malevolence. Jack fired off shots in rapid succession, each one finding its mark. Not all were armed with their own guns, or if they were, they hesitated to fire for fear of hitting each other across the room.

Evelyn was a blur of motion, her small pistol forgotten as her lithe form darted between assailants as she dealt swift, merciless blows with a pair of straight razors. No sane barber would ever think of using them in the way she did.

"Didn't think I'd ever see the day," Jack muttered between clenched teeth as he took down another guard, "when I'd be taking on the mayor's goons with his enemy's daughter."

"Life's funny that way," Evelyn called back, her voice laced with dark humor as she sent another guard toppling onto the cold concrete floor. A stain beneath him.

The relentless onslaught continued, their attackers closing in from all sides. Jack's heart pounded in his ears and sweat beaded on his brow as he considered their dwindling chances for escape.

"Any bright ideas?" he gasped, his breath ragged with the adrenaline rush. He replaced an empty magazine after dropping yet another guard.

"Working on it," Evelyn replied through gritted teeth, her fierce determination shining through the shadows.

As they fought back-to-back, the odds stacked against them, the scent of blood and betrayal heavy in the air, Jack couldn't help but think that this was the kind of danger he'd been born for – a dance with death and darkness. And if it meant bringing down Mayor Hale and his twisted empire, then he was ready to take his last waltz.

Almost as quickly as they had arrived, the few remaining guards peeled back into the shadows. All that was left of them was the faded sounds of running feet echoing in the building. Jack checked the last magazine he had loaded into his gun. He had three rounds left and at least twice that many men were in full retreat. It would not have lasted much longer once the slide on his weapon had locked open, empty. Then again,

Evelyn hadn't pulled her pistol yet. Six shots from a .38 would have been better than no more at all, especially up close.

"Either whoever was leading them gave the order to cut and run or they all got smart at the same time, " Jack said. He bent over, picked up his hat, and punched it from the inside to get it close to its original shape.

"I doubt it was getting smart," Evelyn said. "Guys like that are good at taking orders, not planning them. It means we may see some of them again."

"Yeah," Jack agreed. "We will. This is far from over."

6

Once again, rain lashed the streets, painting the city in shades of dark blues and grays. Jack stood huddled beneath a flickering streetlamp, water streaming off the brim of his hat as he scanned the shadowy alleyways for any sign of Evelyn Marsden and Lt. Rebecca Davis. They had agreed to meet here in the city's underbelly, the only place they could be sure their reluctant alliance would go unnoticed.

"About time," Jack muttered as Evelyn emerged from a shadowy doorway, her beige trench coat pulled tightly around her lithe frame.

She was followed by Rebecca, her uniform soaked through and clinging to her body. Her eyes locked onto Jack's, radiating mistrust and suspicion.

"Let's get this over with," snapped Rebecca, wiping rain from her brow.

"Fine by me," Jack agreed, his voice heavy with weariness. He knew working together wouldn't be easy, but they each held pieces of the puzzle that had ensnared them all.

"Someone's been playing us against each other," Evelyn began, her voice barely audible above the din of the rain. "We need to find out who before we all end up dead."

"Or worse," Rebecca added, casting a wary glance down a nearby alley.

"First things first," Jack interjected, as he felt the weight of their combined knowledge bearing down on him. "We have to decide what our next move is."

"Simple," said Evelyn. Her eyes narrowed. "We take out whoever's behind this. Make them pay for what they've done."

"An eye for an eye?" Rebecca countered, crossing her arms over her chest. "That's your brilliant plan? What happened to justice?"

"Justice," Evelyn sneered. "In this city? You're delusional."

"Enough!" Jack roared, silencing both women. "We're not going to get anywhere if we keep tearing each other apart."

"Fine," Rebecca sighed, relenting. "What do you propose, Callahan?"

Jack paused, considering the weight of his words. "We find out who's pulling the strings and bring them down. Legally, if possible. But if it comes down to it...we do what needs to be done."

Rebecca bristled at the suggestion. "You're talking about murder, Jack. Don't forget that."

"Sometimes there's no other choice," Evelyn interjected, her eyes locked onto Jack's. "Don't tell me you haven't done things you regret in the name of justice, detective."

"Damn it, Evelyn," Jack snapped. "This isn't just about vengeance for your brother and father. This is bigger than all of us."

"Is it?" she challenged, staring him down. "Or are you just afraid of getting your hands dirtier?"

"Enough!" Rebecca yelled, stepping between them. "Arguing won't get us anywhere. We need to come up with a plan. One we can all agree on."

"Alright," Jack said, swallowing his anger. "But we do this my way. By the book, as much as we can. I won't let this city sink any deeper into darkness."

"Agreed," Rebecca nodded.

"Fine," Evelyn conceded, reluctantly. "But if it comes down to it, don't expect me to hesitate any more than I have."

"Let's hope it doesn't come to that," Jack whispered, as they disappeared back into the shadows, rain streaming down their faces like tears for the city they once knew.

A flickering neon light cast a sinister red glow over the trio as they huddled together in a grimy alley. Jack's eyes darted around while Evelyn clutched the scrap of paper and Rebecca clenched her fists, her police instincts fighting against the seedy underbelly they were about to descend into.

"Alright," Jack muttered, his voice barely audible above the pounding of the rain. "This message states: 'When the clock strikes midnight, the serpent will slither from its den.' Whatever the hell that means."

Evelyn squinted at the cryptic note. "Midnight? That's in fifteen minutes. We don't have much time."

"Damn riddles," Rebecca grumbled. "Why can't anything be straightforward in this city?"

"Because then it wouldn't be New Orleans," Jack replied with a wry smile. He racked his brain for any clue as to what the message could mean. Midnight. Serpent. Slithering.

"Wait a minute," he said, snapping his fingers. "The underground casino on Bourbon Street. It's called The Serpent's Den. I've heard rumors about some unsavory dealings going on there. Maybe that's where our real adversary is hiding."

"Sounds like we have our destination," Evelyn said. "Let's go."

"Jack, are you sure about this?" Rebecca asked, concern etched on her face. "We're walking right into the lion's den."

"More like the serpent's," he corrected, but his heart raced just as fast as hers. "But it's the only lead we've got. We'll need to tread carefully."

As they made their way through the damp and treacherous streets, shadows danced around them, every corner a potential ambush. The city's underworld had eyes everywhere, and Jack could feel their gaze boring into him like a thousand needles.

"Keep your wits about you," he warned. "We're not exactly welcome here."

"Never thought I'd be sneaking around with a cop and a detective," Evelyn said, the corner of her mouth curling up in a rueful smile. "Strange times."

"Desperate times call for desperate measures," Rebecca replied, her voice taut with tension. "And believe me, this is as desperate as it gets."

The Serpent's Den loomed before them like a malevolent specter, its front door barely illuminated by the feeble glow of flickering streetlights. As they approached the entrance, Jack felt for the familiar weight of his 45, its cold metal a grim reminder of what might lie ahead.

"Alright, we don't know what's waiting for us in there," he

cautioned, his heart pounding like a jackhammer. "Stick together, watch each other's backs, and keep your eyes peeled for anything suspicious. We walk in, gather whatever information we can, and get out. No heroics."

"Agreed," Evelyn whispered, her face pale but determined. "Let's do this."

"God help us," Rebecca murmured, crossing herself as they stepped into the ominous darkness of The Serpent's Den, not knowing if they would ever see the light again.

The dim light from a single, swinging bulb cast sinister shadows across the grimy walls. A cacophony of hushed whispers and muffled laughter filled the air like toxic fumes. Jack's heart hammered in his chest as they weaved their way through the seedy crowd, every instinct screaming danger.

"Something doesn't feel right," Rebecca muttered, her eyes darting nervously between shadowy figures.

"Stick close," Jack warned, feeling the weight of eyes on them, watching, waiting.

"Maybe we should..." Evelyn began before stopping short, her gaze fixed on a massive figure standing guard at a partially hidden door. Even if it had been completely hidden, the man standing guard at a wall would have given it away. His face bore the scars of countless battles, and his cruel eyes seemed to pierce straight into their souls.

"Looks like we found our obstacle," Jack said, swallowing hard. "Any ideas?"

"Could try sweet-talking him," Evelyn suggested with a smirk.

"Or I could use my badge," Rebecca offered hesitantly.

"Neither will work," Jack answered. He scanned the room for an alternative. "We need a diversion."

"Leave that to me," Evelyn murmured, slipping away before either Jack or Rebecca could protest.

Within moments, shouts and the sounds of glass shattering echoed through the den. The guard's attention snapped towards the chaos, leaving the secret door unguarded.

"Go!" Jack hissed, shoving Rebecca forward. They sprinted

towards the door, slipping through just as the guard began to turn back.

Inside, they found themselves in a narrow hallway, the darkness so thick it felt suffocating. Jack fumbled for his lighter, its flame casting a feeble glow around them.

"Shouldn't we wait for Evelyn?" Rebecca whispered, her voice shaking.

"Can't risk it. We need to keep moving," Jack replied, knowing full well that he might be leaving Evelyn to her fate. His chest tightened with guilt, but he couldn't let it distract him. Not when they were so close.

As they stumbled through the darkness, Jack's mind raced. The cryptic message had led them this far, but what if it was all just another trap? What line was he willing to cross to bring down their true enemy?

"Jack," Rebecca said softly, gripping his arm. He could feel her fear, her uncertainty. They were in too deep now, and there was no turning back.

"Trust me," he told her, though he wasn't sure he trusted himself. "We're going to make it out of this."

"Wherever this leads," she replied, her voice wavering, "I hope it's worth it."

"Me too," he agreed, his heart heavy with the weight of the choices he'd made. But there was no time for second-guessing, not when the shadows seemed to close in around them, hungry and relentless. They pressed on, leaving everything they knew behind them.

Rain still battered the streets, washing away the sins of the city as if trying to cleanse its tainted soul. Hunched in the shadows beneath a rusty fire escape, Jack Callahan lit a cigarette and watched the water flow into the gutter. The acrid taste of tobacco mixed with the dampness in the air, but it did nothing to dull his senses.

He glanced back at the door they had come through. Out of the back of the building into yet another alley. The big man had been guarding an escape route. Jack knew they were being followed.

"Seems like we're not the only ones interested in finding out the truth," Jack muttered, glancing at Rebecca. Her once-pristine uniform was a mess, dark stains soaking through the fabric. She looked like hell, and he knew she felt it too.

"Who is it?" she asked, her voice low. "Someone from the force?"

Jack shook his head, taking a long drag on his cigarette before flicking it into the rain-drenched street. "I'm not sure, but we need to keep moving."

"Wait." Rebecca grabbed his arm, her fingers digging into his skin. "There's something I need to tell you."

"Spill it, doll. We don't have all night."

"Back at the station, when we were going over the evidence... I found something. But I didn't tell you about it because I didn't want to believe it myself."

"Jesus, Rebecca, what did you find?" Jack's pulse quickened, his gut churning with dread.

"An envelope full of cash, addressed to Evelyn."

The revelation hit him like a punch to the gut, leaving him breathless. Of course, it made sense now – the way she'd been acting, the secrets she kept. But he couldn't fathom why she would betray them.

"Are you sure?" he demanded, his voice cracking slightly. "Maybe there's some other explanation."

"Does it look like I'm lying to you, Jack?" Rebecca's eyes glistened with unshed tears, her lips pressed into a thin line. "I wish I were wrong, too. But we've been played. And now we're in this godforsaken place because of it."

Jack stared into the darkness; his jaw clenched as he grappled with the ugly truth. Betrayal from someone he'd trusted – that hurt more than any bullet or blade ever could.

"Alright," he said finally, as determination hardened his features. "We finish this, then we deal with Evelyn."

"Agreed," Rebecca murmured, her voice heavy with regret.

As they resumed their trek through the underbelly of New Orleans, Jack's mind raced with thoughts of vengeance and justice. But beneath it all, he was haunted by the memory of Evelyn's smile, the way she looked when they first met. The woman he thought he knew seemed like a ghost now, an illusion shattered by the harsh reality of their situation.

Jack, Rebecca, and the treacherous Evelyn stood huddled under the awning of an abandoned storefront, their faces drawn and tense. Above them, the sky crackled with electricity as a storm brewed, mirroring the tumultuous emotions that churned within each of them.

"Feels like the end of the world out here," Rebecca muttered, her voice tight with anxiety.

"Maybe it is," Jack replied, his eyes darting between her and Evelyn, the wound of betrayal still raw in his chest.

"Enough with the melodrama," sneered Evelyn, her voice dripping with disdain. "We've got bigger problems to worry about."

"Like what?" Jack snapped, his patience worn thin by her presence.

"Like this," she said, holding up a crumpled piece of paper. "I found it on one of the thugs we took down earlier."

Jack snatched the paper from her hand and scanned the message scrawled in smudged ink. A chill ran down his spine as he realized the implications. The antagonist had orchestrated a catastrophic event – something so big it would shake the very foundations of New Orleans.

"Christ," he breathed. "This can't be happening."

"Believe it, sweetheart," Evelyn drawled with a sardonic smile. "We're in deep now."

The city around them seemed to vibrate with tension. The air was thick with anticipation. As if on cue, a distant explosion echoed through the night, followed by a cacophony of sirens and screams. Panic-stricken people flowed into the streets, their faces twisted in fear as they tried desperately to flee the chaos that was rapidly engulfing their world.

"Looks like our mystery man just made his move," Rebecca said grimly, her eyes narrowing as she surveyed the pandemonium. "We need to find him, and fast."

"Agreed," Jack replied, his jaw clenched with determination. "But first, we need to get out of here. The streets aren't safe anymore."

"Lead the way, fearless leader," Evelyn drawled, her mocking tone grating on Jack's frayed nerves.

"Cut it out, Evelyn," Rebecca snapped, her eyes flashing with barely restrained anger. "You've done enough damage."

"Can't argue with that," Jack muttered as he pushed through the panicked crowd, desperately searching for a path to safety. But with each step, the chaos of New Orleans seemed to close in on them, mirroring their own inner turmoil.

"Over there!" shouted Rebecca, pointing to an alleyway that offered a brief respite from the swelling tide of fear and violence. As they sprinted towards it, Jack couldn't help but wonder if they would ever escape the darkness that had descended upon their lives – or if their fates were already sealed.

In the shadows, Jack's eyes scanned the chaos that had erupted around him. The acrid scent of smoke and fear clung to his nostrils like a leech and left a bitter taste in his mouth. His mind raced as he tried to piece together the puzzle of an enemy that always seemed to be one step ahead.

"Alright," he rasped, his voice barely audible over the cacophony of screams and shattering glass. "We need to split up. Cover more ground."

"Are you out of your mind?" Evelyn spat, her eyes flashing with anger. "That's exactly what they want us to do."

"Maybe so, but we're getting nowhere fast," Jack retorted, his jaw set as he stared her down. "And time's running out for this city."

"Fine," Evelyn muttered begrudgingly, her gaze locked onto his with a mix of defiance and desperation. "But if I don't see you again, just remember – I didn't sign up for any of this."

"Neither did I," Jack replied. "But it's our mess now, isn't it?"

As they went their separate ways, Jack couldn't shake the feeling that he was being watched. After several blocks, he stepped into a dimly lit bar. The bartender glanced at him, eyebrows raised in silent inquiry.

"Whiskey, neat," Jack ordered, his eyes scanning the room as he slid onto a stool. "And any news on who's behind this whole mess would be appreciated."

"News?" The bartender chuckled darkly as he poured the drink. "You won't find any truth here, pal. Just more lies."

"Guess I'll have to take my chances," Jack replied, downing his whiskey in one gulp before slamming the empty glass on the counter. "Thanks for nothing."

"Hey, don't mention it," the bartender called after him sarcastically as Jack stepped back into the chaos outside.

Meanwhile, Rebecca dove deeper into the heart of New Orleans's underground, navigating the labyrinth of sewers and tunnels that lay beneath the city. Her flashlight flickered, casting eerie shadows on the damp walls as she pushed forward, determined to uncover the truth.

"Keep your friends close, and your enemies closer," she mused, her breath echoing through the darkness. "But how can you tell the difference in a place like this?"

As Evelyn wandered the streets, she couldn't help but feel a creeping sense of dread. The city she had once known was now a twisted maze of secrets and lies, each corner more dangerous than the last. And yet, in spite of it all, she couldn't let go of her quest for justice.

"Damn you, Jack Callahan," she muttered under her breath, her eyes glistening with unshed tears. "You've led me straight into the lion's den."

7

Evelyn Marsden stood beneath the flickering streetlight; her face half-hidden in shadows. Her eyes scanned the dark alleyways like a predator hunting its prey. The rain had slowed to a drizzle, leaving the city slick with wet grime, and the scent of damp concrete and stale cigarette smoke filled the air. She focused on the distant sound of footsteps, her heart pounding in time with each heavy step.

"Someone's following you," a raspy voice whispered from behind her. Evelyn tensed, her fingers gripping her revolver tighter.

"Harry," she said icily, recognizing the voice. "You always did have a knack for sneaking up on people."

"Comes with the territory," Harry replied, stepping out from the shadows. His scarred face twisted into a grin, revealing yellowed teeth. "What brings you to this part of town, doll?"

"None of your business," she snapped, trying to keep her own emotions under control. But there was something about Harry that always got under her skin, something that made her want to tear him apart piece by piece.

"Fine, fine," he chuckled. "But maybe I can help you track down whoever it is you're looking for. You scratch my back, I'll scratch yours."

"Last time we tried that, Harry, I ended up with a knife at my throat," Evelyn reminded him bitterly.

"Water under the bridge," Harry shrugged. "Besides, I've been keeping an eye on some rather interesting characters lately. Maybe they're the ones you're after."

"Who?" she demanded, her curiosity piqued despite herself.

"Vincent," Harry whispered, a wicked smile playing on his lips. "He's been meeting with someone who doesn't want to be seen. Now, I don't know about you, but that seems awfully suspicious to me."

Evelyn hesitated, her mind racing. She knew she shouldn't trust Harry, but if he had information that could bring her closer to the truth, she couldn't afford to turn him away.

"Fine," she said through gritted teeth, "but if you try anything, I won't hesitate to put a bullet in your skull."

"Wouldn't dream of it," he replied, his grin widening.

Harry led Evelyn through the labyrinthine streets, occasionally stopping to peer around corners or duck into shadows. She couldn't help but notice how easily he navigated the city's underbelly, as if this were where he truly belonged.

"Here we are," Harry whispered as they reached an unmarked door at the end of an alley. "This is where Vincent's been meeting his mysterious friend. What do you say we take a little peek inside?"

Evelyn hesitated for just a moment before nodding her agreement. Together, they pushed open the door, bracing themselves for whatever lay beyond.

"Stay close," Evelyn warned Harry as they entered, her voice barely audible. "And remember our deal."

"Of course," Harry replied, his tone dripping with insincerity.

As they crept through the dimly-lit room, the tension between them was palpable. Both knew their alliance was tenuous at best, but for now, they needed each other. And as they moved closer to the truth, the stakes only grew higher.

"Something's not right," Evelyn murmured, scanning the empty space for any sign of life. Suddenly, a chilling laugh echoed through the darkness, sending shivers down her spine. The game was just beginning.

Jack moved through the shadows of the city's seediest back alleys, feeling the weight of the darkness pressing down on him. He had been through hell and back in this town, but tonight felt different. Tonight, the air was thick with dread.

"Nice night for a stroll," a voice came from the shadows, dripping with sarcasm.

"Frankie 'Fingers' Malone," Callahan muttered, his eyes narrowing. "What brings you to this charming part of town?"

"Same as you, I reckon," Frankie replied, stepping out of the darkness. "Rumor has it there's a rat scurrying around these parts."

"Must be your lucky day," Callahan shot back, "I'm looking at him."

"Very funny," Frankie said, a hint of amusement in his tone. "But we both know the real filth is still out there, pulling strings."

"Let's cut the chitchat," Callahan growled. "I've got no time for games."

"Fine by me," Frankie agreed, his eyes cold and calculating. "I've heard whispers. Our mutual friend, Vincent, has been meeting some unsavory types in this very neighborhood."

"Whispers won't do me much good," Callahan replied, scanning the area. "I need more than that."

"Right this way, detective," Frankie said, leading Callahan deeper into the alleyways.

As they waded through the muck and grime, Callahan couldn't shake the feeling that he was walking into a trap. He'd never trusted Frankie, but desperate times called for desperate measures. And right now, he needed every lead he could get.

"Here," Frankie whispered, stopping outside an unmarked door. "This is where I last saw Vincent slinking off to."

"Vincent was supposed to be getting me information. Seems he changed his mind. I'll deal with him later. Stay out here," Callahan warned, his hand on the door. "I don't need any surprises."

"Suit yourself," Frankie replied, and leaned against a damp brick wall.

Callahan pushed open the door and stepped inside, his senses were on high alert. The room was dimly lit and reeked of stale sweat and desperation. He could feel eyes watching him from every corner, sizing him up like a piece of meat.

"Looking for someone?" A voice slithered out of the darkness, followed by a group of thugs emerging from the shadows. "You must be lost."

"Maybe I am," Callahan said, tensing for a fight. "But I have a feeling I'm in just the right place."

"Then you've got bigger problems than being lost, pal," one of the thugs sneered, cracking his knuckles. "Nobody comes into our territory uninvited."

"Shame," Callahan replied, his pulse quickening. "I thought we could all be friends."

"Give it up, detective," another thug taunted. "Your time's run out."

"Guess I'll just have to make the most of what's left," Callahan shot back, lunging forward to meet their challenge. There was no time to draw his gun, not that he had many rounds left for it.

Fists flew and bodies collided as the dimly-lit room became a whirlwind of violence. Callahan fought with everything he had, knowing that even if he survived this encounter, there were darker forces still at play in New Orleans's twisted heart. As blood and sweat mingled with the rain outside, he wondered if he'd ever truly escape the city's grasp.

The rain hammered against the windows, its rhythm punctuated by Callahan's labored breathing as he fought off the men. He'd been holding his own, but they just kept coming – a relentless stream of muscle and malice.

"Could use some help about now!" he growled internally, throwing an uppercut that sent one thug reeling into another. But it wasn't enough. He felt himself being pushed back, cornered, and he knew that if something didn't change soon, he'd be done for.

And then, out of nowhere, it came. A gunshot that echoed like thunder through the room, followed by the sudden appearance of a familiar face. Benny "The Blade" Parker, a small-time crook with a talent for getting in and out of tight spots. Jack had crossed paths with him before, but never thought they'd end up on the same side of a fight.

"Looks like you could use a hand, Callahan," Benny said coolly, stepping over the unconscious body of a thug as he made his way toward the melee.

"Or a loaded gun," Callahan grunted, giving Benny a nod of gratitude as he ducked a punch and landed a blow to the gut.

"Got that covered too," Benny replied, tossing a spare revolver to Callahan, who caught it deftly and fired at the remaining thugs without hesitation. The odds were slowly turning in their favor.

"Didn't think I'd ever see the day, Benny," Callahan panted, his voice dripping with both sweat and sarcasm. "You playing the hero?"

"Let's not get carried away," Benny retorted, dodging a wild swing from a goon. "I'm just repaying a debt."

"Whatever your reasons, I'll take it," Callahan thought, finally catching his breath as the last thug hit the floor with a resounding thud.

"Listen, Callahan," Benny said, his tone suddenly serious. "I didn't just come here to bail you out. I got some information that changes everything."

"Spill it, then," Callahan demanded, wiping the blood from his lip and clenching the revolver in his hand.

"Your main target ain't who you think it is," Benny revealed, glancing around nervously as if worried they were still being watched. "I overheard the boss talking. Turns out, he's just a puppet for someone bigger – someone with connections all the way up to the mayor's office."

Callahan felt the room spin as the words sank in, the weight of this revelation threatening to crush him. All this time, he'd been chasing shadows while the true enemy lurked unseen. A twisted game of deception, with New Orleans its hapless pawn.

"Damn it," Callahan muttered, his fists clenched in frustration. "We've been played."

"Looks that way," Benny confirmed, eyes shifting warily. He gave Jack a handful of rounds for the pistol. "But now we know. And knowing's half the battle, right?"

"Something like that," Jack agreed, his mind racing with the implications of this new information as he reloaded. The path forward was unclear – but one thing was certain; the stakes had just gotten a whole lot higher.

A distant crash echoed through the building, followed by

the sound of hurried footsteps approaching their location. The eased out of the building and went in different directions.

Jack slipped into the shadows, his mind a whirlwind of betrayal and anger. The unusually cold New Orleans air pierced through his worn trench coat as he slunk through the damp alleyways, the city's dark underbelly swallowing him whole. He needed to find Evelyn – she had to know what they were up against.

A flicker of movement caught his eye, and Jack tensed, the borrowed revolver at the ready. But instead of an ambush, it was Evelyn, her raven hair cascading down her back as she emerged from the gloom.

"Jack," she whispered urgently, relief etched across her face. "I've been searching for you."

"Likewise, doll," Jack replied, holstering his weapon. "We got a problem."

"Only one?" she quipped, shadowed eyes betraying her concern.

"More like we've been dancing with the wrong partner," he muttered, recounting Benny's revelation. Evelyn's expression darkened as the new information sunk in.

"Damn," she cursed quietly, her jaw set with determination. "What now?"

"Nothing's changed," Jack said, his voice low and resolute. "We find this puppet master and put an end to their game."

Evelyn nodded, then hesitated, the weight of her brother's death heavy on her shoulders. "Jack... thank you. For everything."

"Save it," he replied gruffly, though a fleeting tenderness flickered in his eyes. "We ain't done yet."

Before they could say another word, a crackling sound echoed through the night. A nearby radio sputtered to life, its tinny speaker straining as the antagonist's sinister voice cut through the static.

"Good evening, New Orleans," the faceless enemy crooned, every syllable dripping with malicious intent. "By now, you must realize that your precious city is on the brink of collapse.

But fear not, for I offer a solution. Surrender to my authority, and together we will usher in a new era of order and prosperity."

"Son of a bitch," Jack growled, his knuckles white with fury. Evelyn's eyes flashed with fire as they exchanged a knowing glance.

"Come on," she urged, grabbing Jack's arm. "We need to stop them."

"Agreed," he said, determination hardening his features. "Let's go knock some sense into this puppet master."

As they raced through the treacherous streets, pursued by unseen forces, one thought burned in their minds. The fight for New Orleans had only just begun.

Shadows stretched long and dark under the flickering streetlights. Jack scanned the surroundings, feeling the weight of his revolver in his damp trench coat pocket. Evelyn moved beside him, her face set, eyes narrowed against the downpour.

"Where do you think he's hiding?" she asked, her voice barely audible over the relentless drumming of raindrops.

"Somewhere we ain't lookin'," Jack replied, his jaw tight. "But we need to find him fast. This city's fallin' apart."

They ducked into an alleyway, water cascading from rusted gutters above. The stench of stale cigarette butts mixed with trash and the tang of desperation pervaded every corner of New Orleans. Jack couldn't help but feel that same sense of hopelessness creeping into his own soul. But he pushed it aside – there was work to be done.

"Jack," Evelyn said suddenly, pulling him back from his thoughts. "Over there. That warehouse – something doesn't seem right."

Jack squinted through the rain, taking in the sight of the dilapidated building adjacent to them. A faint glow emanated from a cracked window, accompanied by muffled voices. He nodded at Evelyn, the decision made in a heartbeat.

"Let's check it out."

Creeping toward the entrance, they pressed themselves

against the cold brick wall. Jack reached for the door handle; his hand was steady despite the chill that seeped into his bones. With a silent twist and a shove, they slipped inside.

"Looks like we hit the jackpot," Evelyn whispered, her gaze fixed on the group of men huddled around a table littered with maps and blueprints. Their faces were hard, their intentions darker still.

"Listen up," Jack murmured, his heart pounding in his chest. "We take 'em by surprise. Quick, quiet, and nothin' they can use against us."

"Got it," Evelyn replied, her eyes glittering with determination. Together, they moved stealthily through the shadows, closing in on their unsuspecting prey.

In a blur of motion, Jack and Evelyn sprang into action. Fists flew, bodies crumpled, and the plans for the antagonist's dark scheme clattered to the floor. It was over as quickly as it had begun.

"Looks like we just put a wrench in their operation," Jack said, panting slightly as he surveyed the scene. Evelyn nodded, a grim satisfaction painting her features. She gathered up everything on the table.

"Maybe now we have a chance to save this city."

As they exited the warehouse, the rain continued its relentless assault on the streets of New Orleans. The echoes of victory were bittersweet, tainted by the knowledge of what had been lost along the way. But beneath the weight of their shared burden, a spark of hope flickered in the darkness – a promise that, perhaps, redemption was still within reach.

"Where to now?" Evelyn asked, wiping blood from a fresh cut above her eyebrow.

"Somewhere dry," Jack replied, a wry smile tugging at his lips. "And after that... we'll figure it out. Together."

8

Jack leaned against a brick wall. His trench coat collar was pulled up around his neck as he took a drag from his cigarette. The hazy smoke swirled into the damp air.

"Callahan," a voice said, cutting through the patter of the rain. He turned to see Evelyn approach. Her black hair was plastered to her face as she looked at him with steely determination.

"Got your message," Jack said, flicking the spent cigarette onto the wet pavement. "What's the plan?"

"First, we rally the troops," Evelyn replied, her eyes scanning the shadows for threats. "We need all the help we can get."

"Frankie 'Fingers' Malone?" Jack asked, raising an eyebrow.

"Maybe," she said, hesitating for a moment before adding, "We need someone who knows the ins and outs of this city."

"Fine," Jack agreed, pulling out another cigarette and lighting it. "But if he double-crosses us, I won't hesitate to put a bullet in him and we get someone else."

"Understood," Evelyn nodded. "And Davis?"

"Rebecca? She's with us, but she's walking a thin line," Jack warned. "The department doesn't take kindly to those who buck the system."

"Good enough," Evelyn said, brushing a strand of wet hair from her face. "Now to the plan. We're going up against Mayor Hale, and he's not going down easily."

"They never do," Jack muttered, smoke curling from his lips.

"His guard will be up, so we need to hit him where he least expects it—his charity gala tomorrow night," she explained.

"That's where he'll be vulnerable."

"Sounds risky," Jack said, but a smirk played at the corner of his mouth.

"Desperate times, Callahan," Evelyn replied, her eyes meeting his with a shared understanding of what was at stake.

"Alright," Jack said, flicking his cigarette away and stepping closer to Evelyn. "We get inside, find whatever dirt we can on Hale, and bring him down once and for all."

"Exactly," she agreed, her voice barely audible over the rain. "But first, we need to prepare. Gather our allies, set up a rendezvous point, and make sure everyone knows their part in this."

"Let's get to it then," Jack said, determination setting in as the two of them slipped into the shadows, ready to face the darkness that awaited them in their battle against corruption. They had one shot, and neither could afford to miss.

The rain had stopped, but the damp air hung heavy around Jack and Evelyn as they entered the dimly lit bar, seeking shelter from their own dark thoughts. A sultry jazz tune floated through the haze of smoke, the low tones of the saxophone weaving a somber melody that clung to the room like the mist outside. Jack scanned the faces in the crowd, searching for allies in this den of lost souls.

"Mayor Hale's been cozying up to some dangerous people," Jack said quietly, leaning towards Evelyn so his words wouldn't be carried away by the music. "They say he's got his hands deep in the pockets of the underworld."

"Desperate men make desperate choices," Evelyn replied, her eyes following the movements of a suspicious-looking man near the bar. "He wants power, control over the city. He'll stop at nothing to get it."

"Even murder," Jack muttered, anger simmering beneath his tired eyes.

"Especially that," she agreed, her voice cold as ice.

"Listen, we've gotta—" Jack started, but his words were cut off by the sudden arrival of Frankie "Fingers" Malone, who slid into the booth next to Evelyn with the smoothness of a snake.

"Evening, Callahan, Miss Marsden," Malone drawled, his grin revealing a gold tooth that glinted in the dim light. "Couldn't help but overhear your little chat."

"Of course, you couldn't," Jack grumbled, his hand instinctively reaching for the comforting weight of the gun beneath his coat. He had extra magazines on him now. The borrowed revolver was tucked away in an ankle holster.

"Relax, tough guy," Malone said, waving a dismissive hand. "I ain't here to cause trouble. Fact is, I might be able to help you out with your little...problem."

"Is that right?" Jack asked skeptically, his eyes narrowing as he studied the gangster's face for any sign of deception.

"Believe it or not, I ain't a fan of Hale's either," Malone admitted, his voice barely audible over the mournful wail of the saxophone. "Man like him, he's bad for business."

"Strange bedfellows," Evelyn mused aloud, studying Malone with a mixture of curiosity and disdain.

"Seems we're all in this together," Jack said, a sardonic smile tugging at the corner of his mouth.

"Indeed," Malone agreed, raising an eyebrow as Lt. Rebecca Davis appeared at the edge of their booth, her uniform standing out like a sore thumb among the bar's seedy patrons.

"Thought I'd find you here," she said, her eyes meeting Jack's with a mixture of concern and determination.

"Great, just what we needed," Jack muttered under his breath before addressing her directly. "You sure you want to be seen with us, Lieutenant?"

"Considering the stakes, I think I can risk it," she replied, sliding into the booth next to Jack.

"Welcome to the party," Malone quipped, a wicked grin spreading across his face. "Now that we're all acquainted, let's get down to business."

"Fine," Jack said, his jaw clenched tight as he surveyed the unlikely team gathered before him. "Let's get to work. We've got a long night ahead of us."

"Wish your partner was here too," Rebecca said. "We could use more people."

"Lane is working his own case right now. They paid up front. A lot. He can't just walk away from it. It's bad for business. We got a reputation to uphold you know."

"Hale is who is bad for business," Frankie said.

"I agree. Here's to taking down Hale," Evelyn said, raising her glass in a toast.

"Cheers," the others echoed, clinking their glasses together before downing their drinks, the burn of the alcohol igniting a fire within them as they prepared for the battle to come.

"Alright then," Jack said, slamming his empty glass on the table. "Let's get moving. Time's running out."

The night air was thick, the oppressive heat sticking to Jack's skin like a shroud as he led his motley crew through the dimly lit streets of New Orleans. The city seemed to hold its breath in anticipation, a sense of foreboding settling over the group like a specter.

"Alright," Jack murmured, his eyes narrowing as they approached the entrance to Mayor Hale's palatial estate, a towering symbol of wealth and corruption. "We go in quiet, stick together, and get out fast."

"Like thieves in the night," Evelyn whispered, her voice barely audible over the distant howl of a stray dog.

"Or a pack of rats," Frankie added, his grin visible even in the darkness.

"Focus," Lt. Davis urged, her hand resting on the butt of her service revolver, knuckles white with tension.

As they crept closer to the mansion, Jack couldn't help but feel a chill run down his spine. He knew that what they were about to do would change everything - for better or worse.

Entering the shadowy hallway, the smell of stale cigar smoke and expensive whiskey hung heavy in the air. This part of the house seemed eerily empty, devoid of any life. Jack's heart hammered in his chest, adrenaline coursing through his veins like wildfire.

"Stay close," he warned, leading them through the labyrinthine halls, each step echoing ominously in the silence. "And keep your guard up."

"Trust me," Malone muttered, "I don't plan on getting

killed tonight."

"Neither do I," Evelyn replied, her voice edged with steel.

"Quiet," Jack hissed as they approached an ornate door, the Mayor's private office just beyond it. His gut churned with unease; something felt off, but there was no turning back now.

"Ready?" he asked, meeting the eyes of his unlikely allies, each nodding in response.

"Let's do this," Lt. Davis said, determination etched on her face.

Jack flung open the door, and they charged into the room like a storm, fully prepared to confront their enemy head-on. But what they found stopped them dead in their tracks.

Mayor Hale sat at his desk, a smug smile plastered across his face as he clapped slowly, mockingly.

"Bravo," he drawled, his voice dripping with venom. "I must say, I'm impressed you made it this far."

"Cut the crap, Hale," Jack growled, his hands clenched into fists. "You're finished."

"Am I?" the Mayor sneered, raising an eyebrow. "It seems to me that you've walked right into my trap."

"Trap?" Evelyn spat, her eyes widening with rage and fear.

Before any of them could react, the doors slammed shut behind them, the sound reverberating through the room like a death knell. Lining the walls behind them were many men with drawn weapons. They were trapped, cornered, and utterly vulnerable.

"Did you honestly think I didn't know about your little plan?" Mayor Hale taunted, standing up and strolling towards them, his steps measured and deliberate. "You underestimate me, Mr. Callahan. And now...you'll pay the price."

The room seemed to close in on them with the stench of treachery. Jack's heart hammered in his chest, a bitter mix of anger and dread churning in his gut.

"Quite the predicament we find ourselves in, isn't it?" Mayor Hale sneered, his eyes gleaming in the dim light, like those of a predator stalking its prey. "Or, should I say, the predicament you find yourselves in."

"Enough of your games," Evelyn spat, her voice wavering only slightly as she glared at him. "We're not afraid of you."

"Ah, but you should be," Hale replied, a wicked grin stretching across his face as he took another step towards them, hands clasped behind his back. "You see, I've always been one step ahead of you, Mr. Callahan. And now, here we are – you, me, and your little band of misfits. Along with some of my best men, of course."

"Careful, Hale," Frankie growled, his fingers twitching as if itching for a weapon he no longer had. "You might just find out how much of a 'misfit' I really am."

"Big talk from a man with no gun," the Mayor scoffed, pausing to survey them all with a cold, calculating gaze. "But enough about that. It's time to discuss the matter at hand."

"Which is?" Jack demanded, clenching his jaw as he fought to maintain control over the storm of emotions threatening to erupt within him. He looked towards the large group of men who had taken their weapons from them. They'd even found his 'back up' at his ankle.

"Simple," Mayor Hale replied, his voice dripping with disdain. "One of you will die tonight."

"Over my dead body," Lt. Davis growled, her eyes narrowing in defiance as she squared her shoulders.

"An interesting choice of words, Lieutenant," the Mayor mused, stroking his chin thoughtfully. "Because that can certainly be arranged."

"Go to hell," Jack snarled, taking a step forward despite the weight of dread pressing down on him. "You won't touch any of them."

"Ah, the noble detective," Mayor Hale mocked, shaking his head in mock disappointment. "Such a waste of potential. But I digress. One of you will die, and the rest will be allowed to leave. It's really quite simple."

"Like hell we'll play your twisted game," Evelyn spat, her fists clenched at her sides.

"Then you all die," the Mayor replied, his voice cold and merciless. "I'm not a patient man, so choose quickly."

"Nobody's choosing anyone!" Jack shouted, his blood boiling with rage. "We're not going to give you the satisfaction!"

"Very well," Mayor Hale said with a shrug, his voice as casual as if discussing the weather. "Say goodbye, then."

And it was in that moment, as the room held its breath, that Jack saw the shadow of movement from the corner of his eye. A gunshot rang out, deafening in the silence, and Lt. Davis crumpled to the ground, blood pooling around her.

"Rebecca!" Jack cried, dropping to his knees beside her, his hands shaking as they tried to staunch the flow of blood. "Stay with me, Bec. Stay with me!"

"Guess I didn't make the cut, huh?" she whispered, the hint of a rueful smile on her lips before her eyes fluttered and closed.

"Damn you, Hale!" Jack roared, grief and fury igniting within him like a supernova. "This isn't over!"

"Isn't it, Mr. Callahan?" the Mayor taunted, turning away with a dismissive wave. "It seems to me that you've lost."

"Rebecca," Evelyn murmured, her hand on Jack's shoulder as they stared down at their fallen friend. "We can't let her die in vain, Jack."

"Damn right," Frankie growled, his eyes fixed on the retreating figure of Mayor Hale. "Let's end this bastard once and for all."

"Agreed," Jack said, his voice low and dangerous. He kept pressure on her wound. "For Rebecca."

The rain came down like bullets, pelting the streets of New Orleans with a ferocity that matched the storm brewing within Jack Callahan. He couldn't shake the image of Rebecca, her blood staining his hands as he worked to save her. It was not the first time he had tried to stop someone from bleeding out, but it seemed so different than during the Great War. The memory burned in his skull, fueled by a need for vengeance hotter than hell itself.

"Listen up," Jack growled, his voice barely audible over the din of the downpour. "Hale's holed up in an old warehouse down by the docks. Frankie, you take the back entrance; Evelyn and I will go in through the front. We hit him hard, fast, no mercy."

"Understood," Frankie replied, his eyes locked on Jack's with a fierce determination. "For Rebecca."

"Right," Evelyn whispered, her haunted eyes reflecting the ghosts of her own past. "For my father and brother too."

The trio made their way through the slick, dark streets, thunder rumbling overhead as if heralding the impending confrontation. As they approached the decrepit warehouse, waves crashed against the shore, adding their symphony to the cacophony of the storm.

"Ready?" Jack asked, steeling himself for what lied ahead.

"Let's do it," Frankie said, nodding, before slipping around the corner to the back entrance.

"Good luck," Evelyn murmured, following Jack through the front door.

Inside, shadows danced along the walls, illuminated by the flickering glow of a single lantern. A sinister laugh echoed through the warehouse, cutting through the sound of rain pounding on the roof.

"Welcome, Mr. Callahan," Mayor Hale sneered, emerging from the darkness. "Once again, I've been expecting you."

"Cut the crap, Hale," Jack spat, clenching his fists. "This ends now."

"Does it?" the Mayor taunted, taking a step forward. "You think you can stop me, when I've come this far?"

"Watch us," Evelyn hissed, stepping up beside Jack, her eyes blazing with fury.

"Such sentiment," Mayor Hale scoffed. "You think your pathetic emotions give you strength? Such a waste."

"Enough!" Jack roared, lunging at the Mayor, fists flying.

"Jack, behind you!" Evelyn cried out as one of Hale's henchmen appeared from the shadows, a flash of steel in his hand.

Jack spun around, just in time to dodge the knife aimed at his throat. He grappled with the attacker, their bodies slamming together, their struggle mirrored by the storm raging outside. As they fought, Frankie burst through the back entrance, guns blazing. A hail of bullets found their marks, dropping henchmen left and right.

"Stop him!" Mayor Hale barked, but it was too late. Jack had gained the upper hand on his assailant, sending him crashing to the ground with a sickening crunch.

"Give it up, Hale," Jack panted, sweat and rain mingling on his brow. "It's over."

"Over?" the Mayor sneered, his eyes narrowing dangerously. "This is just the beginning, Mr. Callahan."

"Wrong, pal," Frankie said, appearing at Jack's side, his gun trained on the Mayor. "This is the end of the line for you."

"Maybe so," Mayor Hale conceded, his voice dripping with venom. "But not without taking you all down with me."

"Try it," Evelyn challenged, her own weapon drawn and steady.

"Fine," the Mayor snarled, his hand diving into his coat pocket. But before he could pull out whatever weapon he had hidden there, a gunshot rang out, and Mayor Hale crumpled to the ground, dead.

"Rebecca will be proud," Frankie said quietly, lowering his smoking gun.

"Maybe," Jack muttered, staring down at the lifeless form of the man who had cost the city so much. Hale's hand gripped a Mk 1 grenade. The pin still in place.

"But we've still lost too much."

More rain drizzled down from the dark sky, casting a slick sheen over the streets of New Orleans. The city's sinister underbelly lay exposed, like a fresh wound in the aftermath of Mayor Hale's demise. Jack surveyed the scene, his heart heavy with the weight of loss and victory.

"Callahan," Frankie said, sidling up next to him. "We've got more trouble than we bargained for."

"Seems like trouble's all I ever find," Jack replied, his voice a gravelly rasp.

"Word on the street is, with Hale out of the picture, there's a power vacuum. All the rats are coming out of their holes, trying to claw their way to the top."

"Great," Jack muttered, rubbing his temples. "Just what this city needs – more filth fighting for control."

"Hey, we took down the boss, right?" Evelyn offered, her eyes searching his. "That's something."

"Sure," Jack agreed, but inside he couldn't help but question if it had all been worth it. Had they really made the city any safer?

"Listen," Lt. Davis chimed in, her gaze flicking between the others. One arm was still in a sling. "I know it doesn't feel like much of a win right now, but we've made a difference. If we stick together, we can keep making a difference."

"Rebecca's right," Frankie nodded. "We're the ones who brought down Hale. We can clean up this mess too."

"Maybe you're right," Jack conceded, looking at the ragtag group that had somehow formed around him. They'd lost so much along the way, but perhaps they could still make a stand against the darkness that threatened to consume the city.

"Alright then," Jack said, determination steeling his voice. "Let's get to work."

"Before we do that, Jack," Evelyn interrupted, her voice soft but insistent. "There's something you need to know."

"Spill it," Jack said, not liking the look in her eyes.

"Mayor Hale had a contingency plan. A list of names. People he could use as leverage against anyone who threatened him."

"Where is this list?" Jack demanded, his heart pounding.

"Already being circulated," Evelyn replied grimly. "And your name's on it, Jack. Along with all of us."

"Damn," Jack cursed, his mind racing with the implications of this new revelation.

"Callahan!" a distant voice shouted from down the street.

The four allies turned to see a shadowy figure sprinting toward them, desperation etched onto their face. As they approached, Jack recognized the man as Bill, one of his informants from the seedy bars he frequented.

"Jack!" Bill panted, skidding to a halt before them. "Someone's after you! They found out about –" A gunshot rang out, cutting off his words. Bill crumpled to the ground, his lifeless eyes staring up at the rain-soaked sky.

9

The latest band of rain came down hard on the streets, washing the blood and grime into the gutters. The city was still reeling from the aftermath, bearing its wounds like a cheap suit. Neon signs flickered in the darkness, casting their sickly glow on the damp pavement below. Scattered cigarette butts floated in the puddles, tiny wrecks in a storm-tossed ocean. The scent of stale whiskey clung to the air.

Jack Callahan stood in the doorway of yet another dimly lit bar, his shoulders hunched against the relentless rain. He took a drag from his cigarette, the smoke mingling with the mist that hung heavy over the city. His eyes scanned the street, taking in the faces of those who walked by, each one a story of sin and salvation. Maybe more sin than salvation, he thought.

"Hey, Jack," said a familiar voice, pulling him from his reverie. It was Louie, the bartender. "You gonna stand there all night, or you gonna come in and dry off?"

"Give me a minute, Louie," Jack replied, his gravelly voice barely audible above the sound of the rain. "Just trying to make sense of it all."

Louie shook his head, knowing better than to argue with Jack when he was in one of his moods. He retreated back behind the bar. Jack tossed his cigarette into a puddle and stepped inside.

The bar was another refuge for the lost souls of the city—a place where dreams went to die and hope drowned in a glass of bourbon. It was a local joint. Not one the tourists frequented. Jazz music played softly from an old radio in the corner, adding to the atmosphere of quiet despair.

Jack made his way to the bar, taking a seat on a worn

stool. "Whiskey," he muttered as the bartender approached. Louie poured him a drink, and Jack downed it in one gulp, the burn in his throat a welcome distraction from the pain in his heart.

"Rough day?" Louie asked, refilling Jack's glass.

"Something like that," Jack replied, staring into the amber liquid before him. "Been thinking about the line between right and wrong, Louie. How it's thin as a razor's edge."

"Can't help you there, pal," Louie shrugged. "All I know is people do what they gotta do to survive in this city."

"Survival ain't the same as living," Jack said, taking another drink. "I've seen too much evil in this world to believe in absolutes anymore. Good men go bad, and bad men find redemption. And sometimes, you can't tell which is which until it's too late."

"Sounds like you got a lot on your mind, Jack," Louie said, wiping down the bar with a rag. "But nobody said life was fair. It's just the way things are."

"Maybe so," Jack conceded, finishing his whiskey. "But every time I think I've got it figured out, this city throws me another curveball."

"Welcome to New Orleans," Louie chuckled, topping off Jack's glass. "Now drink up and forget about all that philosophical nonsense for a while."

"Cheers to that," Jack murmured, raising his glass as the rain continued to fall outside.

Jack leaned against a grimy brick wall. Cigarette smoke curled around him like a serpentine accomplice. He didn't have to wait long.

"Callahan," a sultry voice whispered from the shadows. Evelyn Marsden stepped into the pale glow of a flickering neon sign above them, her high heels clicking on the cracked pavement like a ticking clock. "You're a hard man to find."

"Only when I want to be," Jack replied, taking a drag on his cigarette. "What's eating you, doll?"

"Choices, Jack," she said, her red lips twisting into a bitter smile. "I've made my share of bad ones. But tonight, I'm choosing a new path."

"Careful now," he warned, smoke escaping from between his teeth. "Change can be a dangerous thing in this city."

"Maybe so," she conceded. "But it's the only way I'll ever find justice for my brother. The only way I'll ever escape this twisted web of lies and corruption."

"Suit yourself," Jack shrugged, crushing out his cigarette under his heel. "Just remember, there's no going back."

"Who says I'd want to?" Evelyn shot back, her eyes flashing with defiance.

Before Jack could respond, the faint sound of sirens echoed through the alley, growing louder by the second. Lt. Rebecca Davis stumbled into view, clutching at her shoulder where blood seeped through her bandage and her fingers.

"Rebecca!" Jack rushed forward, concern etched across his face.

"Callahan," she gasped, her breath ragged as she leaned heavily against the wall. "They're onto us. They know about our investigation."

"The whole damn department must be crooked," Jack muttered, his jaw clenched in anger.

"Guess that makes me the odd one out," Rebecca managed, half-smirking despite the pain. "I should've been more careful with my loyalties."

"Never thought I'd see the day," Jack said, his voice thick with disappointment. "An honest cop in this cesspool of a city."

"Save the eulogy for later, Callahan," she snapped. "We need to get out of here, now."

"Alright, let's move," he agreed, sliding an arm around her waist to support her as they stumbled deeper into the shadows.

A door slammed somewhere behind them, and the screech of tires filled the air. Evelyn cast one last look over her shoulder, her expression hardening with resolve. "This isn't the end, Jack. It's just the beginning."

"Let's hope we live long enough to find out," Jack muttered as they disappeared into the darkness, the sirens growing closer.

The sun dipped low over the New Orleans skyline, casting long shadows across the rubble-strewn streets. Finally rain free, the air was thick with the scent of sweat, blood, and determination as people clawed their way through the wreckage, trying to piece their lives back together. Jack stood on a street corner, watching the city begin to rebuild itself, embodying both resilience and sorrow.

"Looks like hell, don't it?" a voice drawled beside him. Jack glanced over to find Slim Malone leaning against a lamppost, a cigarette dangling from his lips.

"New Orleans has seen worse," Jack replied, his eyes never leaving the destruction before him. "City's got a knack for coming back stronger."

"True enough," Malone agreed, taking a drag from his cigarette and blowing out a cloud of smoke. "Still, ain't gonna be easy. Especially with all these crooked cops still in play."

Jack frowned, his gaze flickering to Malone. "What do you plan to do about that?"

"Me?" Malone snorted, a sardonic grin spreading across his face. "Ain't much I can do, Jack. I'm just one honest man in a sea of corruption."

"Maybe," Jack said, his voice hardening. "But now's the time to fight, Slim. The city needs us more than ever."

Malone took another drag of his cigarette, surveying the rebuilding efforts around them. "You know, maybe you're right," he conceded. "I've been playing the game too long, trying to stay afloat in this cesspool. Maybe it's time to stand up and make a difference."

"Good," Jack said, clapping him on the shoulder. "We'll need all the help we can get." They watched as a group of volunteers hauled away a pile of debris, revealing a battered storefront beneath.

"Hey, Jack," Malone said, flicking his cigarette butt into the gutter. "What happened to that lady cop you were working with? Rebecca, was it?"

"Rebecca Davis," Jack confirmed, his jaw clenching at the memory. "She's recovering. Turns out she was one of the few honest ones left."

"Damn shame," Malone muttered, shaking his head. "You two made a good team."

"Maybe we still will," Jack mused, his eyes locked on the slowly rising cityscape before them. "We've got our work cut out for us."

"True enough," Malone agreed, pushing away from the lamppost. "Well, I'll let you get back to your brooding, Jack. Just remember, you ain't in this fight alone."

"Thanks, Slim," Jack said, nodding as Malone walked away. He turned back to the rebuilding city, his heart heavy but determined. It was a new day in New Orleans, and nothing would ever be the same again. A sudden crash echoed through the streets, followed by shouts of panic. Jack tensed, his hand instinctively reaching for his gun. Trouble was never far away in this town.

The smoky tendrils of twilight curled around the ruins of the city like a mournful lover, clinging to the remnants of what once was. Jack stood on the street corner, rain-soaked fedora pulled low on his brow, eyes narrowed in thought. As the shadows lengthened, New Orleans seemed to breathe an uneasy sigh.

"Jack!" A voice pierced the thick air, and he looked up to see Evelyn Marsden approaching, her heels clicking against the pavement like a metronome ticking down to midnight. She held a damp envelope in one gloved hand, the other gripping her purse with white knuckles.

"Didn't expect to see you out here," Jack said, keeping his voice even despite the sudden thud in his chest.

"Thought I'd find you brooding in the shadows." Her lips twisted into a bitter smile that never reached her eyes. "You've got a knack for it."

"Comes with the territory," he replied, inclining his head towards the envelope. "What's got you so riled up?"

"Someone left this in my apartment," she said, thrusting the envelope towards him. "It seems we didn't uncover everything, Jack."

Jack took the envelope, his fingers brushing against hers -

an electric jolt that sent shivers down his spine. He tore open the seal, pulling out a single sheet of paper covered in hurried, jagged handwriting. As he read, his jaw tightened.

"Seems there's still some rats in the walls," he muttered, crumbling the paper in his fist.

"Figured you might want to know," Evelyn said, shifting from one foot to the other, her gaze flickering over his face as if searching for something.

"Thanks," he replied, tucking the crumpled note into his coat pocket. "I'll look into it."

"Jack, I..." Evelyn hesitated, swallowing hard. "I'm leaving New Orleans."

"Leaving?" Jack forced a wry smile. "Finally got sick of the sleaze and grime?"

"Something like that," she admitted, her eyes dark with secrets and sorrow. "Not for good though. Just for a while."

Jack stood in the rain-soaked street, the last echoes of Evelyn's footsteps fading into the night. It wasn't storming. It was more of a constant drizzle this time. The damp air clung to his skin like a shroud, and he drew in a deep breath. He smelled bourbon and cigarette smoke intermingling with the scent of fresh rain on cracked pavement.

"Damn it all," he muttered under his breath, turning away from the alley where she had vanished. His thoughts churned like the muddy waters of the Mississippi, the lingering thread of conspiracy gnawing at him like a rat on a sinking ship.

In that instant, Jack made his decision. He couldn't let the city continue to crumble under the weight of its own sins. He would find the truth, expose the rot for all to see. Maybe then, New Orleans could begin to heal.

"Time to pay my respects," he murmured, adjusting the brim of his fedora as he strode through the rain toward the heart of the city.

The streets teemed with life despite the late hour, mourners and revelers alike crowding the sidewalks. Jack soon found himself outside St. Louis Cathedral, its spires reaching skyward like grasping fingers seeking deliverance from the darkness below.

A hush fell over the crowd gathered inside the candlelit nave, their whispered prayers echoing like sobs among the shadows. Jack took in the faces around him, many worn and haggard from years of hard living, others fresh and innocent, yet tinged with the same desperate hope.

"Here's to you, fallen ones," he muttered, raising an imaginary glass to the flickering candles illuminating the names of the dead. "May your souls find peace, even if this city can't."

"Jack." A voice cut through the silence like a knife, and Jack turned to find himself face-to-face with Rebecca, her eyes rimmed red from tears.

"Rebecca," he replied, his voice low and gruff. "Didn't expect to see you here."

"Neither did I." Her gaze flickered over his face, searching for something. "But we all have our ghosts, don't we?"

"Seems that way," Jack muttered, the weight of his own past heavy on his shoulders.

"Jack, I've made my choices, and I'll live with the consequences." Rebecca swallowed hard, her fingers gripping a rosary so tight her knuckles turned white. "But whatever you're planning, be careful. There's more at stake here than just your own life."

"Thanks for the warning." He sighed, meeting her gaze for a brief moment before turning back to the candles.

"Good luck, Jack," she whispered, her voice barely audible above the rain outside.

"Thanks." He nodded, but as he left the cathedral, he couldn't shake the feeling that luck had long since abandoned New Orleans. The shadows seemed to tighten their grip on the city, a palpable sense of foreboding settling over the streets like a shroud.

The neon sign cast a red glow over Jack's face as he leaned against the brick wall, a cigarette dangling from his lips. The smoke twisted and turned like the thoughts in his head, swirling up into the night sky. It was raining, but not the kind of rain that washed away sins; this was the kind that made it harder to breathe, leaving a heavy dampness hanging in the air.

"Jack," came Rebecca's voice, cutting through the fog of his thoughts. She stepped out of the shadows, wearing her police uniform like an armor that never quite fit. Her eyes were tired but determined, and even in the dim light, they seemed to burn with a restless fire.

"Rebecca," he said, taking a drag from his cigarette. "I didn't think you'd come."

"Didn't think I could let you just walk away without saying goodbye, did ya?" she replied, a hint of a smile tugging at the corner of her mouth.

He shrugged, flicking the ash from his cigarette. He wondered how she knew what he had been considering. "I suppose not."

"Jack, what are you going to do now?" she asked, her tone serious. The rain had plastered her dark hair to her face, but she didn't seem to notice.

"Damned if I know," he muttered, staring down the wet streets that seemed to stretch on forever. "I want to fight. Fight the corruption, the decay from within but, maybe it's time for me to leave this place. Find a new city, one that isn't so full of ghosts."

"New Orleans isn't all bad, Jack," she said softly. "There's still some good here, buried beneath the muck."

"Maybe," he conceded, his eyes scanning the rain-slicked sidewalks. "But the muck's getting pretty deep these days."

"Is there anything I can say to make you stay?" Rebecca asked, a note of desperation creeping into her voice.

"Rebecca, you're the best thing this city's got going for it," he said, finally looking her in the eye. "But I can't answer that...Yet. Stay. Go. Who knows? I'm trying to keep what little sanity I've got left."

"Then I guess this is goodbye," she whispered, her eyes glistening with unshed tears.

"Goodbye, Rebecca," he said, his voice rough, aching with the weight of things left unsaid. The rain was coming down harder now, drowning out the sounds of the city, the hum of the neon sign above them.

"Take care of yourself, Jack Callahan," she said, reaching out and touching his arm. It was a brief, fleeting moment of connection, but one that spoke volumes.

"Same to you, Lieutenant Davis," he replied, taking one last drag of his cigarette before flicking it into a puddle.

And as they parted ways, each walking towards their own uncertain future, the rain continued to fall, washing away the traces of their final meeting, leaving nothing behind but the lingering scent of damp earth and tobacco smoke.

10

The rain fell like daggers, slicing through the thick air as Jack walked away from the alley, his coat collar turned up against the chill. The streetlights cast a faint, sickly glow, making the wet pavement shimmer like spilled oil. He moved through the shadows with the ease of a man who had seen too much darkness, the city's secrets heavy on his brow.

As hot as the spring and summer was in New Orleans, Jack kind of wished they would come sooner. He was tired of all the rain. The city was gloomy enough at night as it was.

"Help me," a voice whispered, barely audible over the patter of the rain. Jack stopped in his tracks, his eyes scanning the dimly lit street for the source of the plea. Huddled beneath a tattered awning, a young woman stood, her face pale and her eyes wide with fear. She clutched a battered suitcase to her chest, as if it were her lifeline.

"Hey, what's the matter?" Jack asked, his tone gruff but not unkind. The woman hesitated, her gaze darting back and forth between him and the shadows beyond.

"Someone's after me," she stammered, her voice cracking with terror. "I don't know what to do."

"Alright, calm down," Jack said, his instincts kicking in. "Let's get you somewhere safe." He offered her his arm, which she took without hesitation, and guided her down the rain-slicked streets.

"Who's chasing you?" he asked, his eyes scanning their surroundings for any sign of danger.

"His name is Mickey O'Sullivan," she replied, her voice trembling. "He works for... someone powerful. I stole something from him, and now he wants it back."

"Ah, one of the city's many bottom-feeders," Jack mused,

his grip on his gun tightening. "Don't worry, I've dealt with his type before."

"Thank you," she whispered, her eyes full of gratitude. A faint blush crept into her cheeks, and for a moment, Jack saw the ghost of a smile.

"Name's Jack," he said, tipping his hat in a brief gesture of gallantry. "Jack Callahan."

"Grace," she replied, her voice steadier than before. "Grace LeClair."

As they walked together, something stirred within Jack - a feeling he hadn't experienced in years. It was as if a door had opened, ever so slightly, revealing the possibility of something more than the cold, lonely existence he had come to know.

"Once we've shaken off your pursuer, Grace," Jack said, determination in his voice, "maybe you and I could grab a cup of coffee. You know, when things settle down."

"I'd like that, Jack," she replied, a genuine smile playing at the corners of her lips.

Suddenly, in the distance, a gunshot rang out in the night, shattering the fragile peace. Jack pushed Grace behind him, drawing his gun in one fluid motion. The city's shadows seemed to close in around them, hiding the unseen threat.

"Stay close," he warned her, his voice low and urgent. "We're not out of the woods yet."

The streets of New Orleans were slick with rain, the neon lights reflecting off the wet pavement like a twisted carnival. Jack, his eyes scanning for danger, kept Grace close as they navigated through the damp shadows. The air was thick, heavy with the scent of stale cigarettes and sins left unspoken.

"Looks like you've made yourself quite popular around these parts," Jack quipped, glancing at Grace's worried expression. "Seems to be a pattern in this city."

Grace grimaced, her gaze darting between the dark alleyways. "Evelyn Marsden is back and has been shaking things up lately. She's got half the town on edge."

"Ah, Evelyn," Jack mused, memories of the femme fatale flickering through his mind like scenes from an old movie. "Haven't seen her in a while. What's she got herself into now?"

"Word is she's working with the new mayor," Grace said, her voice trembling. "Trying to clean up this place, but she's stirring up more trouble than good, it seems."

"Cleaning up New Orleans," Jack scoffed, a bitter laugh escaping his lips. "Now there's a lost cause if I ever heard one."

"Maybe, but people are taking notice," Grace insisted. "Even if it's just making the rats scurry out of their holes."

"Rats have a nasty habit of biting back," Jack replied, his hand gripping his gun beneath his coat. They turned a corner, and he caught sight of a figure lurking in the shadows, watching them intently. "Speaking of which..."

"Who is that?" Grace whispered, fear evident in her eyes.

"An old acquaintance," Jack muttered, tensing as the figure approached. "Just can't shake some people."

"Remember me, Jack?"

The voice was all too familiar. It belonged to Vincent, a man he had crossed paths with during the war. They hadn't parted on good terms; in fact, the last time they saw each other, Callahan had left him for dead in the trenches.

"Vincent?" Jack muttered.

"Surprised?" The man stepped out of the shadows. "You should be. You thought I was dead, didn't you?"

"Can't say I'm happy to see you." Jack's hand inside his jacket tightened around his pistol grip.

"Neither am I, Jack," Vincent snarled, his eyes flashing dangerously. "But here we are."

Jack shook his head, trying to make sense of the situation. He couldn't help but wonder if Vincent was a real threat or just another pawn in a twisted game. The weight of the gun in his hand was both a comfort and a burden, reminding him of the lives he'd taken and the lines he'd crossed.

"Look, Vincent," Jack said, his voice cracking with exhaustion. "I don't know what you want, but let's not do this dance again."

"Too late for that, old friend," Vincent sneered, waving his knife. "You made your choice back in the trenches. Now it's time to pay."

As the two men circled each other, Jack's thoughts raced. He knew he couldn't trust Vincent, but he also knew that killing him wouldn't solve anything. The city was a cesspool of corruption, and if Vincent wasn't the mastermind behind it all, someone else was. Jack had lost too many allies to keep fighting this battle alone.

"Vincent," he said, lowering his hand slightly. "We've both been through this. We don't need to be enemies."

"Nice try, Jack," Vincent spat. "But I'm not falling for your tricks again."

"Damn it, Vincent!" Jack shouted, his frustration boiling over. "We can either kill each other here in the street or we can live to see if it get's any better around here!"

For a moment, the rain seemed to drown out everything else, leaving Jack and Vincent locked in a silent standoff. Then Vincent lowered his knife, a bitter laugh escaping his lips.

"Fine," he growled, sheathing his weapon. "It was a long time ago and we both had been in the wine. Let's agree to not try and kill each other again."

"Deal," Jack replied, holstering his gun. "Besides, you brought a knife to a gun fight. This isn't like the last time when we both held a bayonet."

Vincent raised an eyebrow. He had not noticed that Jack hadn't pulled what he had under his coat out yet. The expression on his face revealed he now knew it wasn't a blade.

"You're still playing the hero, I see."

"Wouldn't be me if I didn't," Jack shot back, his eyes narrowing. "What do you want, Vincent?"

"Thought you might like to know your old pal Evelyn's been stirring up more than just trouble," Vincent said, a malicious grin spreading across his face. "She's got something big planned, and it's gonna change things forever."

"Empty threats and vague predictions," Jack retorted, unimpressed. "You'll have to do better than that, Vincent."

Vincent chuckled, stepping back into the shadows. "Just remember, Callahan, in this city, there's no such thing as a clean slate. And when the next storm hits, don't say I didn't warn you."

As Vincent vanished into the darkness, Jack felt a shiver run down his spine, though he refused to show it. The haunting words echoed in his mind, leaving him with an uneasy feeling that lingered long after the sinister figure had disappeared.

"Jack?" Grace asked, her voice wavering. "Do you think he's telling the truth?"

"Hard to say," Jack admitted, his jaw clenched. "But one

thing's for sure - in New Orleans, the shadows never sleep. We're not out of the woods yet."

"Will we ever be?"

"No," he said.

Epilogue

Jack's '32 Ford rumbled through the dark night, its wheels screeching on the wet cobblestones of the French Quarter. Yellow halos surrounded the streetlights that cast dim shadows across his tired, unshaven face. Few people braved the cold rain, leaving the sidewalks empty of all but the locals, barren streets that seemed like a fitting metaphor for the desolation within his soul.

"Can't run from yourself, Jack," he muttered under his breath, taking a swig from the battered flask that had seen him through many a rough night. The bitter taste of cheap whiskey burned his throat, but it was a familiar pain, one he'd come to embrace as part and parcel of the life he'd chosen. Turning right, he pulled to a stop down the block from Prima's Shim Sham Club at 229 Bourbon Street. Normally he couldn't get near the place, even after 1:00 a.m., but that night only the hardest core roamed the streets.

His thoughts drifted back to Rebecca, her tear-streaked face haunting him like a specter. She'd begged him not to leave her, but Jack knew he was no hero, just a man with too much blood on his hands, seeking redemption in a world that offered none. She was better off without him.

"Maybe she'll find someone better," he mused, allowing himself the tiniest flicker of hope for her future. "Someone who can make her happy."

Riley the Bartender looked up as Jack came in. So did a woman drinking alone at a nearby table.

"Where are you headed?" she asked from across the aisle, her green eyes filled with curiosity. She was young, beautiful, and not unlike a certain femme fatale who'd once stolen Jack's heart. She'd steal his heart too... for the right price.

"Yeah," Riley said. "What she said. I heard you was leavin'."

"I was. Now I'm not."

"No?"

"When you've got New Orleans in your blood, you can't ever leave. Tried another place once. Spent a few years in the Windy City. It wasn't the same."

Riley nodded, like that made perfect sense. "Your partner's in the back, the usual table."

Jack pointed with his thumb. "I'm headed back there," he said to the young woman, pausing to realize that whatever her profession might be, she really was good looking. *Damned good looking.* He added, "for tonight. Catch me some other time. I'm here every night."

"*Every* night?"

"Mostly, yeah. Some nights a grab a bite at that new place, Mother's, but then I come on over."

"I'll make that a point," she said.

The End

In the shadow-drenched alleyways of 1938 New Orleans, skeptical private investigator Lane Walsh is thrust into a twilight world of cults, spectral entities, and dark omens, where his pursuit of answers entwines his fate with the supernatural, challenging not only his firmly-held beliefs but also the very fabric of his being.

BLUES, BOOZE AND BULLETS

A Delta Private Investigations Book

WILLIAM ALAN WEBB

And

KEVIN STEVERSON

BLUES, BOOZE AND BULLETS
Copyright © 2023 by William Alan Webb and Kevin Steverson

All rights reserved. No part of this book may be reproduced in any form or by any means without written consent, excepting brief quotes used in reviews.

This book is licensed to the original purchaser only. Duplication or distribution via any means is illegal and a violation of International Copyright Law, subject to criminal prosecution and upon conviction, fines and/or imprisonment. No part of this book can be reproduced or sold by any person or business without the express permission of the publisher.

Thank you for respecting the hard work of these authors.

This is a work of fiction. Names, places, characters, and events are entirely the produce of the author's imagination or are used fictitiously, and any resemblance to persons living or dead, actual locations, events, or organizations is coincidental

1

Rain spat against the windows with a vengeance that suggested personal animosity, while Lane Walsh leaned back in his chair, feet propped up on the desk. He glanced at the clock on the wall... ten to four. The afternoon was crawling by like a drunk snail. He fingered the cigarette between his lips and lit it, taking a long drag. New Orleans in 1938 was a city of smoke, jazz, and secrets, and he knew them all. The problem was nobody wanted to pay for them.

Delta Private Investigations wasn't exactly a five-star establishment, but most of the time it paid the bills. Lane shared the cramped office with his partner Jack Callahan, a man who could've been mistaken for a rhinoceros if you squinted just right. But damn, he was good at what he did.

The door to the office slammed open, startling Lane from his musings. A woman hurried inside, her hat askew, her coat shedding rainwater on their floor. She was distraught, her eyes wide like a rabbit caught in headlights.

"We need to get a secretary," Lane said to Callahan.

"You going to pay her salary?"

The woman spread her hands like a preacher asking for a tithe. Lane recognized her as Clara Redwood, a face and name that had laid cash on their desks more than once.

"Mr. Walsh, you have to help me," she said, hands coming together in supplication. "It's my husband, Claude. He's vanished into thin air."

"Again, Clara?" Lane said.

"No, this time he *vanished*."

"Vanished?" Lane asked, lifting an eyebrow. He dragged on his cigarette, blowing out a plume of smoke. "Sounds like a magic trick gone wrong."

Across the room, Callahan's eyebrow arched in a silent gesture that screamed *knock it off, we need her money!* Clara didn't seem to notice, her voice quivering as she described bizarre, shadowy figures and attempted abductions reported by her now-missing husband.

"Where was he last seen?"

"I don't know."

Based on previous work they'd done for the high-strung Clara Redwood, mostly also involving Claude having gone missing, her husband had likely gone off on a prolonged bender to forget the biggest mistake of his life, namely marrying Clara. She was the kind of woman that could break any man's heart... an intricate and delicate beauty, masked behind her gaudy façade. Too much makeup caked her face, and she wore jewelry that glittered and sparkled like diamonds embedded in ice, but which Lane strongly doubted were real. As glamorous as she appeared, it only served to mask what lay beneath the surface, rather than flaunt it. The whole package screamed 'problem.'

"Please, Mr. Walsh, something's not right. People are disappearing left and right. It's like they're being swallowed by the darkness itself."

"People?"

She nodded. A single blonde curl escaped a flat-brimmed hat tilted to one side, concealing part of her left eye and ear. "Yes, people," she replied, completely missing Lane's sarcasm.

"Swallowed by darkness, huh?" Lane mused, tapping ash into the tray on his desk. "Sounds like the kind of case you'd find in one of those cheap detective novels."

"Mr. Walsh, this isn't a joke," Clara cried, her desperation nearly palpable. "I don't know who else to turn to."

Lane studied her for a moment, weighing his options. The phone book had dozens of PIs listed, but business had been slack lately, and they certainly needed the money. And while he wasn't a man to shy away from the inexplicable, shadowy abductions sounded like something out of a dime store pulp. Still, there was something about the raw terror in her eyes that tugged at a buried part of him, the part that wanted to help those in need. At least, that's what he told himself. Lane also knew from experience that Clara Redwood paid cash.

In advance.

"Alright, Mrs. Redwood," he said, stubbing out his cigarette. "I'll look into it. But I can't make any promises. If you're expecting miracles, you've come to the wrong place." "

"Thank you, Mr. Walsh," she breathed, relief washing over her face. She reached for her purse.

"How much do you need?"

"This could take a while."

"Is two hundred dollars enough?"

Across the office, Jack Callahan nearly choked.

Lane reached across the desk and took the offered cash from her trembling hands. "That will be fine," he said, not having to force a grin. The scent of desperation hung heavy in the air, but money had a way of making it more tolerable. "Tell me everything you know about Claude's disappearance, every detail. Don't leave anything out."

As Clara told her tale, Lane took notes with a stubby pencil, asking questions until he was satisfied with her answer. When finished, he flipped the notebook closed and slid it into the inside pocket of his brown suit coat.

"I'll call you with what I turn up. I believe we still have your number."

As Clara left the office, Jack sauntered over to Lane's desk, looking as unconvinced as before.

"That woman is trouble," Jack said. "Expensive trouble. Her answers were gibberish."

"Two hundred dollars can buy a lot of better answers, Jacky," Lane said with a wry grin. "Or at least, they can buy the right questions."

"Whatever you say," Jack replied, shaking his head. "I just hope you know what you're getting yourself into."

"Since when have I ever known that?" Lane retorted, rifling through the mess on his desk for any the keys to his car. "But hey, isn't that what makes life interesting?"

"But shadowy abductions?" he asked, sneering. "Last I heard you hate that kind of thing. You don't believe her, do you?"

"I believe in Ben Franklin," Lane said, pulling another cigarette from the pack. "Especially when he's twins."

Jack lit a smoke of his own. "At least we can eat meat this week."

"To answer your question, no, I don't believe the bit about

shadows and vanishing into thin air. If I had to guess, I'd say Claude either took off with a waitress or got mugged looking for one. But even the strangest tales have a kernel of truth. And if there's something going on—"

"What's going on is that Claude Redwood took a powder."

"If something *is* going on," Lane repeated, "we're gonna find it."

He struck a match and lit his cigarette, inhaling deeply before exhaling the smoke. Outside, the rain continued to pour, as if mourning the city's lost souls. So much water was unusual for New Orleans, and Lane couldn't shake the feeling that they were about to stumble onto something big, something lurking just beneath the surface.

"Let's get to work," he said, determination creeping into his voice. "We've got shadows to chase."

"Not we, *you*. I'm meeting a client in half an hour, remember?"

"I forgot. Me then."

"You sticking around or going home?"

"Sticking around. I'm going to see what I can dig up on Claude Redwood."

A thin layer of dust covered the top of the office's only file cabinet. Lane rifled through the archives to find the folder marked *Redwood, Clara*. His eye caught the emergency bottle of Bacardi stashed in the corner. The seal was cracked and it was three fingers light. A dollar bill underneath allowed for them to buy more real Bacardi, not the fake label stuff that most people drank. There were two things he and Jack never skimped on: booze and bullets. Coffee came in a close third. Their only disagreement came over music; Jack was a Jazz man, while Lane loved the Blues.

Temptation made him lick his lips, but the sooner he found Claude Redwood, the sooner he could feel right about pocketing Clara's two hundred bucks. Whether it was a lot of money to her or not, that kind of cash bought damned near three weeks of his time, and while it might have been good for business, Lane wasn't as crooked as people believed.

Angling the desk lamp to shine against encroaching night, Lane opened the file in its glaring puddle of light. By reflex he stuck a cigarette in his mouth, flicking the Zippo lighter given him by a grateful client.

Two hours later the smoke had still not been lit, as Lane stared at the same few pages over and over again. Something didn't add up. Claude Redwood had some lousy habits for sure, from gambling to working girls, any of which could have led to him leaving New Orleans to restart his life somewhere else.

Snapped out of his reverie by the office door opening. It was Jack Callahan.

"I was driving by and saw the light on. You had supper?"

Lane shook his head. "Not hungry. I thought you were working a case."

"I'm done for the night. Go home, Lane. Or better yet, let's go to that new place, Mother's. It's some fine eatin'."

"They're still open?"

"Pretty sure, yeah."

"You go on, I might catch up later. I'm gonna go through the old newspapers."

Stacked in a corner was six months of unread local papers, a subscription in the name of Delta Private Investigations for 'research.' Mostly, they did the crossword puzzles.

"Sure. See you there."

Jack left. Lane spun the wheel on the Zippo and lit the Lucky Strike. Then he plunged into scanning the newspapers.

It didn't take long for his practiced eye to pick up on an unsettling thread. Over the past few years, there'd been a handful of other missing persons cases, all of them seemingly unconnected, yet bearing striking similarities to Clara's husband's disappearance. At first glance, they were just your garden-variety runaways and lost souls, but as Lane read between the lines, something darker began to emerge.

"Hey Jacky, take a gander at this," he said, forgetting that Jack left. Instead, he scribbled a note and tossed it onto Callahan's desk along with the newspapers in question.

I think we might have company, the note read.

He didn't need to hear Jack's response in person, though. They'd gone through the trenches of France together, and been inseparable ever since.

"Company?" Callahan said, raising an eyebrow as he flipped through the pages. "You mean to tell me there's more of these shadow-grabbers running around?"

"Could be," Lane mused.

"Right, and I'm the mayor of this fair city," Callahan snorted, tossing the papers back onto Lane's desk. "But if you're right, and there is something going on, what do we do about it?"

"First things first," Lane said out loud, as if Jack was in the room. Grabbing his hat, Lane headed for the door. "We follow the shadows."

Opening the middle desk drawer, his finger brushed the P08 Luger, but grabbed the 1911 Colt .45 instead. If war taught him anything, it was the value of stopping power. He and Jack had connections for a lot of things, one of them being US Army issue ammunition. If Lane had to use the gun, he wanted to be judged by twelve, not carried by six.

The night air was thick with fog and the stench of stale booze, sweat, and sin, which the recent rains had done little to wash away. As Lane Walsh made his way through the twisted streets of 1938 New Orleans, he felt like a moth, charmed and cursed in the same sputtering flicker of a deceptive flame. Something drew him deeper into what was becoming more than he'd bargained for. He'd spent the better part of the day tracking down families affected by these strange vanishings, and each new tale only served to deepen the shadows that clung to the case.

Driving to his next appointment, he rolled up his windows against the strong odors coming from the Thompson-Hayward Chemical Company, one of the chief employers in Gert Town. Fifteen minutes later he stopped at the address jotted in his notebook.

"Mrs. Dupont?" he asked, as a weary woman in her late forties opened the door to a dilapidated house. Her eyes were rimmed in red, the dull ache of loss etched into her face. She's probably once been pretty, but life and loss had taken their toll.

"Y-yes," she stammered, clutching a handkerchief.

"Name's Lane Walsh, ma'am." He passed her a business card. "I'm a private investigator looking into some recent disappearances. May I have a moment of your time?"

"O' course, Mr. Walsh," she replied, leading him into a dimly lit sitting room. Her voice had a typically thick Louisiana lilt. The air inside was heavy with grief and the smell of old cigar smoke.

"Your son, Tommy, vanished last month, right?" Lane asked, scanning the room for any hint of the boy.

"Tommy... my sweet boy." A tear rolled down Mrs. Dupont's cheek. "He went down to Gehrke's one evenin' and never came back. Neighbors said they saw shadows movin' strangely around him before he disappeared. I went out lookin' for him myself, I found nothin' but more questions."

The last came out as *Ah foun nuttin' but mo' questions.*

"Shadows, huh?" Lane mused, tapping a finger against his chin. It wasn't the first time he'd heard the word 'shadows' that day. "How about you, ma'am? You ever see anything... unusual?"

"Nothin' concrete," she murmured. "Just glimpses of dark figures in the corner of my eye, you know what I mean? Whispers in the middle of the night, that sort of thing. I thought it was just grief playing tricks on me, but..."

"Tell me about Tommy."

Mrs. Dupont related the story of a thousand teenage boys like Tommy. Bert City crushed souls, including those of its children. Tommy hung out down at Gehrke's General Store, like most of the locals, but soon fell in way a bad crowd.

"Haitians," she said, "you know 'em right off, with their damned accents and weird way of talkin'. They got their own creole language, don't you know? Not like Americans, different, you can't hardly understand anything they is sayin."

"Haitians," he said, writing it down in the notebook. It wasn't the first time he'd heard that word, either.

"Thank you, Mrs. Dupont," Lane interrupted, not wanting to let her dwell too long on the pain. "I'll do everything I can to find out what happened to your boy."

"You will?"

"Yes Ma'am."

"Forgive my askin', Mr. Walsh, but... why? Why you do that for me?"

Good question.

"I'm working another case, Ma'am, one with some similarities to your Tommy's disappearance. If I can find an answer for you, I will. But Mrs. Walsh, I have to warn you, in my experience these things don't often end well. I'm not trying to scare you–"

She reached over and touched his wrist. "God be with you, Mr. Walsh," she whispered, her voice barely audible over the distant wail of a saxophone. Nodding to the back, she added, "my husband George."

"Tommy's father?"

"No. George is my third husband."

She walked him to the door. He stepped back into the murky night.

Lane stopped by a few more homes during the indefinite period when period got home from work, and before they had to turn in to begin the grind all over again. Each bore the same haunted expressions and whispers of shadowy figures. The stories were starting to wear on him, like ice water dripping down his spine, but he couldn't let it show. He was supposed to be the tough guy, the one who could stare down the barrel of a gun without flinching. At least, that was the reputation of Delta Private Investigations, *Tough Guys for the Tough Cases.*

"Hey, Walsh!" a voice barked from behind him. Lane turned to see Detective James Barnett leaning against a lamppost, a sneer plastered across his face. Under the harsh glare of the streetlight, the beefy cop looked like a dime-store gangster caught in the harsh prologue of a forgotten tragedy, his contours throwing hard-edged shadows on the pavement as the dim glow painted him in greys and stark whites, crafting a specter of disillusionment amid the heavy night. His eyes, cold and distant, betrayed tales of once-trusted ideals soured by too many nights wading through the city's unbridled corruption, and now, they were little more than bitter echoes trapped in a hulking frame that teetered on the brink of melancholy and menace. "What brings you to this side of town, huh? Looking for a stiff drink or a good time?"

"Neither, Barnett," Lane shot back, his eyes narrowing. Barnett wasn't the worst cop on the NOPD, but Lane preferred not to trust him too far, either. "I'm working a case. Missing persons."

"Really?" Barnett said, pushing away from the lamppost and sauntering closer. "I heard something about that. What makes these so special?"

"You heard?"

"Word gets around."

Huh.

"Shadowy figures, sudden vanishings," Lane replied, watching as Barnett's smirk faltered for a moment before returning in full force.

"Ah, so you're chasing ghosts now? That's cute, Walsh. Real cute."

"Maybe I am," Lane said, his voice steady. "How'd you know where I was?"

"Pure coincidence."

"I don't believe in coincidence."

"Too bad."

"I'm gonna find out what's going on, Barnett. You'd better believe I am."

"Good luck with that," Barnett snorted, walking away. "You'll need it."

"Thanks. I always appreciate a little encouragement from those whose job I'm doing for them."

Barnett waved over his shoulder, vanishing into the night shadows.

Vanishing...shadows.

The fog seemed to thicken, swallowing the streetlamps' feeble glow as Lane stared into the darkness. He couldn't shake the feeling that he was being watched, but every time he turned to look, there was nothing there.

As always happened, Lane Walsh found himself back in the French Quarter. Dampness clung like a second skin as he strolled down Decatur Street toward Café Du Monde, his footsteps echoing off the cobblestones. Instead of whiskey, what he needed most was coffee and time to think. A stray cat slunk into an alleyway, its eyes glowing with suspicion and hunger. Neon signs flickered overhead, casting a sickly glow on the empty streets.

"Damn phantoms," Lane muttered, shoving his hands deeper into his trench coat pockets. "It's just shadows and light playing tricks, that's all it is."

As if in response, a sudden movement caught his eye – an unexpected shadow danced at the edge of his peripheral vision. He turned sharply, heart pounding, but saw only an empty street corner, bathed in the dim light of a nearby lamp.

"Evenin', Lane," a familiar voice called from behind him. Lane spun around, hand instinctively reaching inside his coat for the Colt, before recognizing the greasy smile of Benny, the local newsstand owner.

"Jesus, Benny, don't sneak up on a man like that," Lane snapped, his pulse racing.

"Sorry, boss," Benny said, holding up his hands defensively. "Didn't mean to startle ya."

"Never mind," Lane sighed. "What do you want?"

"I heard you was pokin' around. Thought you might be interested in this," Benny said, producing a crumpled newspaper from his pocket. The headline screamed about another mysterious disappearance. "Seems like there's something goin' on in this city of ours. Real spooky stuff."

"Spooky how?"

"People vanishing. That ain't normal. Anyway, I thought maybe you'd want to know."

"Hey, how'd you know I would be here?"

Benny shrugged as he ambled back toward his newsstand, leaving Lane with his question unanswered.

Lane scanned the article, feeling a chill creep down his spine as he read about yet another lost soul. He shook off the sensation, attributing it to stress and the psychological impact of the tales he'd been hearing all day.

"Shadows don't snatch people off the street," he called into the darkness after Benny. Crumpling the paper he tossed it into a nearby trash can. "There's gotta be a logical explanation for all this."

"Logical explanations?" a voice whispered from the shadows, sending a shiver through Lane's body. "You won't find them here, Mr. Walsh."

"Who's there?" Lane demanded, laying a hand on the Colt while scanning his surroundings. The street was empty, the whisper nothing more than a memory carried away on the wind. With a frustrated growl, Lane released his weapon and stalked toward Café du Monde. Beignets weren't much of a dinner, but powdered sugar and strong coffee would keep him going a while longer.

Mosquitoes swirled around his face as Lane Walsh approached the last known location of Clara's husband—the corner of St. Ann and Chartres Street. Approaching midnight under leaden skies made the French Quarter feel like a forgotten graveyard, its ghostly inhabitants lurking just out of sight. A light rain began to fall.

Lane pulled his trench coat tighter around him, shivering from an unsettling chill that had nothing to do with the weather. As he reached the shadowy corner, Lane sensed something *off* about the place. Several lamposts were not shining. No doubt their bulbs had burned out. Yet it was as though the inky darkness itself radiated an eerie menace, causing the hairs on the back of his neck to stand at attention. He shook off the feeling, reminding himself that it was the cold, hard facts that Jackered—not some half-baked supernatural hokum.

"Alright, Mr. Redwood," he said, "let's see if you left any breadcrumbs for ol' Lane Walsh to follow."

He scanned the area, noting the shuttered storefronts and barred windows for signs of anything unusual. The wind seemed to whisper secrets as it danced through the narrow alleys. More than once he turned to see if somebody had spoken.

"Get a grip, Walsh. You're turning into one of those loony spiritualists," he chided himself. But even as he tried to focus, the shadows cast by the flickering streetlights seemed to twitch and weave unnaturally. Alone in the night, with even late-night revelers inside against the rain, Lane couldn't help but recall the chilling consistency in the tales he'd heard, of shadowy figures and sudden vanishings.

"Hey, mister!" a voice called out, making Lane jump despite himself. An elderly man stood nearby, leaning on a cane and eyeing him with curiosity. Shabby clothes and deep eye sockets marked him as a wino. "You lookin' for somethin'?"

"Maybe," Lane replied cautiously, his heart rate slowing as he recognized the man as human—not some otherworldly specter. "You seen anything unusual around here lately?"

"Unusual?" The old man scratched his head, considering the question. "Well, there was that fella who disappeared last week. Just up and vanished into thin air. That's pretty unusual, I'd say."

"Vanished, you say?" Lane couldn't help the shiver that ran down his spine. Despite his determination to cling to logical explanations, it seemed fate was determined to test his resolve.

"Yep," the old man confirmed, nodding sagely. "Like he stepped off the edge of the world or somethin'. Real strange, if you ask me."

"Strange indeed," Lane muttered, his eyes drawn once more to the unnerving shadows. Desperately clinging to logic, he knew he had no choice but to follow the trail, wherever it might lead. With a nod of thanks to the old man, he ventured further into the darkness, his every step weighed down by the growing dread gnawing at his gut.

"Could you maybe spare a dime for a guy down on his luck?"

"What else can you tell me about the missing man?"

"Just what I heard."

"Heard from who?"

"Huh?"

"If you didn't see the man for yourself, who told you he vanished without a trace?"

"Oh, I see what you mean. One 'o them fellas out o' the Caribbean... Jamaican, Haitian... yeah, Haitian I'd say."

"Thanks." Lane dug two nickels out of his pocket and handed them to the man.

"You be takin' care, Mister. They's been some odd stuff in the Quarter lately."

"It's the Quarter," Lane said, "odd things are normal."

Rare cold weather brought with it lingering rains. The chill seeped through his trench coat as he prowled deeper into the alley where Clara Redwood's husband had last been seen. His shoes splashed in murky puddles, their echoes swallowed by the narrow passage.

He should have brought a flashlight. There was one in his car, but that was three blocks away. The darkness seemed to thicken around him, suffocating the faint glow of the streetlights at either end of the alley. A soft whisper rustled through the air, momentarily freezing Lane in his tracks. It sounded like a woman's voice, pleading for help. Then it stopped, leaving the investigator doubting his own senses. He continued his slow march deeper into the shadowy corridor, his eyes scanning for any sign of Clara's missing spouse. Black doorways lined both sides of the ancient brick buildings that flanked the alley. As he walked, the whispers returned, more insistent this time. They swirled around him like vengeful spirits, their cries piercing the relentless drumbeat of the rain.

"Please, someone help us..."
"Where did they take him?"
"Who will save us now?"

Lane gritted his teeth, cursing the desperate edge these voices had given his thoughts. He fought against the creeping tide of doubt that threatened to consume him, clinging to logic like a drowning man grasps for a lifeline.

"Alright, enough!" he barked, his voice cracking with a mix of anger and fear. "There's no one here but me and my own damn imagination. Now, shut up and let me work!"

The whispers fell silent, leaving only the faint scurryies of rats to fill the void. Lane focused on his breathing, willing himself to regain control over his fraying nerves. He knew there had to be a rational explanation for these disappearances, some common thread that would lead him to the truth. But as he stood there, soaked to the bone and shivering, the whispers returned, more menacing than ever. They clawed their way through his carefully constructed defenses, leaving a chilling seed of doubt buried deep within his soul.

"Who are we, Mr. Walsh? What do we want?"
"Perhaps you'll join us soon."
"Only time will tell..."

The voices faded once more into the night. As much as he

tried to deny it, something about this case defied logic, taunting him with its eerie ambiguity. And in that moment, he knew he could no longer dismiss the shadows as mere figments of his imagination.

"God help me," he whispered.

"Bondye te abandone w, mesye Walsh."

Lane froze. He knew enough creole to recognize the words had a difference; it was Haitian Creole. Worse, he understood them.

"God has forsaken you, Mister Walsh."

2

The next morning, Lane's hangover came from too much coffee and too little sleep, not too much alcohol. Any other day he would have slept it off. Instead, he showered, brushed his teeth and put on a clean shirt and suit. The other ones needed cleaning after a night of being soaked by the rain.

After a breakfast of eggs, bacon, toast, grits, tomato juice and coffee at the Vieux Carré Café, he dropped the still-wet shirt and suit at a dry cleaner and headed for NOPD headquarters. A request for the case files for the various missing persons cases met with a stony face from Sergeant Touissant at the front desk. Lane knew the expression didn't mean 'no', it meant 'what's it worth to you?' A five-dollar handshake later Lane had what he needed. Touissant pointed him to an empty interrogation room, since the files could not leave the premises.

The dim room smelled of stale smoke and lost hope, a haze of tobacco fumes lingering like ghosts in the air. A dented metal ashtray overflowed with cigarette butts, a few of which had lipstick. Walsh adjusted a long-necked lamp and hunched over the stack of police reports. The only sound was the faint tick of his wristwatch and the occasional turn of a page.

What he found was not what he'd expected. The reports all had strange drawings in them, near the last known location of the missing person. He hadn't known to look for signs in the alley where Claude Redwood disappeared, and made a note to return in daylight to look for them.

For now, the eerie symbols he traced with his finger had an unnerving effect. Any native of New Orleans would recognize them as Voodoo symbols. And one name came up over and over again: a self-styled Haitian Voodoo Priest named Papa Ghana, who had strong ties to the city's criminal underbelly. His organization was one Lane had heard of, but never encountered.

"Head of the Mas Nwa, huh?" Lane said, raising an eyebrow. "And Voodoo to boot."

There were other files to go through, but Lane had read enough. Restless, he handed them back to Touissant, and asked to use the phone.

"God a nickel?" Toussiant asked.

Fishing in his pocket, Lane held up a coin. Touissant pointed at the door.

"There's a pay phone in the hall."

Vivian Moore was at home. She told Lane to come on over.

During the drive, his methodical, rational mind fought against the cryptic, seemingly supernatural clues left behind. What had begun as a simple husband-run-away case, was growing into some much bigger.

Memories of childhood encounters with the occult and horrors witnessed on the battlefields in France during World War One gnawed at him, threatening to erode his skepticism. Lane recalled his numerous friends entwined with the alternate religions of the city, like Vivian Moore, the enigmatic Voodoo priestess who always seemed to know more than she let on. He usually avoided seeing her because she made him feel naked, as if she could read his mind. Lane did not like the feeling.

The day had a freshness after the rains. He heard the low murmur of jazz music drifting from the open windows of local bars on Royal Street. The unseen undercurrents of The City That Care Forgot whispered their secrets as he drew closer to Vivian's place. Old steps led to the door of Moore's shop, *Vwal & Veso: Founiti Vodou ak Mistik*, filled with potions, roots, icons, and anything else needed to practice Voodoo.

As he arrived at Vivian's door, he hesitated. He couldn't help but wonder if he was about to take a step into darkness from which there'd be no return. But without taking risks, answers would remain forever out of reach. She opened the door before he could knock.

"You late, Mister Walsh," she said, drawing out the word 'Mister.' Her Haitian accent sounded thicker than the last time he'd heard it.

"Now I'm *Mister Walsh*?"

She grinned. Perfect white teeth centered between a petite nose and high cheekbones reminded Lane of earlier time.

"You here as a client?"

"I'd prefer to be here as an old friend."

"Me too, but you didn't answer my question. Don't Jacker one. You are also late."

"I drove here as fast as I could."

"You was expected yesterday. Come in."

Lane didn't know what to say, so he stepped into the small foyer. To his right was the door to her shop. Directly ahead was a flight of stairs that led to Moore's personal apartment. He knew that because he'd climbed those stairs more than once. She went first.

"How could you expect me yesterday?"

"Do you forget who I am?"

"Oh, right. The reincarnation of Marie Laveau."

"Not 'xactly correct, but not 'xactly wrong, neither."

Like most people from New Orleans, Vivian left the 'h' silent so that 'neither' came out as 'neatuh.'

The doorway of her apartment had numerous signs and sigils around the frame. Much had changed since the last time he'd crossed that portal.

The living room beyond bore the essence of another world, shrouded in mystery and veiled in a haze of frankincense that hung in the dimly lit space. Vivian spent a moment lighting candles throughout the room, leaving Lane to wonder how she'd managed to so far avoid setting fire to the whole building. Tethered to the tangible yet beckoning to the ethereal, every nook seemed to cradle shadows that fluttered with murmurs of long-passed spirits and forsaken souls. The walls, an eclectic tapestry of time-worn charms and cryptic symbols, ensnared his gaze, leading it to an altar intricately adorned with candles flickering like lonesome stars in a forlorn sky, their light caressing the contours of sacred figurines and vials of enigmatic concoctions. Dried herbs and curious artifacts dangled from the ceiling, creating a spectral canopy beneath which the Priestess navigated her sacred, spectral ballet. On a modest table, a skull gazed through vacant sockets toward a future it would never see, beside a worn deck of cards, perpetually poised to unveil destinies yet unwritten. The air, thick with the mingling scents of herbs and a perpetual, melancholy resonance, seemed to pulse with the energies of realms unseen, forever ensnaring the apartment in a timeless embrace between the earthly and the divine.

Vivian Moore was really good at setting the mood for her clients. Removing the light robe she wore over tight pants and a sleeveless shirt, Vivian sat on a plush couch while Lane took a chair. Both lit up cigarettes.

"I *am* glad you are here, Lane. I hoped you would come. You are in danger."

"Yeah?"

"Yes. Moore's smile faded, replaced by a solemn expression. "You're not the first man to come asking about them."

"Them?" Lane raised an eyebrow. "Them who?"

She laughed softly. "You know who. You just didn't say the words."

"Alright Viv, then what's the skinny on these bogeymen?"

"Many have sought their secrets, Mr. Walsh. Few return with answers, and even fewer with their sanity."

"Sounds like my kind of party," Lane said, smirking. "So, you gonna tell me who beat me here?

"Silver Dollar Sam Carollo was here. One o' his men go missing," she said, the words seeping into his consciousness, unwelcome but impossible to ignore. "You might want to talk to him."

"Carollo and I ain't exactly bosom buddies" Lane said. "But why did he come to you?"

"The same reason you did."

"Reading my mind again?"

Her smirk accented high cheekbones. "The mind of a man is easy to read, they always thinking of the same thing." The smirk faded. "But this time, yeah, Carollo have same questions as my beautiful Lane do."

"You know, Viv, sometimes you give me the creeps."

"And the other times? What do I give you then?"

As much as he wanted to, rather than pursue that path Lane swung the conversation back to business.

"Carollo was looking for a missing man, and so am I. You said you knew why I was here, so tell me what you think you know and I'll fill in the rest."

"Voodoo. You here to ask about Voodoo for a case you workin'. But they is more... you are scared, Lane." Vivian paused, then her words acquired urgency.

"You in danger, Lane. You in big danger!"

He threw out the name he'd come to ask her about. "From Papa Ghana?"

She paused, relaxing just a little. Her lips drew in smoke in a way that made him wish he was the cigarette.

"I see you been workin'."

"You were right, I have a client."

"She must be a 'she'. You don't work that hard for no 'he.'"

He ignored her.

"Tell me about Papa Ghana, Vivian. He's Haitian, I know that much."

"She's a *she* alright. She pretty?"

"What do you care, Vivian?"

"You forget me that easy, Lane?"

"I couldn't forget you if I wanted to, but that was a long time ago."

"Not to me."

"Papa Ghana?"

"If I tell you that, I won't see you again for another three years?"

"I'll come by, I promise."

"Make sure you do. You askin' 'bout Papa Ghana... you already know he a Haitian man, but did you know he's a Voodoo Priest too? It's true. But Papa Ghana, he's more than that. He runs a gang what are called *Mas Nwa*... masque noir."

"Black Mask."

"Qui. Mas Nwa is much feared in Port Au Prince. Papa Ghana, he uses Voodoo to help confuse people, know things he shouldn't know, blackmail, that sort o' thing."

"Kidnapping?"

She shrugged. "Sure."

"What about murder?"

"The government don't kill you no deader for murder than for kidnapping."

"I'll take that as a 'yes.'"

She nodded.

"Papa Ghana sounds like a swell guy."

"I know you're jokin', Lane, but Papa Ghana, he nothing to joke about."

"What's he doing in New Orleans?"

"What *everybody* doin' in New Orleans? He schemin' and scammin'."

"What do you make of these?"

He handed her his pocket notebook, open to the page with the symbols he'd sketched from the police reports. Vivian reached for it, then drew back her hand.

"Where did you get those?"

Lane lit another cigarette off the butt of the first one.

"The police are investigating a spate of recent missing persons cases. Those symbols were scrawled near the last place the victims were seen."

Vivian looked away for a moment. "Those be a mixture of warnings, and prayers to saints."

"What kind of prayers?"

She met his eyes. "Prayers to accept a sacrifice."

"Voodoo allows human sacrifice?" he said, stunned. Although not a practitioner, everybody in Louisiana had at least a passing knowledge of the basic beliefs of Voodoo. Animal sacrifice was expected, but human sacrifice was strictly taboo. Or so he thought.

"No, it does not," Vivian said. "But that do not mean some people don't practice it anyway. Rumors from both Haiti and Cuba about it... if Papa Ghana be doin' that, he needs to die."

"I'm not a paid killer, if that's what you're suggesting."

"No, not you, sweet Lane, not you." Vivian looked over his shoulder at nothing, her eyes roaming somewhere else.

"You know I don't much believe in Voodoo, Vivian. We've had that talk enough times in the past, so take this question the wrong way... can Voodoo summon shadows, or watch and talk to people without anybody actually being there?"

"Mister Lane Walsh," Vivian said, once again using her pearly whites to best advantage. "I might make a believer outa you yet. Yes, Voodoo can do those things. It take a powerful *Oungan* to do it, but it can be done."

They talked a few more minutes, but Lane had a powerful need to type up everything he'd learned. It was how he pieced these together. Vivian Moore didn't try to get him to stay, but as he stood in her doorway let her touch linger on his hand.

"You me make a promise, you best keep that promise," she said. Waggling a finger, she went on, "don't make me use no spell on you, *Mister* Lane Walsh." She stood on tiptoes and kissed his cheek. "An' you'd best stay alive, too. Remember, I can speak with the dead."

Walking back to his car, Lane wasn't sure she was joking.

"Remember, my love," Moore called after him before he was out of earshot, "the shadows have eyes."

"Shadows always do," he muttered under his breath, striking a match and lighting his smoke. "Question is, whose side are they on?"

Jack wasn't there when Lane returned to the office. He pulled a blank sheet of paper closer, rolling it into place on his typewriter. Then he stopped. Setting aside the machine, he grabbed a pencil instead, and slowly began to sketch the symbols he'd written in his notebook, one by one.

As his pencil traced their arcs and lines, a visceral shiver coursed through him, as if the symbols themselves were alive, writhing beneath his fingers like living shadows. He understood why Vivian shied away from touching them. Up close, the symbols took on a sinister quality that sent a chill down his spine.

"Charming work of art, isn't it?" Lane remarked aloud, trying to dispel the oppressive quiet of the office. The empty room offered no response.

Finishing the last symbol, he leaned back in his chair, studying his handiwork. The symbols seemed to stare back at him, malevolence lurking within their twisted forms. He could almost feel them weaving an unseen net around his world, drawing tighter with every passing moment.

The talk with Vivian Moore only worsened the feeling of being watched as it crawled along his skin. When he looked up, there was nothing but sharp shadows cast by the desk lamp. His rational mind rejected any thoughts of Voodoo magic or stalking ghosts, yet even as he tried to dismiss the sensation, the sketched symbols seemed to seep into his surroundings, their dark influence stretching out to touch the very walls of the room.

Lane hadn't intended to move on to his next stop until morning, but it was barely past seven pm, so he pulled out the phone book and called Dr. Arthur Greaves. The professor answered on the third ring. At first the interruption annoyed him, until Lane explained the reason for his call. Delighted that someone had called for his professional expertise, Greaves invited Lane to join him in his office that very night.

Once again going through the ritual of putting on coat, hat and pistol, Lane picked up the notebook. Before putting it in a pocket, he took another look at the symbols.

"Alright, you bastards," he said. "Tell your boss if he wants a fight, I'll give him one."

"Damn academics."

Lane Walsh stalked through the darkened hallways of Tulane University, his footsteps echoing off the gleaming floors. Only a janitor with a mop greeted him. When he asked for the office of Dr. Greaves, the man pointed down hall.

"Fourth door on the left."

He hesitated for a moment. Something about the name nagged his brain like an itch he couldn't scratch. Unable to think why the name 'Greaves' seemed familiair, he knocked anyway. The door creaked open, revealing a man who seemed to have been put together from spare parts: hair sprouting in odd directions, glasses askew, and a suit that hung off his frame like a scarecrow's rags.

"Dr. Greaves?" Lane asked. The man nodded, his eyes darting around the room like trapped butterflies.

"Mr. Walsh, I presume," the doctor replied, his voice a whisper. "Come in, come in. You've come to discuss your... symbols?"

"That's right," Lane said, stepping into the cluttered office. Books and papers were piled high on every surface, casting strange shadows on the walls that made him shudder. He pulled out his sketches and handed them over, watching

Greaves' fingers tremble slightly as he took them.

"Have you seen anything like these before?"

"Oh my," Greaves murmured, studying the symbols with a frown. "Goodness... but I must ask, how did you come across them?"

"Long story," Lane replied, leaning against a bookshelf that groaned under his weight. "Let's just say they've been popping up in some unexpected places."

"Really?" Greaves looked up, his eyes suddenly sharp and alert. "Please tell me more."

"Look, Doc," Lane said, rubbing the back of his neck. "I don't want to hold you up longer than necessary. I've already caused you to come all the way back to your office. Just tell me if you know anything about these symbols or not."

"That was no bother, I only live two blocks from here," Greaves said. "And for something this interesting it was worth the walk. These symbols remind me of certain...ritualistic markings. Possibly Voodoo in origin. Or Santeria. But without further research, I can't be sure."

"Voodoo, huh?" Lane said. "That's what Vivian Moore said."

"Vivian Moore? You've spoken to her about this?"

"Yes, earlier tonight."

"Then why did you come to me if you already know what they mean?"

"I don't take anything for granted during an investigation."

"I see. Did she tell you these were warnings?"

"Yes."

"Did you she tell you the nature of these warnings?"

Lane folded his arms. "No, she didn't."

"Mr. Walsh," the doctor said slowly, meeting Lane's gaze through the twisted frame of his glasses. "The path you're on is a dangerous one. Are you prepared for what it might lead you to discover?"

"Doc, I've seen things that'd vibrate your nerves like piano wire," Lane replied, though his heartbeat raced at the thought of what he might uncover. "I can handle whatever this city throws at me."

"Miss Moore may have been trying to spare you unnecessary worry, or perhaps she did not know... and mind you, I cannot be certain... but these are warnings to stay away from the business of the Saints, meaning Voodoo or Santeria, lest you share the fate of the missing."

"Damn."

"Yes. It is a warning not to interfere in the business of forces you cannot control, or even comprehend."

"In other words, beat it, and forget you ever saw it?"

"In current vernacular, yes, that would be accurate."

"Can you tell me who might have left these warnings?"

"Not specifically, no. But I do have contacts of my own in the local occult community. If you'd like I will reach out to them. May I keep these markings?"

"We can make a copy, but I'd prefer to speak with them myself, Doc. No offense. It's just you can tell a lot about what people might be leaving out by watching their expressions."

"It has taken me years to gain their trust, Mister Walsh. I cannot risk those relationships by giving you their names. I am sorry. I hope you understand."

"Sure, Doc, I get it. I have my own informants who wouldn't appreciate me telling the cops about their activities."

"Yes, precisely," Greaves said, nodding. "I'll see what else I can find out about these symbols, and who might have left them. There is a new presence in New Orleans, a Haitian organization that is said to be engaging in petty crime and performing certain rituals–".

"Mas Nwa?"

"Oh my, you *have* done your homework. If you ever decide to take college courses, I would love to have you as a student. Yes, Mas Nwa. I presume you know the name Papa Ghana, then?"

"I do."

"But remember, Mr. Walsh: some doors, once opened, can never be closed."

"Thanks for the warning," Lane replied, heading for the door. "I'll keep that in mind."

As Lane stepped out into the hallway, he couldn't shake the feeling that he'd set something in motion, something that couldn't be stopped.

"Damn," he whispered, lighting a cigarette and watching the smoke curl through the air like a wraith. A grid of lightpoles cast deep shadows across the Tulane University campus. Walking to his car, Lane heard footsteps on the pavement. Black figures, darker than the night, flitted in his peripheral vision, but every time he snapped his head around they were gone.

3

The next day, Lane held off conducting further interviews to hear back from Dr. Greaves. He spent the day at the main library, researching Voodoo, Santeria, and anything else that seemed relevant. Several times he sensed people watching, but could never catch them staring his way. Except for one woman about his age, with black hair and a heart-shaped face. She didn't look away when their eyes met.

Lane didn't mind being watched by her. As a general principle he never objected to pretty ladies noticing him. In fact, he didn't object enough to walk over to her table and slip her his business card along with his best smile. To his surprise she handed him a card back; Beatrice Robicheaux, Attorney at Law.

"What kind of law do you practice?" he said.

"Ssshhh!" said an older woman sitting nearby.

"What kind do you need?" she whispered back.

"Maybe we should talk about it over a drink?"

"Maybe we should."

He promised to phone her, smiled again, and went to call Greaves from a phone booth outside the main entrance. Greaves answered on the first ring.

"Walsh? Meet me at The Toast, on St. Phillip St., near Decatur."

"I know the joint. When?"

"As soon as you can get there."

When the city renamed Gallatin St. to French Market Place three years earlier, demolition began soon thereafter on what had been the heart of vice and violence in the French Quarter. During the 19th and early 20th Century, just walking the streets after dark could get you killed. Once the derelict buildings started coming down, the remaining criminals migrated to places like The Toast, only a few doors down St. Phillip Street from their old haunts across Decatur St.

The murky streets of New Orleans seemed to swallow Lane as he walked side by side with the ghosts of all those who'd come before him. Banks of putrid fog rolled off the nearby Mississippi River, and the air hung thick with humidity, as if the city was sweating out its sins. His hand never strayed far from the butt of the .45 in his shoulder holster.

Moments after exiting his car, Lane found himself pushing opening a glass door under a neon light that flickered like a dying firefly. When lit, the sign read 'The Toast.' He'd only been there once, years earlier, but the place reeked of desperation, a tomb for lost souls.

Inside, a bartender with arms the size of steel cables on the new Ansemen bridge looked him up and down to see if trouble had walked into the bar. Veins snaking underneath the skin were like a roadmap to every shady deal and bar fight the man had ever known. The bartender's left hand disappeared out of sight, no doubt fingering the trigger on a sawed-off shotgun under the bar.

Lane decided to put the man at ease. Laying four bits on the counter he ordered a Sazerac.

"We have a serious drinker in the house tonight," the bartender said, sliding the quarters through a puddle of water and out of sight. Turning, he pulled a bottle of Absinthe off the top shelf behind the bar.

"Do you make it with rye or Cognac?"

That brought raised eyebrows. "I can do it either way, but most people they want rye."

"Rye is fine."

Three ice cubes added to the combination of Peychaud's Bitters, Rye Whiskey and Absinthe formed an amber liquid that refracted the room's few lamps like diamonds in a tumbler. Lane took a sip and nodded to the man. The drink was delicious.

"You want your change?"

"Keep it. You know a Dr. Arthur Greaves?"

The huge man's tone changed to one of suspicion. "You a cop?"

"Private. And Doctor Greaves called me to meet him here.

My name's Walsh."

Lane handed the man a card.

"Sure, okay. Doctor Greaves he a regular. He's in the backroom."

"Thanks. You got a name? Anybody who can make a Sazerac like this is a genius in my book."

"I'm Lou. They call me Barge."

"Barge? Would that be Barge Barone?"

He grinned. "The one and only."

"I saw your fight against Tucker, back in... what, 28?"

"Twenty-seven."

"You were great, Barge. There was thunder in your fists. I can't talk now, but I'll be back again for some fight stories and more Sazeracs."

It was a lie, but bartenders made for terrific confidential informants, so it was best to be their friend. Lane found Dr. Arthur Greaves waiting for him in a small room with one table, near the Men's Room, nursing a watery glass of whiskey.

"Evenin', Doc," Lane said as he slid into the seat across from Greaves. "This ain't the kind of joint I figured you for."

"Good evening, Mr. Walsh," Greaves replied, his voice hardly more than a raspy whisper. "This establishment fits my budget. Unfortunately, a doctorate does not necessarily bring with it a commensurate salary."

"Existence hangs heavy, a worn overcoat on the bony shoulders of the inevitable, each thread a frayed testament to the daily drudgery and nocturnal whispers of regret."

Greaves leaned back, eyes wide. "I am in the presence of a philosopher par excellence."

"I'm a PI, Doc, we're all philosophers. What have got for me?"

"I've done some digging, and what I've found..." He paused, staring into his drink as if it held the secrets of the universe. "It's like nothing I've ever encountered before."

"Sure, okay... but what does that mean?"

"Those symbols you showed me are very specific... they're connected to a cult that's been operating in the shadows for centuries. They engage with the evil Loa, Mr. Walsh, Kalfu in particular. They practice an ancient form of voodoo that can warp a man's soul, if not outright destroy it."

"Sounds like a lovely bunch," Lane said, but his gut

churned like the muddy waters of the Mississippi. Any other time, in any other place, he would dismiss talk about evil Loa and warped souls as stories to frighten children, like monsters under their beds. But in that moment it didn't seem ridiculous at all. After another slug from the Sazerac, he said, "and this Papa Ghana mook? He's their leader?"

"Indeed he is," Greaves confirmed. "But he's more than that. He's a practitioner of the darkest voodoo, using it to manipulate and control those around him. Some even say his power comes from a pact with the devil himself."

"Great," Lane muttered, rubbing a hand over his face. "Just what this city needs: another goddamn monster."

"Mr. Walsh, I must warn you," Greaves said, leaning in closer. "The deeper you delve into this world, the more dangerous it becomes. There are forces at play here that few can comprehend, let alone control."

"Doc, I've stared down German machine guns and walked away," Lane replied, trying to mask his growing unease. "I think I can handle some hocus-pocus hoodoo."

"Remember, Mr. Walsh," Greaves cautioned, as he drained the last of his whiskey. "There is no turning back once you set foot on this path. You may find yourself changed in ways you never imagined."

"Change ain't always a bad thing, Doc," Lane said. "Sometimes it's just what a man needs to survive in this rotten world."

"You *do* like to talk, Mister Walsh."

"Yeah? What of it?"

"I mean no offense. I distrust a close-mouthed man. He generally picks the wrong time to talk and says the wrong things."

"Huh?"

"Nothing. It's from a book I like. Good luck, Mr. Walsh," Greaves said. "You're going to need it."

"Thanks, Doc. I'll put that right next to my rabbit's foot and four-leaf clover. I appreciate your help."

Greaves held his empty glass. One side of Lane's mouth lifted in a half-smile. "Sure, Doc. And thanks again."

"I'm here if you need me again," Greaves said. "I frankly find all of this a bit thrilling. Frightening, but thrilling."

"Yeah, it's great," Lane said, not bothering to hide his sarcasm.

Before leaving, Lane slid another fifty cents across the bar to pay for Greaves' whiskey refill.

4

He'd barely made it five steps from the front door when something made Lane stop and turn. A figure materialized in the alley to his right. Its form seemed impervious to the dim light spilling over from the street, remaining impossibly dark and insubstantial. Lane squinted, trying to shake off the vision, but the figure stood rooted in place, undeterred by his disbelief. Reaching for the Colt might provoke a reaction he didn't want.

"Alright, pal," he said, taking a deep drag of his cigarette, "you got my attention. What's your angle?"

The figure didn't respond, didn't so much as twitch. It just floated there, an enigma wrapped in darkness and silence. Lane clenched his jaw, frustration mounting alongside his unease. But before he could challenge the apparition further, it vanished as abruptly as it had appeared, leaving him standing alone in the alley. Faint traces of mist looked like the tendrils of some forgotten nightmare.

"Damn..." With a shake of his head, he wondered if the stories about absinthe causing hallucinations might be true. Checking his watch, he decided it was high time to pay Carollo a visit.

Lane eased into the driver's seat of his '34 Dodge Sedan, coaxing the engine into a growl, like an ancient beast stretching, bitter about being summoned from its mechanical dreams into the drudgery of the night's work. He guided the car out of the French Quarter past bars and clubs where blues music spilled into the night. One marquee outside a dump on Decatur Street announced "Mississippi" Melvin Dupree and Lucille "Blue Note" Carter on the same bill. Lane took of the place. He loved the blues, and had heard good things about those two musicians. Meanwhile, the loud revelry of the living was a stark contrast to the shadowy world he'd stumbled into.

He drove out to Avondale, the restaurant named Nonna's Kitchen and Trattoria looming in his thoughts like an ill omen. The joint was a well-known hangout for the New Orleans Crime Family, the kind of place where secrets were traded like currency and loyalty was measured in blood. If Carollo had been sniffing around about Papa Ghana, there was a good chance that Lane would find him there.

"Alright, Silver Dollar," Lane muttered as he pulled up to Nonna's, killing the engine and taking one last drag of his cigarette. "Let's see what you know about shadows and voodoo dolls."

Lane expected guards out front and wasn't disappointed. A man in a black suit and a face that dared the world to cross him stood under a porch light next to the front door. His eyes were twin orbs of cold steel, the kind that had seen too much and weren't about to let anything, or anyone, slip by unnoticed. Lane eyed him back. An instant, unspoken dislike sprang up between them. The man put out an arm to stop him.

"Tell Mr. Carollo that Lane Walsh wants to discuss his missing man."

"Who the hell is Lane Walsh?" the man said, his voice dripping with the kind of sarcasm intended to make lesser men shiver.

"Your boss didn't tell me I was gonna get the third degree from one of his goons," Lane said, the lie coming easily to his lips. "Tell him I'll come back when that's squared away."

The sentry squinted, trying to decide if Lane was lying. He half-turned to leave when the door to Nonna's opened with a creak. Lane moved forward without looking at the door guard.

"I'll see you around," the man said as Lane passed him.

"Talk's cheap," he answered.

The moment Lane stepped inside, the aroma of simmering tomato sauce and garlic swept him through his senses like a beautiful woman in a red dress. It clung to the air, wrapping him in sensuous arms, and whispered promises of culinary delights yet to come. Somewhere in the background, the sizzle of meat on the grill sang a low, lusty tune, promising satisfaction for the hungriest of souls. Diners would know right away they were in for a night of tangled flavors and mysteries, where every bite held the key to another layer of intrigue.

Unfortunately, he wasn't there to eat.

A lean man with graying temples and a bowtie asked if he would be dining alone.

"I'm here to see Mr. Carollo."

Bowtie nodded once and stepped back. A gorilla-size bouncer frisked him. Beefy hands lingered on Lane's pockets like they were searching for a lost love. They stopped when they came to the holstered pistol. Shorter than the man outside, the inside man was half again as wide, and none of it was fat. When Lane reached to pull out the pistol, four men in black suits with gray pinstripes surrounded him. The handsy frisker reached past Lane's hand and pulled out the Colt. A slim man with a pencil mustache took it from him.

"I want that back when I leave."

"*If* you leave. What do you want?" he said.

"Please tell Mr. Carollo that Lane Walsh would like to discuss his missing man. I was referred by a mutual friend. I'm a private detective working a case that might be related to whatever happened to his man."

"Wait here."

The man disappeared through a door at the back of the main dining room, where patrons pointedly ignored the commotion near the front door. Lane stood for several minutes, waiting for whatever Carollo's verdict Carollo. It was a dangerous game, dealing with the Mafia, but Lane had never been one to play it safe.

Moments later the man reappeared, beckoning for Lane to follow him into the back room. Cigarette smoke hung below a ceiling of decorated copper tiles. Carollo sat at a table with several other men his own age, while younger men stood against the walls. Carollo eyed Lane with a mix of suspicion and amusement, a wolf sizing up its prey.

"Mr. Walsh," he drawled, "I am Silvestro Carollo. You have information about Marco Dantoni?"

"Could be," Lane replied cautiously. "I am investigating a

missing person named Redwood, and my case seems to have many similarities to Mr. Dantoni."

"You have my attention."

Succinctly, Lane filled him in on the basics of the case. Since Carollo wasn't his client, he left out some of the details. He also danced around the identity of Vivian Moore, referring to her only as 'an expert on such Jackers known to both of us.' Being unaware of the exact nature of Vivian's relationship to Carollo, Lane didn't want to expose something the Mafia boss might have wanted to keep quiet. For his part, Carollo seemed to appreciate his discretion.

"Your reputation is well earned, Lane. May I can you Lane?"

"Sure." *This guy's heard of me?*

"Thank you. Marco's got four kids, ya see," Carollo said, his oval face momentarily showing genuine concern. "I feel responsible for seeing to their needs until he's found. It's a... a *family* thing. So let me propose this to you. I'll give you a thousand bucks if you can figure out what happened to him, an' if somebody's behind it, you give me their name. I'll take it from there."

"That's a lot of money."

"I pay a man what he's worth."

Lane paused, weighing the danger against the potential payoff. Finally, he sighed and nodded his agreement, knowing full well he was dancing with the devil himself.

"Alright," he said. "You've got a deal. Can you fill me in on what you know?"

Carollo glanced up someone standing behind Lane, gesturing with his right index finger.

"Albert has the details," Carollo said, "he can fill you in outside."

Obviously dismissed, Lane nodded and followed the tall man into the darkness. On the way out, one of the black suits handed him the .45 butt first. Lane held it pointed at the floor and checked the chamber; still loaded. Stepping through the front door, he gave the man outside a sideways glance. A bright moon peeked from behind scudding clouds. Albert walked out of earshot. Lane followed. Both men lit a cigarette. Without warning Albert started speaking.

Marco Dantoni vanished in broad daylight during what

Albert called his 'rounds' at the markets and bars near the Port of New Orleans. The time was around three in the afternoon. Several people saw him come out of a butcher shop named 'Leo's', turn left, and stop at the entrance to an alley, listening, like somebody called out to him. He stepped into the shadows of the alley and was never seen again.

"How much time passed before somebody went looking for him?" Lane asked.

"The people around there said only a minute or two, but you know how that goes."

"Yeah... coulda been ten minutes or two hours. Would Marco have been carrying a large amount of money at that time of day?"

"If you mean enough to tempt a robber, that would be a 'yes.'"

"Does Mr. Carollo have any..." Lane paused, thinking of how to phrase *fellow gangsters* so as not to get shot. "Competitors, who might think stealing from Marco Dantoni easier than earning their own cash?"

"No."

The word came out flat and harsh. Lane didn't pursue it.

"Was anything painted on the walls or street?"

Albert squinted, taking a long drag to delay his answer. "Yeah, weird looking stuff. How'd you know?"

Lane ignored the question. "Did anybody copy them down, or maybe take a photograph?"

"What, I look like some ink jockey to you? Like I carry a camera around?"

"I meant no offense. Last question. Is there any chance Marco Dantoni skipped with the money? Maybe with a girl, you know, go start a fresh life somewhere else with a shapely blonde?"

"No chance. For one, Marco ain't that kind of guy. For another, you don't do that in our line o' work. Mr. Carollo, he'd take that as a personal betrayal. You couldn't run far enough where he couldn't find you."

Lane finished his smoke and tossed it in the gravel.

"Thanks for your help, Albert."

"I didn't do it for you, I did it 'cause Mr. Carollo asked me to. But Walsh... find Marco, yeah? He's a good earner."

"I'll do my best."

"Mr. Carollo said to give you this."

Albert held out a wad of hundred dollar bills. Lane didn't bother counting them; whatever the amount, he wouldn't accuse Carollo of trying to cheat him. That was a fast way to get a Chicago overcoat.

Lane crunched through the gravel parking lot back to his car, wondering again what the hell was going on. A nearby street light helped him fit his key into the door's lock, and he went to sit down, then stopped. Something was in the seat.

Lane's fight or flight reflex leaned heavily toward the brawling side of the equation. The Colt slid from its holster as he executed a deft spin, scanning the dimly lit surroundings for any lurking shadows with ill intentions. Nonna's lay nestled well away from the main drag, surrounded by an eerie emptiness... no close-by structures, just a vast expanse of gravel-laden parking lot. Shadows filled the space on either side of the restaurant. Were figures moving there, in the darkness, or was he imagining it?

Lane had chosen to plant his car near the lone sentinel of illumination, a streetlight that flickered with the weariness of years spent watching the secrets of the night unfold. It was his feeble attempt to deter tire thieves, though boosting tires parked in a mobster's den would have been a brand-new level of audacity. Yet, as seconds ticked away and no immediate peril emerged from the darkness, Lane dipped beneath the seat and came up with a flashlight to inspect the object in his seat.

A petite pouch, akin to a clandestine cache, lay swathed in a drab, musty-gray fabric, reeking of mold and decay. A black string kept the contents from spilling out. His probing fingers detected pliable forms, yielding to his touch like some dark, forbidden knowledge begging to be uncovered.

How it wound up in his locked car, Lane didn't know. Maybe a top-notch lockpick could have done it, and maybe not. Nor could Lane say exactly what it meant, although he could make an educated guess. About all he knew for certain was its origin: Voodoo.

Despite the late hour, down the block he used a phone booth to call Dr. Greaves. Standing exposed, Lane kept his head on a swivel as the phone rang and rang. The night had grown darker, the city's shadows stretching across the streets like grasping fingers reaching for their next victim. Lane couldn't shake the feeling that he was being watched. So far during the case he'd brushed those feelings off as a case of the heebee-jeebees from all the Voodoo stuff, but not anymore. Somebody *was* following him, and Lane wanted to know why.

"–lo..." said the groggy voice of Arthur Greaves.

"Doc, it's Walsh. I got somethin' I need to show you."

"Mister Walsh... it's past one a.m., can't it wait until tomorrow?"

"No, sorry, it can't. I need answers tonight."

"You mean this morning, don't you?"

"I'll be there in twenty minutes."

The address was for a one half of a modest duplex bungalow near campus. Arthur Greaves greeted him at the door in a robe, with a raised eyebrow and a finger to his lips.

"My landlady lives next door, and she hates for me to have late night company."

"Get dressed, I know an all-night diner."

"I have a class at eight-thirty."

"You're gonna want to see this."

Greaves fully woke up at Lane's tone of voice. Ten minutes later they sat in a run-down Cajun place frequented by sailors and riff-raff, that served the strongest coffee and most delicious gumbo Lane had ever tasted. Despite being spooked by the night's activities, he ordered both and encouraged Greaves to do the same.

"Just coffee," Greaves said. "I'm afraid the whiskey earlier precludes mixing it with gumbo and having a happy outcome."

"Suit yourself."

While waiting for the food and coffee to show up, Lane eyed the assortment of characters filling up the place. Every single one of them looked like suspects for a crime.

"Not that I don't enjoy your company, Mr. Walsh, but would you please tell me why we are here?"

Lane took the bag out of his coat pocket and laid it on the table.

"This is why we're here."

Even across the table and above the din of the diner, Lane heard Greaves' sudden intake of breath.

"I'm guessing there's no Christmas card inside there," Lane said.

"Put it away, Mr. Walsh. Please. This is not the place to display such things."

"What thing? What is it?"

The waitress carried a few extra pounds, which Lane thought suited her. She put down the coffee mugs, slid Lane's gumbo off a tray along with a spoon and napkin, and gave him flirty smile before walking away.

"That is a gris-gris," Walsh said. "Perhaps you've heard of them?"

"Only in passing."

"They are totems against evil, or to bring good luck... usually. But they can be harbingers of evil, or warnings that you are delving into something best left alone."

"Let me guess, this one's the latter?"

"I can't say for certain, that would depend on what's inside—"

"Let's find out." Lane started to untie the bag, until Greaves reached to stop him.

"No! Not here, and not without protection from whatever is inside."

"Come on, Doc," Lane said, "Do you really believe all this mumbo jumbo?"

"Believe it?" Arthur replied, his eyes serious and unflinching. "I fear it."

As the words hung in the air, a shiver ran down Lane's spine, a cold, foreboding sensation that whispered of truths best left buried. Part of his mind rejected such Voodoo as being nothing more than a ghost story, but there was another part that didn't so easily reject the supernatural. He'd seen things in France that he could never forget... or explain.

"You need to go back and see Vivian Moore," Greaves said. "She's the only one I know who might protect against whatever is inside that gris-gris."

5

Jack Callahan stepped out the office door for Delta Private Investigations as Lane Walsh approached in the hallway.

"Bankers have been at work for an hour," Jack said.

"Late night," Lane said, wishing the two aspirin he'd gulped would take effect. "You still on that same case?"

"Yeah."

"I got a new client."

"Make it fast."

"Silver Dollar Sam Carollo."

That stopped Jack in his tracks. "We're deaing with the Mafia now?"

"For a thousand bucks, yeah, we are."

Jack whistled. "In advance?"

Lane pulled out the hundreds and peeled off five. Handing them to Jack, he said, "don't spend it yet. Let's see if I find the guy I'm supposed to find."

"Sure." Jack pointed at the office using his thumb. "She's in there."

Lane didn't have to ask who 'she' was.

Vivian Moore sat in one of the two straight-backed chairs facing his desk, wearing a fine but plain dress with a floral pattern, and a wide-brimmed hat with veil. A large purse rested in her lap.

"Good morning, Angel," he said. "What lured you into my lair?"

"Show me," she said.

He didn't need to ask what she meant. Using his right hand, Lane reached into his outside coat pocket and laid the gris-gris on the desktop. Vivian leaned forward and lifted the veil. Studying the small bag for nearly a minute, she finally sat up straight again.

"Somebody warning you to stop lookin' into that missing man," she said. Her words disturbed Lane less than her tone, which held genuine fear. "This gris-gris call evil spirits into your life if you don't."

"You can tell that just from looking at it?"

"No need for me to open it, my love. Marie Laveau, she make plenty like it, which means I know what it is. The bag be's a death shroud. Inside they is a toad with one eye, the heart of a rooster, an' the little finger of someone who killed theyself."

"Sounds grim. Is that why it stinks?"

"The smell attracts evil spirits. This gris-gris meant for Baka."

"Baka? What's Baka?"

"Not what, Baka be a 'who.' Bad loa, Baka like death. He angry. Only powerful *houngan* can call on Baka."

"Like Papa Ghana?"

Vivian nodded to her left, a variation of a shrug. "If he as powerful as they say he be, yes, like Papa Ghana."

"If?"

"I said what I said."

Lane needed definite answers about Papa Ghana, who he was and what he was, so he sought out the only one man who could give them: Adrien Gandil, an Algerian soldier serving with the French Army that Lane Walsh and Jack Callahan met during the war. The two PIs were instrumental in helping Gandil immigrate to Louisiana in the war's aftermath. Gandil now ran a network of shoeshine stands that doubled as an informal network of informants whenever Walsh and Callahan need information. If anybody had a line of what was going on, it was Gandil.

He found the wiry Algerian in front of a barbershop on Claiborne Street. Hard faces stared as Lane got out of his car. Several younger men moved to block his way as he strode down the sidewalk, but Gandil threw out his arms in greeting. The others backed off.

"Monsieur Lane! C'est si bon de te voir!"

"It's good to see you too, Adrien. It's been a while."

"Yes, much too long. What brings my old friend to Claiborne Street?"

"Can we talk alone?"

"Of course!"

Lane expected to move down the street, but instead Gandil waved the others away and they moved off. Once alone, Lane mapped out the information he needed from Gandil.

"For my old friend I will do anything," Gandil said. "I have heard of this Papa Ghana. He is not a good man, Lane, but I will find out what happened to the missing man. What was his name?"

"There's at least two of 'em, Claude Redwood, and Marco Dantoni."

Gandil's face fell into a scowl at the latter name. "D'Antoni?" he said, using the original Sicilian pronunciation that Americans found so difficult. "He is part of the Carollo Family, no?"

"That's right."

"Yes, him I already know about. He tried to shake me down, to take a percentage of the earnings my boys and girls make from shoe-shines. They work hard for that money. I told him no, and he didn't like that. But his car had unfortunate things happen to it, and he left me alone. When he disappeared, I did not cry."

"How did you hear about it?" Lane said. "I didn't know there was much call for shoeshines down around the port."

"I know nothing about the port. Ever since he tried to steal from me, my boys been looking out for him. If he enters the area where I do business, I hear about it. D'Antoni showed up in the Quarter one day not long ago, walking fast. My boys followed him. They said he looked scared. He went into an alley, and never came out again."

"In the Quarter?"

"Oui. Vieux Carre. The alley off Rue Dauphine."

"You're sure of that?"

"Yes."

Was Sam Carollo lying to him? Or...

"You said Dantoni looked scared. Could somebody have been following him?"

Gandil shrugged. "I wasn't there, Lane. I can ask my boys."

"Please do that, Adrien. Call me at the office day or night. If I'm not there, leave a message with the answering service. Just a simple 'yes' or 'no' will be fine."

"For you and Jack, anything, anytime."

The weight of the .45 comforted him as Lane stood at the corner of Dauphine and Dumain Streets, waiting for Arthur Greaves. The streets were swollen with faces, but somewhere in that shuffle, eyes had him pinned. He felt the itch of being someone's mark. Across the way stood a knot of men who would have looked suspicious anywhere else, and their eyes were all pegged on him. Lane stared back until they looked away. Arthur Greaves picked that moment to push through the crowd, face flushed, mopping his cheeks with a handerkerchief.

"I think I'm being followed," he said, through heavy breathing.

"What makes you say that?"

"Every time I turn around the same two men are behind me. They've been there since I parked over on Royal."

"Do you see 'em now?" Lane said.

Greaves looked back the way he'd come, trying to see through the constant stream of bodies.

"No, I can't them."

"Come on and show me what you called about."

"I'm sorry to drag you down here like this–"

"It's okay, but let's get going. I have a feeling we don't want to still be here after dark."

The warm weather made them forget it was still winter. Sunset came early in February. In the harsh late-afternoon sunlight the French Quarter's shadows stretched like black cats on a moonlit prowl as Lane and Arthur Greaves navigated through the crowds toward Dumain St. The days of immersing himself into New Orleans' Voodoo heritage had begun to take their toll on his nerves. The whispered tales and shadowy figures were enough to fray the jagged edges of reality, threatening to unravel the world Lane once considered familiar. The strong beliefs of Vivian Moore and Arthur Greaves had begun to undermine his innate skepticism.

"Arthur, how much further?" Lane asked, his voice tight with unease.

"Just up there," Arthur replied, his eyes scanning the way ahead. "There's something you need to see."

They turned into half a block before Dumain, where in the gathering gloom ghostly gas lamps cast an eerie glow over the hunched figures that lurked in doorways. Lane caught snatches of conversation... sinister murmurs, desperate whispers... and he couldn't shake the feeling that those people could see right through him.

"Here." Arthur stopped abruptly before a grimy window, the glass opaque with years of grime. "Take a look."

Lane peered through the muck, squinting to make out the scene within. The small room was packed with oddities - shrunken heads, jars of pickled creatures, ancient books bound in what might have been human skin. He felt a cold sweat break out across his brow, his stomach churning with repulsion.

"Jesus, Arthur," Lane muttered. "What in God's name is this place?"

"Uncharted territory for the likes of you and me," Arthur replied, his voice barely above a whisper. "But I've got it on good authority that this is where Claude Redwood was last seen."

"Who's your source?" Lane asked, unable to tear his gaze away from the grotesque display. Adrien Gantil mentioned an alley in the Quarter where Marco Dantoni disappeared. Could he and Redwood have both vanished from the same place?

"I don't know," Arthur said. "I found a note slid under the door of my classroom this morning. It told me what I'd find here."

"Great," Lane grumbled. "Just what I need, more half-baked riddles from shadow-dwellers."

"Look, Lane," Arthur said, his voice taking on a rare note of urgency. "You wanted my help, and I'm giving it to you. Frankly, I find all of this both terrifying and invigorating. But you've got to be willing to push past your skepticism. There are things in this world we can't explain, forces that defy reason."

"Is that right?" Lane shot back, his voice dripping with sarcasm. "Well, excuse me if I don't start believing in the bogeyman just because somebody's husband took off, or a two-bit hood goes missing."

"Suit yourself," Arthur shrugged. "But you might want to keep an open mind. You never know what's lurking around the next corner."

"My mind's a lot more open now than I ever wanted it to be when it comes to Voodoo. The truth is, he finally admitted, eyeing the decrepit people watching them. "I don't know what to think anymore."

"Good," Arthur replied, his eyes meeting Lane's in a moment of shared understanding. "Because, my friend, I have a feeling we're about to step through the looking glass."

Lane walked Greaves back to his car, trying to make sense of what he'd seen. The Professor wanted to stay, but instincts told Lane that a fight was coming, and if it did, Greaves would only be a liability.

"Perhaps you should consider dropping this case," Greaves said.

"Listen, Arthur," Lane said, his voice firm. "I don't care if we're up against the devil himself. I'm not backing down until we find that poor sap and put an end to whatever sick game is being played here."

"Brave words," Arthur replied, a hint of admiration in his voice. "But don't forget, courage can be a double-edged sword."

"The PI who gives up because of a few ghost stories doesn't deserve his license," Lane snapped, frustration boiling up within him. "I've had enough riddles and spooky mumbo-jumbo to last me a lifetime. You want to help me find this Papa Ghana character, fine. But we do it the old-fashioned way: with guns and fists, not candles and incantations."

Once alone, Lane shook his head, trying to dispel the doubts that gnawed at his resolve. Lane Walsh didn't believe in ghosts and goblins. He believed in truth and justice, in the power of a well-aimed fist or a well-placed bullet. With nothing more to accomplish, Lane headed for his own car.

As he rounded a corner, Lane's heart skipped a beat. There, standing in the middle of a suddenly empty street, was a figure shrouded in darkness. It seemed to defy the very laws of nature, its form an ever-shifting play of light and shadow.

"Who are you?" Lane demanded, his voice barely betraying the fear that clawed at his insides. He wished he could get a better look at the figure... at the *man* he told himself, but the gloom was thickest at that point. Then it did something unexpected.

The figure chuckled, low and sinister, and stepped forward into the dim light of a flickering streetlamp. For a moment, Lane thought he saw the face of a long-dead friend, but then it was gone, replaced by a stranger's mocking grin. Whoever, or whatever it was, it was alive and not a ghost.

"Names are such fleeting things," the figure said, its voice as smooth as silk. "But you may call me... an ally."

"An ally?" Lane snorted, his skepticism rearing its ugly head once again. "And why should I trust you?"

"Because, Mr. Walsh," the figure replied, its eyes narrowing. "I can offer you answers to the questions that plague your restless nights. Together, we can unravel the web of lies that has ensnared you."

"Web of lies?" Lane's thoughts raced. Could there be some rational explanation for the bizarre series of events that had led him here?

"Think about it," the figure continued, its voice like honeyed venom. "What if everything you've seen, everything you've experienced, is merely the result of someone pulling the strings behind the scenes? Someone manipulating you for their own nefarious purposes?"

"Go on," Lane said, his curiosity piqued despite his misgivings.

"Ah, but first," the figure replied, a wicked smile playing across its lips. "You must prove your worth. You must show me that you are willing to walk this dark path, wherever it may lead."

"Fine," Lane growled, his resolve hardening. "I'll play your game. Just don't expect me to start holding hands with ghosts and goblins anytime soon."

"Very well, Mr. Walsh," the figure said, stepping back into the shadows. "Remember my words, for they may be the key to your salvation... or your doom."

And with that, the figure turned and walked off, leaving Lane alone in the darkened street, his mind a whirlwind of questions and doubts. Only the distant wail of a saxophone player running the scales while warming up filled his ears, like the mocking laughter of shadows. Then something slammed into the back of his head.

A cold drizzle soaked his clothes when Lane woke up in the gutter of St. Peter Street. The soft patter of rain mingled with the distant sound of a blues band. Staggering to his feet, he felt a knot on the back of his skull that matched the pain lancing through his brain. An overhanging balcony provided cover from the rain as he checked to see what the mugger had stolen.

Nothing. Not even the Colt. So who hit him if not a thief? Or had someone frightened his assailant away before he had a chance to rob his victim? Lane checked his watch... past nine. He'd been out for hours. Sick to his stomach from the blow to his head, experience taught him that what he needed was a hot shower and rest. This time, though, he drew the Colt, not caring who spotted him with a gun. If anybody wanted to hit him again, they'd get a bullet for their trouble.

Feeling for his cigarettes, he shook one out of the pack. It drooped from being water-soaked. Now, adding to his troubles, he had to stop and buy more smokes before going home. Only then did he realize that he'd lost his fedora.

6

The next morning's headache was no worse than the hangover from a batch of Trenchfoot Whiskey, the stuff they'd distilled in bunkers back during the war. Ingredients included anything that would ferment, with potatoes producing the alcohol least likely to make you go blind. The worst part was losing his hat.

Lane stayed in bed, staring at the ceiling. He'd sweated enough to dampen the sheets, which made him fear a concussion, but when he finally sat up his vision remained steady, not swimming, so a concussion seemed unlikely. Walking slowly into the apartment's tiny kitchen, he brewed coffee and smoked the day's first cigarette. Then the phone rang.

"Hello?"

"Lane, do not go back."

"Uh, good morning to you, too Viv."

"Yes, good morning. Do not go back. The same thing happen to you. Then I have to get involved."

"Vivian," he drawled into the phone, trying to sound awake and alive, "you've never called me before, and I'm really not in a mood for more riddles. Where is it I'm not supposed to go, and what happened to who?"

"You not heard yet? Dr. Arthur Greaves, he was attacked last night on Dauphine Street."

That gained Lane's full attention. "Dauphine? When, how? How do you know all this? Is he alive?"

"Dr. Greaves be known to many of my friends an' clients. Where Voodoo concerned in the French Quarter, I hear everything. Since he a prominent man, the police they come, take him to hospital. I hear he go home later, beat up but otherwise not hurt. I hate to see the same thing happen to my sweet,

sweet Lane."

Damn. Apparently he and Greaves had gotten too close to somebody. Just as obvious, Greaves had not gone home but headed back to the place off near Dumain.

"What do you know about–"

"Do not go back."

"How do you know what I was going to ask you?"

"You know how I know. To answer the question you ain't yet asked your beloved Vivian, it be a portal to a place nobody want to go, a place from where nobody comes back."

Vivian explained that until last night she didn't know about the apartment they'd seen the day before. It had been hidden from her, which could only be by someone as powerful in Voodoo as she was. Now that she know, Vivian was fighting her own private battle to get rid of it, and the power behind it.

"Is that Papa Ghana?"

"I know you want to help the love o' your life, my beloved, but you cannot. You have you own fight…" Vivian hesitated before continuing. "You might hear about a meeting tonight o' Mas Nwa. Stay away, Lane," Vivian's voice was silk spun around the warning, "this ain't you world, and you don't want no part in it."

"Where is this taking place?" he said, putting a hint of demand behind the words, "you know I'll find out anyway. I just want to see what all the fuss is about."

"I won't be the cause o' you funeral," she replied, and hung up.

Lane slipped the phone back into its cradle, drummed his fingers on the receiver, and called Arthur Greaves.

Lane questioned him on what happened, but all Greaves could remember was scraping on the cobblestones and dark shadows in his peripheral vision. After the first few punches, he fell, and someone said "next time you stop breathing" in a heavily accented voice.

"Haitian?" Lane asked.

"If I had to guess, yes, Haitian." Something about the words sounded different, until Lane realized Greaves must be talking through swollen lips.

Greaves gave up the location of the Mas Nwa meeting only after Lane made it clear he was going alone. Beat up or not, the pudgy acamedician still wanted to tag along. To his own surprise, Lane found genuinely himself worried about his new friend's well being.

"You're not going, Doc, and that's the end of it."

After Greaves reluctantly told him the address, Lane asked how he'd gotten it.

"Why, Miss Moore gave it to me," he said.

Lane had to laugh; it was so much like Vivian to give potentially dangerous information by using a proxy.

"Stay put until you hear from me."

"Where else would I go?"

"Based on what you did last night? Somewhere dangerous, and no offense Doc, you're not equipped."

Night had fallen by the time he arrived. He parked several blocks away, filled his fist with the .45, and used shadows and cover to approached a crumbling warehouse without being seen. Surviving thirteen months on the Western Front honed his reflexes enough so he remained unseen until across the street from the meeting site.

The place reeked of trouble; an abandoned warehouse by the river where shadows seemed to breathe their own secrets. He could hear the distant hum of voices and drums as he crept closer, heart pounding in his chest like the rhythm of the city itself. Within a minute he'd spotted the only guard, standing near a rollup door. The tip of a cigarette glowed orange as the man inhaled, making him an easy target; he wouldn't'have lasted thirty seconds at the front lines. Instead, he only suffered a crack behind the ear from Lane's pistol barrel. Lane tied up the unconscious guard using his own laces and belt.

Through a crack in the rollup door, Lane caught sight of something unlike anything he'd seen before. Several hundred people stood watching a dozen women twisting and waving their arms as if possessed by manic spirits. At its center stood a huge man with glistening skin garbed in a black tuxedo coat, pants and top hat, with no shirt. White painted gleamed on most of his face as he orchestrated the macabre performance.

He could only be Papa Ghana.

Lane believed to his core that it was all nothing more than theater, a grotesque pantomime designed to ensnare the weak-minded. But the strange odor wafting from the incense burners made it hard to hold onto that conviction. He could feel himself teetering on the edge of some hypnotic abyss, fighting with every ounce of willpower not to tumble into darkness.

A shake cleared his mind; the smoke must have contained a hypnotic drug. After covering his mouth with a handkerchief, Lane returned to watching. He studied the ritual with a mix of fascination and revulsion, unable to tear his gaze away from the scene unfolding before him. Someone passed a wicker basket, into which the watcher put money.

Off to one side he spotted a young man in his 20s showing children how to pick pockets. Elsewhere, partly hidden by a steel support column, another man demonstrated how to cut purse straps without being noticed. And everywhere there were arcane symbols painted on the walls and floor. Piecing together the strange symbols, the demonstrations, and whispered fragments of conversation that swirled around the ritual chamber, he began to understand what was going on, and what probably happened to Claude Redwood.

The Voodoo rituals were real enough, and the acolytes participating believed in their leader, Papa Ghana. But Papa Ghana was nothing more than a painted-up gangster. The only difference between him and Silver Dollar Sam was how they dressed. He knew better than to underestimate them though. Men like Papa Ghana were looking to muscle their way into the city's drug and prostitution rackets, currently the territory of the Carollo Family. If true, Claude Redwood might have been looking for a fix or a trick in the wrong place, at the wrong time. Given the icy piece of work he was married to, Lane couldn't blame Claude for anything more than picking the wrong moment to cheat.

The last question Lane faced was whether he would tell what he'd learned to NOPD, since chances were good that somebody was getting paid off. With no hard evidence, only theories, they wouldn't listen anyway. But he'd stumbled into the beginnings of a simmering war between Mas Nwa and the Mob, which although he didn't care if they wiped each other out, good riddance to both, innocent bystanders would also surely die.

It was a hard call.

Dr. Greaves would ask for every detail, as would Vivian Moore. He'd tell them the Voodoo stuff, the sights he'd actually witnessed, and keep his conjecture to himself. Then the air seemed to crackle with an energy that felt as sinister as it was seductive, and Lane knew he had to get out while he still could.

It was that moment when he spotted the knot of men on the far side of the warehouse, standing with arms folded, nearly invisible in their dark suits. Four men flanked a fifth, older man, two on each side. Lane recognized three of them... the outside guard back at Nonna's, Albert, and the oval-faced man in the middle was none other than Silvestri Carollo, aka Silver Dollar Sam.

Papa Ghana wasn't Carollo's enemy, he was Carollo's business partner.

I've stayed too long, Lane thought, backing away from the door as quietly as possible. Despite knowing the whole thing was a charade, something still itched at the back of his mind, like unseen spirits watched his every move. But as he turned to leave, a sudden scraping noise stopped him in his tracks. The shadows seemed to close in around him, tightening their grip like a noose.

"Jean-Baptiste, ki kote w ye?" called a voice, rough as gravel and twice as dangerous.

"Damn," Lane cursed under his breath, "This is gonna get ugly."

Three men in black slacks and shirts emerged from the darkness, armed with knives and clubs. They blocked the path back to his car. Streetlights near that close to the river rarely had working bulbs, and those around the warehouse were no exception; in the moonless night, they might have been shadows looking for prey.

"Jean-Baptiste?" said the one in the middle, stepping closer. "Si w ap dòmi, papa ap dezòd ou."

Lane didn't speak Haitian Creole, but he understood enough French to get the gist... *if you're asleep, Papa's gonna mess you up.*

Lane crouched, waiting for them to get close. Three on one was bad odds, even for a veteran of the Great War who'd seen his share of hand-to-hand combat. He could shoot them, and maybe get away before the others could catch him, but then again maybe not. So in a flash he lunged forward, connecting a fierce right hook to the first thug's jaw. Frozen for half a second by surprise, the others took a step back. Lane moved like quicksilver, dodging and striking with ruthless precision. Within moments, two of them lay sprawled on the pavement, while the third trembled in Lane's iron grip. Nobody from inside seemed to have heard the commotion.

"If you try to scream, I swear I'll kill you," he growled, tightening his hold on the man's throat, "Now talk. What's your boss planning to do with Mas Lwa? Why is he in my city? How long has he been teamed up with the Mob?"

"Please!" the man gasped, "I don't know nothin', misye! Papa Ghana he keepin' all that to hisself!"

"Wrong answer," Lane snarled, slamming the man's head against the pavement. The man went limp, unconscious.

"Looks like I'm gonna have to do this the hard way," Lane said as he trotted back to his car. He had to find out just how deep the rabbit hole went before it swallowed him whole. The enemies he'd made so far all had guns, while his allies had words and symbols.

"Carollo, you've got some explaining to do," he said out loud while driving away. He lit a cigarette, thinking it was a good night for a drink or three.

Lane nursed a second rum and cola at a bar on Royal, one he'd never yet been to. It was hard to hide his bruised knuckles. After beating up the Haitians, it was safer to avoid his usual haunts in case anybody guessed who'd assaulted the gangsters and went looking for revenge. Staring into his drink, he thought through what to do next. What had started out as a simple missing husband case had become something far moe dangerous. Each step he took now brought with it the weight of a moral and existential dilemma, a battle waged within his own soul between the truth he sought and the cost of finding it.

Carollo's wrapped up in the disappearances, I can feel it, but why the hell would he hire me to look into Marco Dantoni's disappearance if he wants a piece of Mas Lwa's action?

The answer flashed into his mind: *if things went sour with Mas Nwa, Carollo would claim he was only trying to find his missing employee.* It was a weak alibi, to be sure, but when the DA and most of the judges were in your pocket, it didn't take much to get you off. Given the possibility of a war between his family and Mas Nwa, Carollo was playing both sides.

Suddenly tired, Lane left at a little past two a.m., headed home. His thoughts were interrupted by the distant patter of footsteps echoing through the night. Plenty of people roamed the streets at that hour, derelicts and working girls mostly, but none of them worried about making noise. Someone trying to be quiet could only be up to no good. He ducked into a narrow space between two buildings, pressing himself against the cold brick. Fingers touched the Colt's grip.

"Watch your back, Walsh," came a voice from the shadows, smooth as silk and twice as deadly. The accent was European, not Haitian. It took a few seconds to place it as either Spanish or Italian. "You're getting closer to the heart of darkness and some people don't take kindly to unwanted guests." A figure emerged from the gloom, a black figure backlit by a streetlamp, his face hidden beneath the brim of a wide hat. "You would do well to forget what you have seen and heard. The path you tread leads only to ruin.""

"Is that supposed to be a threat?" Lane replied. "Or are you trying to save my soul? Because, quite frankly, I think that's a lost cause."

"Consider it a friendly warning," the shadowy figure said, his tone chillingly calm. "There are forces at work here that you cannot hope to understand or control. Turn back now, while you still can."

"Sorry, pal," Lane said, stepping out from his hiding place, his eyes gleaming with defiance. "But when it comes to the truth, I'm a bit of a glutton for punishment."

"Then you leave us no choice." The figure raised a gloved

hand and snapped his fingers. From the darkness crept more cloaked figures, like wolves ready to ensnare their prey.

"Hope you brought your dancing shoes, boys," Lane quipped as he drew the Colt, its weight adding to the choices he'd made and the ones yet to come bearing down on him.

Lane aimed at the speaker, bracing the big pistol in both hands. In response the man held up a hand, freezing the others in mid-step.

"You have escalated Jackers, Mr. Walsh."

"It's not my fault if you brought knives to a gunfight."

"One shot, and people will flock to the scene."

"One shot, and people will run like hell away from the scene. In case you didn't notice, we're in New Orleans. So listen closely... you ain't no Haitian, but that doesn't mean you're not working for Papa Ghana. Or Mr. Carollo, or maybe a third party I ain't come across yet. I don't care. I'm tired of threats. I'm tired of being followed, and I'm tired of lugging this gun around without using it. I'd rather be judged by twelve than carried by six, so the next time somebody like you threatens me, you'd better shoot first and ask questions later. But before you do, remember this... a lot of Germans tried that... I'm still here, and they're not."

It was another short night, one where Lane Walsh relied on coffee, cigarettes and breakfast to replace sleep. You could only do that for so long before your body called in that debt.

Outside his window a streetcar rumbled past, its wheels screeching against the rails like a banshee's wail. He pulled a crumpled cigarette from the pack on his desk, flicked the Zippo to life, and inhaled the hot smoke. As the clock ticked toward ten a.m., the fact that nobody had followed or attacked him seemed like a good start to the day.

"Who knew that looking for Claude Redwood could be so hazardous to one's health?" Lane mused out loud.

A knock at his office door brought him out of his chair. Through the frosted glass stood a small shadow. He thought about grabbing a gun, decided not to. Lane opened the door to see a young newsboy holding out an envelope.

"Mr. Walsh?"

"That's right."

"Got something for ya, Mister. Came special delivery."

"Thanks, kid," Lane said, taking the envelope and flipping the boy a nickel. "Buy yourself something nice."

"Sure thing, Mister," the kid replied, catching the coin with a grin before disappearing down the hall. Lane looked both ways before closing the door.

Back at his desk Lane tore open the envelope, revealing a single sheet of paper. As he read, his eyes narrowed, and his jaw tightened. It was from Mas Nwa.

In cursive English script, Papa Ghana offered a truce. If Lane quit investigating Mas Nwa, Papa Ghana would call off the curses laid on Lane's soul, including the gris-gris. As a gesture of goodwill, the letter stated that Claude Redwood reneged on payment for 'services', and would 'not be returning to this life.'

He had already come to that conclusion, but now Lane had proof for his client. Rather than give in to his first impulse to crumple the letter, he held it up to the light pouring in through the window at his back. Pen pressure could be judged by depth of the indentation made by the nib, along with the amount of ink spreading from each stroke. Along with the flourishes of the letters themselves, Lane deduced that a man had written the letter. But not someone who wrote English as a second language, there was no hesitation anywhere on the page. That either meant Mas Nwa had non-Haitians in its ranks, or knew a native-born American willing to write such a document.

Someone, say, from a certain New Orleans crime family.

Common sense told him to close the Redwood case, give Carollo his thousand bucks back and beg off finding Marco Dantoni, and maybe take Vivian Moore to Mexico for a few weeks of fun in the sun while things calmed down in New Orleans. That was the safe play.

The moral implications of his decision weighed heavily on his conscience, but he brushed them aside. One thing nobody had ever accused Lane Walsh of doing was playing it safe. In New Orleans, there were rarely any good choices, only ones that kept you alive or got you killed.

"Protection and secrets, huh?" he said to any spirits who

might be listening. "Tell your boss that if he thinks I'm gonna be his lackey, he's about find out how wrong he his. No one pulls Lane Walsh's strings."

During his childhood, Lane had never gone to his older brother or parents when trouble arose, which it frequently did. He'd been a late bloomer, growing eight inches in six months, and until that happened bigger kids used to pick on him. But they only did it once. Lane Walsh didn't ask for help or mercy, Lane Walsh got even.

Yet there were limits to what he could accomplish alone. Even if Jack wasn't working a case, neither of them carried a badge. The time had come to call in the cops... if he'd known of any not likely to be on Carollo's payroll. The problem was, there was only one for certain he knew to be clean, and she was a she.

Lt. Rebecca Davis.

Davis was probably the best cop he knew. She was definitely the most honest. That's why he hated calling her if he didn't have to, she would dive into the case like a dog digging for a mole, and there was a good chance she'd get hurt. If some corrupt meathead took a bullet, Lane wouldn't think twice. Rebecca Davis, though... besides, he liked her. Jack did too, although neither had ever said so out loud.

So he held off, hoping he'd never have to drop that nickel until he could hand over enough evidence to tie up Papa Ghana with a neat little bow. The Mob boys he couldn't do anything about, but the Haitians didn't have the political cover the Carollo Family did. Not yet, at least.

That night he headed for another notorious dive bar hidden in an armpit of the French Quarter, a place where the unsavory sought refuge, and secrets were traded like currency. The kind of place where an honest cop looking for answers would find a whole lot of people who didn't know anything about anything, but a PI with an iffy reputation might hear a few things of interest.

Duffy's Place made The Toast seem like a palace. Farther north and across the street from old Gallatin Street, legends said more than 100 people had died inside the bar and onetime brothel. It served cheap liquor cheap, patronizing to people who went unnoticed by the society whose laws they ignored.

In a far corner, a skeletal old man with a scarred guitar sat on a stool playing Delta Blues. Lane knew right off he was the real deal. Two fingers on his left hand slid the glass neck of a bottle along the strings, in a way that came straight from the soul. During a trip through the Mississippi River lowlands once, he'd watched the process of how players first removed a bottle's neck, followed by them filing away the sharp edges of the glass so they could use it to produce sounds that could break a strong man's heart.

Unlike most places where the bartender kept his sawed-off shotgun out of sight under the bar, at Duffy's it was in the hands of a bouncer with a bowling-ball shaped head sitting at the far end of the bar. Holes here and there in the brick walls showed why having it ready for instant use made sense.

"Hey, Walsh," greeted Sal, the bartender with a crooked smile that matched his twisted morals. "Long time no see. What brings you to our humble abode?"

"Information, Sal," Lane replied, taking a seat at the bar. "Can't always rely on the grapevine."

"Ah, you know I'm your man for that." Sal leaned in conspiratorially, his eyes darting around the room. "What's got your interest this time? Missing dames, backstabbing mobsters, or something more... supernatural?"

"Right on the money, Sal," Lane said, lighting a cigarette. "I need the lowdown on Mas Lwa. You hear anything?"

"Mas Lwa, huh?" Sal rubbed his chin, feigning deep thought. "That might cost you. Papa Ghana ain't somebody to mess around with."

"Will a sawbuck do it?" Lane replied.

"That depends. What exactly do you want to know?"

Sal looked over Lane's shoulder, staring through a squint. Lane turned to see a bent man with a thin beard pick up his hat and move for the door. A nod to the bouncer sent him following the man outside.

"Skip on his tab?" Lane said.

"Aint' nobody gets credit here. He was payin' too close attention to our conversation."

"I doubt he heard anything."

"No he didn't, but that ain't the point. Around here, listenin' too close ain't welcome."

Sal leaned forward on crossed forearms. "Tell me what you want to know."

"Bunch of folks gone missing in the past few months. Mas Nwa seems behind a lot of them. Why? What's the angle? They couldn't all owe Papa Ghana money."

Sal shook his head. "You want the whole mouthful, huh? Sawbuck ain't gonna cover that."

"How much?"

"Double it."

"Alright."

"Soon as we're done, I'ma start yelling for you to get out and never come back, okay? Just in case somebody notices what we're talkin' about."

"I thought you said we couldn't be overhead."

Sal shrugged. "Can't never be too careful. It's for both our protection."

"But mainly yours."

"They know where to find me."

"Trust me, they know where to find me, too. Let's hear it."

Papa Ghana thought bigger than Lane had given him credit for. In a few sentences, Sal laid out a plan that surprised even the cynical PI. The disappearances served two purposes. First, to scare people into thinking that evil Voodoo spirits stalked the streets of New Orleans, snatching people at random, except in areas protected by the magic of Papa Ghana and Mas Nwa. They, and they alone, could fight the spirits.

But there was more to it. Some of the missing people had been targeted on purpose, either to be held for ransom, or murdered.

"What about Carollo?"

"Carollo?" Sal lifted an eyebrow. Lane studied him face for tells of lying, saw none. "What about him?"

"He's in it with Papa Ghana."

"Yeah? I'll be damned... but I can see where that makes sense, y'know? Farm out his wet work to the Haitians."

Lane lit a cigarette to hide his surprise. Why hadn't he thought of that? It made perfect sense for Carollo to use the Haitians against his enemies.

"We done here?" Sal whispered.

"I think so."

"See ya' around, Walsh." Sal cleared his throat, and then half-climbed over the bar. "Pay for the booze and get out! Don't never come back, y' hear me?"

Lane threw a three bills on the bar, a twenty sandwiched between two singles. The bouncer stood in the doorway, glaring, but when Lane got close the man smiled.

"See ya 'round," he said.

7

Cool air carried hints of rain as Lane picked a well-lit phone booth to call his partner. If something happened to him, he wanted Jack to know what he'd found. More to the point, he wanted to know whether or not to contact Rebecca Davis.

"Listen, Jack," Lane said, blowing out a stream of smoke as he spoke into the receiver cradled against his ear. His right hand dangled at his side, holding the Colt ready but out of sight. "I've been digging into this Mas Lwa business, and it's bigger than I thought. Carollo's definitely mixed up in it, which means so are some high-ranking city officials."

"How high ranking?"

"I don't know that part for sure."

"Christ, Lane," Jack Callahan sighed on the other end of the line, the sound tinny and distant. "I'd like to help, but I'm up to my neck in my own case right now. Give back that two hundred dollar retainer you got, and walk away from this one."

Lane scowled, flicking ash onto the wet pavement. "You know I can't do that, Jack. There's something rotten going on here, and I can't let it slide. Besdies, I already solved that part."

"Claude what's-his-name?"

"Yeah. It looks like Claude was probably diddling the wrong girl."

"I'm shocked, shocked I tell you."

"There's a slim chance he was made an example of, wrong place, wrong time, all of that. I doubt there's a body to be found."

"Look, if you want give it up, watch your back, okay?"

"Always do," Lane replied, hanging up the phone with a heavy clunk. He crushed the spent cigarette beneath his heel and made for his car a few feet away by the curb. The first drops of rain plinked on his bare head, reminding him to get a new hat.

As he went to open the car door, Lane's instincts screamed at him, sensing danger before his mind could fully comprehend it. A muzzle flash lit up the darkness, and Lane dove to the side, narrowly avoiding the bullet that whizzed past his ear. Bracing the Colt on the Dodge's hood, he returned fire in the direction of his would-be assassin.

He heard a yelp. The shooter scrambled out from behind a column and bolted down the street. Lane caught a glimpse of dark clothes and a shadowed face before the figure disappeared into a waiting car. The engine roared to life and the vehicle sped off, leaving Lane standing in the darkness, heart pounding in his chest.

Sirens wailed in the distance, growing louder as they approached. Lane frowned. The NOPD *never* responded that fast so near the river, especially in the middle of the night. By reflex he picked up the spent casing from the three shots he'd fired. As flashing lights approached, he slid the pistol into its holster, folded his arms and leaned against the front passenger door.

Lt. Rebecca Davis stepped out of a squad car and scanned the scene as light breezes tossed her blonde hair. A man in the standard off-the-rack brown suit worn by detectives around the country, lit a smoke and stood around looking bored. Rebecca Davis paid him no attention. She crossed the street, stopping in front of Lane. He didn't mind at all. Her skirt and blouse fit perfectly.

"You got here fast," Lane said. "He shot first."

"Shot?" she said. "Who shot what?"

Lane scratched his lower lip, playing for time. "Nobody, nothing. What can I do for you, Lieutenant?"

"You're out pretty late in a dangerous part of town, aren't you?"

"I don't have *you* to come home to."

She wasn't amused.

"We got a call about a dead body at this location. Yours. Know anything about that?"

"You mean aside from me not being dead?"

"What about those shots you mentioned?"

A flashlight materialized in her left hand. She swept the beam back and forth over the sidewalk and nearby street. Once again Lane's Army service saved him from answering a lot of awkward questions, and probably taking a ride downtown.

"Looking for something?"

"I smelled gunpowder when we drove up."

"Probably smoke from passing freighter. We *are* near the river."

"Alright, smart guy. Word on the grapevine is that someone's got it in for you, Walsh," she said, her voice low and serious. "Watch yourself."

"Thanks for the tip, Lieutenant," Lane said. "I can handle myself."

"So I've heard."

Lane cocked his head, wondering what that meant.

"Hey Lieutenant Davis, would you do *me* a favor?"

"Maybe. Depends on what you want."

"Watch your own back. New Orleans needs about a hundred more just like you, but for now you're all we've got."

Now suspicion filled her tone. "What does that mean? Are you flossing me?"

"No. I didn't mean because you're a girl, I meant because you ain't bought and paid for. There's a lot of people who don't like that kind of thing... honest cops. It crimps their business." Lane nodded with his head, indicating her partner across the street. "I'm betting shovel-face over there is one of those."

"I can handle myself," she said, smiling as she sent his own words back at Lane. "But thanks."

As the police car sped away to the next urgent call, Lane couldn't help but uneasy being alone again. He wasn't sure who was trying to kill him or why, but one thing was certain: the case was far from over, and he'd be damned if he was going to back down now.

It was clear as day now; all pretenses were dropped. Perhaps the gunman had murder on his mind, or perhaps it was just another charade to rattle his cage. Either way Lane was beyond caring. Because once lead started flying, it usually found its home into the dirt, often inside of somebody's guts.

None of the locals had bothered to get involved, but Lane expected that. People getting robbed and killed barely raised an eyebrow in that part of New Orleans. Once home, he went inside with pistol drawn, as if clearing a German bunker back in France. Satisfied that nobody waited inside, he locked the doors and windows, closed the curtains, and doused all but one lamp. Dropping two ice cubes into three fingers of dark rum, he settled on the couch to think. The Colt kept the seat warm next to him, within easy reach.

The only picture in the whole place stood in a silver frame on top of his RCA cabinet radio. It showed a pretty young woman in her late teens, with dark hair and dimples, smiling and trying to look older than she really was; Mary Bennick, his high school girlfriend. When he left for France they agreed to get married when he came home. The Spanish Flu took her while he was in the trenches.

"Maybe I'm going nuts, baby," he said to the image. "Jack told me once I might be tempting death so I can be with you again. If I thought that could happen, he would be right. I'd already be dead. But I don't believe that. I just don't. There's got to be another angle."

The case had taken a violent turn. Now that lead had started flying he couldn't involve Arthur Greaves or Vivian Moore, it was too dangerous. Besides, what could they do? They were experts in Voodoo, and he'd figured out that the whole Voodoo angle was hokum to cover a new criminal enterprise. He'd never believed in it anyway... not really.

The phone rang. It startled him so badly that he nearly shot it off the wall. A glance at his watch showed four minutes past two in the morning. Who would call at that time of night?

"Yeah?"

"You don't need ta worry about me, my beloved," purred Vivian Moore. "I am the Voodoo Queen o' New Orleans. The Loa, they protect me."

The back of Lane's neck felt like somebody touched it with a live electric wire. *How could she have known he was thinking about her?*

"You're up late," was all he could think to say.

"Oh dear Lane, you ain't trickin' me. You *cain't* trick part o' you own soul. You been thinkin' about Vivian, an' she been thinkin' 'bout you. Come see me in the mornin'. I made somethin' special just for you, lover."

She hung up, leaving him staring at the phone, open-mouthed.

Lane half-expected Vivian to be naked when she answered the door, but at five past ten the next morning he found her in the shop, re-arranging tiny bottles of powders and leaves and roots. Several shoppers milled around inspecting shelves filled with strange and arcane objects.

"Bonjou, Misye Walsh," she said. "I have you order ready behind the counter."

"Good morning to you, Rèn Vivian," he said.

Rèn was the Haitian Creole word for 'queen.'

She beamed, the whiteness of her smile all the more striking in the sunlight pouring into the shop. "You been studyin' again."

Once they were both at the counter, he dropped his voice to a whisper. "I won't be around again for a while. Somebody took a shot at me last night, and I don't want to put you in danger."

"I know, but this my fight too."

"No, it's not. This fight uses knives and bullets. You stay out of it."

"Sure Lane, I will," she acquiesced, reaching into a drawer and pulling out a small, cloth-wrapped bundle. "This a special gris-gris, imbued with protection against Papa Ghana's magic. I use my own hair for it. Steam it, breathe in the fumes. Light a cigarette an' blow smoke into the steam. It calls good Loa to shield you from harm."

Lane took the bundle, skepticism clear in his eyes. "You expect me to believe this hocus pocus is gonna keep me alive?"

"You not have to believe for it to work, just do it," she replied. "Do it for the one you love, do it for you Vivian. But remember, when you walk the tightrope between life an' death, sometimes faith is all we have left."

"Thanks for the advice, *Votre Majesté*," he drawled, pocketing the gris-gris despite his doubts.

That brought a laugh, reminiscent of the windchimes on his family's back porch back when Lane was a kid.

"You ever decide to give up this fortune-telling gig, you could make a killing as a philosopher."

"Don't you laugh at Voodoo," she said, wagging her finger in his face. "The shadows watch you every move, and not all o' them are you enemies. You lover Rèn Vivian, she ask Dumballah to watch over you. You meet him once already."

"What d'ya mean I met him?" Lane said, but deep down he *knew*. The dark figure who came to him a few nights back... but how could Vivian know about that? Then his brain finished thinking it through. Voodoo magic had nothing to do with it; whoever the man had been told her after the fact.

"You not believe me anyway, Lane. Just you know, Rèn Vivian fight this fight her own way. Papa Ghana think he the King of Voodoo in New Orleans, but he about to learn different."

"Vivian, I don't want you involved!"

The closest customer turned at Lane's raised voice. Vivian patted his cheek.

"My fight not with bullets," she said. "Now go. Do what I tell you with the gris-gris. Later, you show me thanks."

Lane stepped outside into a shaft of sunlight that caused him to shield his eyes. In the past few days he couldn't shake the feeling that he was walking the road of no return, but somehow Vivian's ardent belief in her religion gave him hope. He didn't buy one word of it, his skepticism was his armor against the supernatural world, and yet... regardless, there was no turning back now. The only way out was straight through the heart of darkness. And he'd be damned if he didn't see it through to the end.

A stop by the office found a note on his desk from Jack, asking what he'd said to Rebecca Davis. Apparently, she mentioned to Lane's partner that he'd been discussing her. Lane smiled. Part of him enjoyed giving his best friend the business, and another part wouldn't mind if Rebecca Davis started paying attention to Lane instead of Jack.

Grabbing a pencil, he flipped the note and wrote on the back, *boys will be boys.*

The answering service had three messages from Clara Redwood for Lane to return her call. First he smoked a cigarette, stalling, thinking exactly what to tell her. He'd barely finished dialing when she answered.

Instead of 'hello', she said, "Mr. Walsh?"

"Yes, Mrs. Redwood. The service said you called for an update on your husband's whereabouts?"

"Yes, have you found him?"

Something about her tone sounded off. A certain breathlessness was to be expected, but Clara Redwood seemed almost... *eager.*

"I'm still working the case, Mrs. Redwood—"

"Please, call me Clara."

That's the last thing I want to do.

"I think we should keep this on a professional level, Mrs. Redwood."

"Oh, yes, of course. I see what you mean. Until the case is over."

Lane looked at the receiver, then out the window, wondering what she'd meant by *that.*

"Uh... sure. I'm afraid I have some bad news. I haven't found out the details yet, but I'm pretty certain that Claude won't be coming home."

"Have you found his body?"

If Lane had been inside a fire station the alarm bells in his head couldn't have been louder.

"No, not yet. I'm not even one-hundred percent sure he's dead."

"What's taking so long?" Clara Redwood said, starting to sound angry. But then her tone changed again, making Lane feel like a pendulum clock. "I mean, do you have any details?"

"No. Listen, I've got another appointment, Mrs. Redwood. I'll call you back when I've got more concrete information."

He hung up before she could reply.

Lighting another cigarette, he leaned back to wonder what

he'd missed. Minutes passed. He lit a second smoke off the first, and a third off the second.

Was Claude Redwood cheating on his wife? Probably. Was she cheating on Claude? Probably. Was Claude now dead? Probably. Was she upset by that news? Not even a little bit.

Clara Redwood wasn't worried about her husband, that much was clear, she was only worried about finding his body. The next question had to be whether or not Clara had a life insurance policy on her husband, to which the answer was another 'probably.' That only left one final question for Lane to answer: did he care about any of that?

Rather than make a decision, he filled the dented metal coffee pot in the Men's restroom down the hall, and put it on the office hot plate to boil. Nonsense or not, he intended to follow Vivian's instructions on using the gris-gris she'd made for his protection. It couldn't hurt, and men in the trenches clung to any superstition or talisman they could find, praying to anybody who was listening to keep them safe. You could have made a fortune selling them gris-gris. Lane's only question was the price he would eventually pay Vivian Moore for his gris-gris. He doubted she wanted money.

Mardi Gras came late that year, leaving the streets of the French Quarter mostly empty of tourists. After completing the gris-gris ritual, Lane made sure to leave no trace for Jack to find. His partner would never let Lane hear the end of it; for the rest of his life, Lane would have to listen to bad jokes about believing in Voodoo.

Early evening murk settled over the streets like fog hanging close to the Mississippi River. Light rain drizzled down on Lane's fedora, beading up and trickling off the brim in ropes of water. A grumbling stomach reminded him it was time to eat.

"Chasing ghosts is hungry work."

In one movement the Colt filled his hand as Lane crouched and spun, aiming at a black figure standing in a dark alley to his left.

"Surprising people like that is a good way to get killed," he said.

"So is sticking your nose where it doesn't belong."

"If vague warnings is all you've got, then be on your way, bud. You delivered your message, and now I've got business to attend to."

Despite his words, Lane's mind raced with possibilities. Who was tailing him? Were these people really part of some unholy alliance, or just pawns in a larger game? And who was pulling the strings?

"Mr. Walsh," the voice said, although deeper, heavy with menace that truly scared him. "You tread dangerous ground. You have made powerful enemies. I have protected you so far, but I can only do so much."

"Yeah? Okay, I'll play along. Who's trying to kill me, and why? And what is it to you?"

"Ever the skeptic," the voice whispered, and suddenly an entity appeared before him, neither fully spectral nor entirely physical. It seemed to be made of shadows itself, its form shifting and flickering like a dying candle flame.

"Who the hell are you?" Lane demanded.

"Someone who knows the darkness that lies ahead," it said, "turn back now, or face the consequences."

"Thanks for the travel advisory," Lane shot back, swallowing his fear with a heaping dose of sarcasm. "But I'm not the type to take the scenic route."

"Then you will suffer," the entity threatened, its voice like ice on the wind. "And all you hold dear will be lost."

"Big words from a shadow puppet," Lane snarled, his eyes narrowed. "You say you're guarding me, but all I get is tricks in the shadows and ominous words, riddles and games. Either lay it out plain, or take a hike. Which will it be?"

"You're a fool."

"Like I thought, you're bluffing. Go back to whoever you work for. Tell him that guys who walked through clouds of mustard gas, with German machine guns trying to cut them in half, don't scare easy. Got that, or should I write it down for you? I can only die once. Now get out of my way before I find out if shadows can bleed."

"Remember this moment, Mr. Walsh," the entity warned, as it melted back into the shadows. "For it is the beginning of your end."

"We've all got endings, friend. Just depends on who writes

the last chapter," he shot back, the weight of his tone more telling than any threat.

A sheet of heavy rain swept down the street. When it slacked off Lane found himself alone in the glare of a lamplight. But instead of being scared off by the latest encounter, he was angry, and tired of people trying to push him around.

He needed a drink, and if that made him a target, so be it. But if somebody wanted to rub him out, they'd better see him first, because the Army made sure that Lane Walsh knew how to kill.

After driving down Bourbon Street, he parked under a lamplight near Barracks Street. Two wiry kids leaning against a brick wall turned away, eyeing the Dodge without appearing to be eyeing the Dodge. Lane smiled. He recognized them as being part of Adrien Gandil's crew.

"Stoney Joe, right?" he said, pointing at the taller of the two. "I'm Lane Walsh, a friend of Adrien's."

"Mister Walsh, sure!" the boy said, perking up. The other maintained a surly expression until Stoney Joe slapped him on the arm. "Mister Adrien, he told us to be listening for your name, you know, keep our ears open."

"Did he? Heard anything?"

"You got some folks riled up, sure enough."

"Anybody in particular?"

"Heard tell some Haitian's ain't your best friend."

"They scare me," said the other boy. Lane couldn't place his name.

Stoney Joe nodded. "They been pushing 'round the ladies, fighting their protectors." 'Protectors was a euphemism for 'pimps.' "They're trying to move into the Quarter."

The other boy cut in, "not just them."

"That's right, Silver Dollar Sam, some o' his people been through here lately. Guess they're trying to cash in on the tourists gonna be coming in for Mardi Gras. Gonna be a lot o' rich folks down here soon. You need a shine, Mister Walsh? I can go get my kit. Or anything else?"

"No, you've already been very helpful. You boys gonna be

around a while?"

"We can be."

Lane dug two quarters out of his pocket. He passed one coin to each of them.

"Watch the car, will you? I'll be at The Blue Parrot. Come get me if you see anybody suspicious, but *don't* try to stop them or tail them."

The harsh lights of Bourbon Street flickered and cast their garish hues upon the wet cobblestones. Echoes of car horns, swing music from Prima's Shim Sham Club and others like it, cries from assorted characters huddled under storefront awnings, all of them competed with the patter of raindrops for Lane's attention as he headed for his and Jack's favorite bar, The Blue Parrot. The city seemed to close in around him, like a suffocating embrace.

Flashes of insight raced in Lane's mind. A picture was coming into focus, still fuzzy, but sharper than it had been before he spoke with the boys. He glanced backward, feeling an uneasy weight settle between his shoulder blades.

Something blinded him, like the flash of a camera. A sting in his neck caused Lane to drop to his knees. Suddenly, the world tilted and blurred. The buildings around him stretched skyward, their windows dark and empty, yet somehow alive with malice. The once vibrant streetlights dimmed into ghostly shadows, casting an eerie pall over the streets. New Orleans had become a spectral city, its citizens trapped in a purgatorial limbo, their faces contorted in mute agony.

"Sweet mother of mercy," Lane whispered, staring at the nightmare vision before him. He felt the cold grip of fear tighten around his chest, threatening to squeeze the life from him.

"Las' warning," a voice rasped in his ear, little more than a breathless, heavily accented whisper. "Nex' time you don't get up."

Lane lay on the sidewalk, staring up into the black and rainy sky. And just like that, the vision shattered, leaving behind nothing but the ordinary, if somewhat sinister, streets of the French Quarter. Pushing to his knees, groggy, Lane pulled his Colt as a lithe figure ran his way.

"Don't shoot, Mister Walsh, it's me, Stoney Joe. The man, he went that way!" The boy pointed back toward Barracks Street. He got into a car and drove away."

Lane pulled a tiny pin from under his left jaw, and slid it into a pocket. Getting the drop on Lane Walsh wasn't easy, meaning his attacker had been fast and experienced. Whatever drug they'd used had been carefully measured to wear off quickly. Shaking his head to clear it, Lane had enough wits to say, "describe the car."

"Big, black, new...shiny."

Haitians didn't usually drive big, black, shiny new cars... but mobsters did. He felt the icy tendrils of doubt creeping through his mind. What the hell had he gotten mixed up in? Lane couldn't shake the feeling that there was something real, something terrible lurking beneath the surface of this city he thought he knew so well.

So far, he could write off every attack as an attempt to get him to drop the case, but now he sensed that was over. Even the gunshots could have been intended to miss. The latest warning he took seriously; next time they would kill him.

"Alright, you sons of bitches," he growled, his resolve steeling within him like a coiled spring ready to snap. "If it's a fight you want, it's a fight you'll get."

The Colt filled his right hand. Maybe the cops would give him a hard time if they saw it, and maybe they wouldn't. But from now on, Lane would shoot first and ask questions later.

"Hey, buddy!" a rough voice called from under a nearby awning. "You look like you could use a drink!"

"Or seven," Lane called back. The man leaned against the grimy brick wall, a bottle of something brown and potent clutched in one meaty hand.

"Name's Eddie," the man said, grinning through stained teeth. "Whaddaya say? You in? Dime a swallow."

"Look, pal," Lane replied, his tone dripping sarcasm, "The last thing I need right now is a swig of whatever rotgut you're peddling."

"Suit yourself," Eddie shrugged, taking a swig for himself. "But don't say I didn't offer."

"Thanks, but no thanks," Lane said, already turning to leave. He couldn't afford any more distractions; time was running out, and he needed answers before the darkness swallowed him whole.

8

Through the large windows of Chez Antoine, Lane admired the new Art Deco building going up at 900 Canal Street. The neon signs displayed the word 'Walgreen's' in red script. Canal Street was a wide thoroughfare, unlike those French Quarter, so breezes kept night fog from gathering as thickly. That allowed the flickering street lamps outside to provide full lighting for traffic and pedestrians.

Inside was a different story, where a haze of cigarette smoke hung beneath the ceiling. The low hum of conversation and the clinking of glasses provided a soundtrack that was as familiar to Lane Walsh as the beat of his own heart. Chez Antoine was a classier joint than he was used to, but not that much classier. He sat across from Rebecca Davis, her dark eyes meeting his.

"Alright, Lieutenant, here's the scoop," he said, leaning in close, "I need your help gathering evidence against Papa Ghana and Silver Dollar Sam Carollo. And I need it yesterday."

"You and your partner seem to think I work for you, not the NOPD."

"Yeah? Jack never tells me anything," he said.

Rebecca raised an eyebrow, a smile tugging at the corner of her mouth. "You're a worse liar than he is. Does this have anything to do with that phone call about you being dead?"

"I don't know for sure, but yeah, probably," he replied, taking a sip of his rum, letting the burn slide down his throat and warm him from within. "But this time, I'm up against something bigger than I ever imagined."

She sipped coffee. "I've heard a lot of that kind of talk lately."

"My lips are sealed."

"So Jack *did* tell you?"

"Is that important?"

"I guess not at this point. Look," she said, lowering her voice as she leaned in closer, "I know you're good at what you do, but you've got to realize that I've got eyes on me all day, every day."

"What does that mean?"

"I'm a woman–"

"I noticed."

"–in a boy's club that doesn't want women hanging around."

"You're worse than that... you're not just a lady cop, you're an *honest* lady cop."

"So you know how careful I've got to be."

"Careful enough not to do your job?"

Rebecca leaned back, anger in her eyes. "You want me to leave?"

Lane lit a cigarette for both of them, handed one to her. "Sorry, I'm a little tight. That was uncalled for."

"What exactly do you want from me, anyway Lane?"

"Information to start. You've gotta hear things."

"Sometimes. What is it you think you know?"

"There's been a series of disappearances in and around the French Quarter, right?"

"More than usual, you mean? Yes. And other places, too. Gert Town, the Ninth Ward, even a few from the Central Business District. You know something about them?"

"I think so, yeah. I think Mas Nwa is behind them. They use Voodoo to scare people, and make them think there's some kind of hocus-pocus behind it all."

"So what *is* behind it then?"

"I don't know yet, that's what I'm trying to find out, but I can tell you Silver Dollar Sam is involved somehow."

"Huh," Rebecca said, drawing on her cigarette. "That seems like an odd fit. The Carollo Family told Al Capone to buzz off, I can't imagine them hanging around with some Haitians. I think you might be wrong about that."

"I saw them together with my own two eyes."

Rebecca's eyebrows up. Lane tried not to stare at her lovely face.

"There's a story there, and as a cop, I'm not sure that I

want to hear it."

"I won't tell it to Lieutenant Rebecca Davis. I *will* tell it to civilian Rebecca Davis."

"I'm sorry, Lane, I can't separate the two. However, now something I heard might make sense. The night somebody phoned in with the tip that you were dead? After you left, my partner said something I didn't understand at the time–"

"You mean your playmate, Joe E. Brown?"

"Lay off, Lane, he's better than some and no worse than the rest. And he covered me during the recent... problem."

Lane mouthed words but didn't speak them. "The Mayor."

"I *knew* Jack couldn't keep his mouth shut!"

"We lived together in a trench for over a year. He knows I would never betray his confidence."

Still irritated, Rebecca pressed on with her story.

"The tipster said you knew too much about something you shouldn't know about, and that made you a target for the mob. I pressed him for more, but he hung up."

"The target part I'm aware of," he said with a wry smile. "The rest of it though..."

"There's more," she said, her expression serious now, "I overheard your name mentioned down at the station. I didn't catch the details or who said it, but they were talking about you. Even with everything else going on, they were talking about *you*. You might want to back off, Lane. Lay low, stay alive."

Lane's hand tightened around his glass. His eyes scanned the room, watching for any sign of danger lurking in the shadows. All he saw was other patrons huddled around tables, and waiters navigating through the maze of chairs. "Thanks for the heads-up, but I can handle myself."

"Can you?" she asked, her eyes narrowing. "Because from where I'm sitting, it looks like you're playing with fire, and sooner or later, you're going to get burned."

"Maybe," he admitted. "But I didn't get into this business to play it safe, any more than you became a cop to get rich. I'm here to find the truth, no Jacker the cost."

"Even if the cost is your life?".

Lane met her gaze and held it, the weight of her words heavy in the air between them. "Now? Yes, even then. They've made me mad, Rebecca. That's not easy to do, but once it's done, there's no turning back."

"Look," Rebecca said, "you need to gather hard evidence if you're going to protect yourself. Evidence that will stand up in court. Not hearsay, not vague rumor, *hard evidence.*"

"I intend to get it."

"Then be careful, Lane," she warned, reaching across the table to place a hand on his. "I don't want to see you end up like all those other poor mugs who thought they could outsmart the mob."

"Nor me," he answered, pressing her hand with a firmness that tried to speak of comfort. "But sometimes, there's a path a guy has to tread, no Jacker how rough the road."

"You asked for my help. If I can, I will."

"You're the best."

With that, he tossed back the last of his rum and stood up, throwing a handful of bills onto the table. He knew that Rebecca was right, he was in too deep, and the danger was growing by the minute. But as he walked out into the sultry New Orleans night, one thing was for certain: Lane Walsh wasn't backing down now.

Sleep came hard. Before coming outside the next morning, Lane Walsh cleaned the Colt and loaded two extra magazines. Better to have it and not need it than the other way around. Then he checked the street for out-of-place cars and strangers.

The first light of day had barely begun to creep through the narrow streets of New Orleans when he stepped out onto the sidewalk, newspaper tucked under his arm and a steaming cup of chicory coffee in hand. The city was still shaking off the cobwebs of another sultry night, the air thick with humidity blown up from the Gulf of Mexico by an incoming storm front. He paused for a moment, inhaling the heady mixture of fried food that wafted from the all-night diner down the street.

"Another day in paradise," he muttered, adjusting the fedora on his head before taking a sip of the bitter brew.

As he prepared to cross the street to his parked car, the distant roar of an engine caused Lane to whirl. Squinting into the half-light, he saw a black sedan tearing around the corner, tires screeching against the damp pavement. The barrel of a gun stuck out of the passenger window.

"Aw, hell."

Lane dove for cover behind a low brick wall as the Tommy gun opened fire. Bullets ripped into the wall and the building beyond, zipping overhead as Lane hugged the ground. Shards of glass and splinters of wood rained on him as the ripping of the sub-machine gun tore through the morning quiet. Drawing the Colt, he waited for a pause in the gunfire before popping up on one knee and squeezing off six shots in quick succession. Three shattered the car's rear window. One found its mark in a back tire, sending the car careening sideways into a lamppost.

Lane switched for a fresh magazine and cautiously approached the wreckage, pistol first. Smoke and steam billowed from the crumpled hood, mingling with the scent of gasoline, burnt rubber, and fear.

Three men in dark pants and sweaters scrambled out of the wreck, their panicked footsteps echoing in the shattered silence. They didn't even bother to glance back at the fourth, who lay groaning in the twisted metal. Lane approached with every instinct on high alert.

"Stay put," he growled. Holding the pistol in his right hand, he yanked the injured man from the wreckage, his grip like iron on the goon's arm. Blood ran from a dozen wounds to the man's face. He groaned when Lane dropped him to the pavement. "You're gonna tell me everything you know, or I'll make sure that bullet wound is the least of your worries."

Through split lips, the man said, "cops'll be here soon... I'll talk to them, not you."

Lane crouched over the man. A few curious onlookers ducked back inside when Lane noticed them. Gathering a handful of shirt, Lane pulled the man close and pressed the barrel of the Colt between his eyes.

"Do I look I'm going to take 'no' for an answer? Spill your guts, or I'll spill 'em for you."

"Who the hell are you?" the man said, sweat and blood mingling on his pale face. His eyes darted around, searching for an escape that wasn't there.

"I'm the guy you just tried to turn into Swiss cheese." Lane leaned in closer, his voice a low snarl. "Now start talkin', pal, I'm losing my patience real quick."

The man met Lane's gaze. Panic filled his voice.

"You wouldn't shoot a man in cold blood!"

"You really don't know me, *do* you?"

"Fine, fine!" The man's bravado crumbled under the weight of Lane's glare. "But I don't know nothin' about who hired us! I swear!"

"You're off to a bad start."

Distant sirens told Lane the clock was ticking.

Lane dug through the man's pockets, feeling around for anything that could give him a clue. His fingers closed around something cold and smooth - ten silver dollars. "What do we have here?"

"Those ain't mine!" the man protested, his voice rising an octave.

"Wrong answer." Lane slammed the butt of the gun into the man's forehead, forcing a gasp from his lips. "I've had enough lies to last a lifetime."

"Okay, okay!" The man wheezed, tears streaming down his face. "Papa Ghana and Silver Dollar Sam Carollo want to work together. They're tryin' to take over the drug, gambling, and prostitution trade in the lower class neighborhoods. That's all I know!"

"Thanks for the bedtime story," Lane sneered, but the instant he heard the words, he knew they rang true. Another piece fell into place when he thought back to the thousand dollar retainer from Carollo. A bribe, disguised as a legitimate job. Why hadn't he seen it earlier? Carollo teaming up with some street-level Haitian Voodoo guy? Why? What was Carollo's angle? Turning back to the injured man, Lane inspected him more closely. Blonde hair cut short, blue eyes, high cheekbones. "Who are you? You're not Sicilian, and you sure as hell aren't Haitian."

The injured man's eyes widened, a flicker of genuine fear cutting through the haze of pain. "That Voodoo stuff... It's real, man," he stammered, sweat beading on his brow. "Silver Dollar Sam's scared of it, too."

"Voodoo?" Lane scoffed, the word like venom on his tongue. "That's what you're gonna hang your hat on?"

"I swear it," the man insisted, desperation seeping into his voice. "I've seen things... things I can't forget. Everybody's spooked, it's why Papa Ghana's driving the bus."

Lane leaned close to study the man's face, weighing the sincerity in his eyes. He was about to press for more when the sharp crack of a gunshot echoed through the air. Something hissed past Lane's jaw, missing him by inches. The man's head snapped back, a crimson bloom spraying from the exit wound as life fled from his eyes.

Reflexes took over and Lane dove behind the wrecked car, heart pounding in his ears. Pistol at the ready he pressed against the warped steel of the car's roof, waiting for more shots.

None came.

As sirens wailed in the distance, Lane kept low, scanning the rooftops and windows for any sign of the shooter. But whoever had pulled the trigger had vanished like a ghost, leaving only the echo of death in their wake.

The police cruisers screeched to a halt around the corner, tires squealing on the slick pavement. Lane tensed, watching as a group of unfamiliar uniforms spilled onto the scene. They were young, tough-looking guys with cold eyes and clenched jaws. No friendly faces there, only the kind of cops who wouldn't think twice about roughing up a private investigator who'd gotten himself tangled in the mob's web. For all Lane knew they were on Carollo's payroll.

"Hey!" one of them barked, leveling a pistol at Lane. "Hands where I can see 'em!"

"Easy there, cowboy," Lane said, raising his hands in mock surrender. "I'm just a working stiff like you."

"Working stiff, huh?" Another cop sneered, grabbing Lane by the arm and yanking him to his feet. Holding up the Colt, the cop said, "what's your job, smart guy, button-man?"

"Door-to-door salesman," Lane shot back, wincing as the cop tightened his grip. "They wanted a refund."

"Oh, we got us a joker here do we? We'll see how you laugh off a murder rap, old man."

Old?

"Maybe we should teach him some manners," a third officer suggested, cracking his knuckles with cruel intent.

"Much as I'd love a lesson in etiquette," Lane replied, his voice dripping with sarcasm. "I've got places to be. So, if you don't mind—"

"Shut it," the first cop growled, shoving Lane hard against the wrecked car. "You better watch yourself, Walsh. You're playing with fire, and you're gonna get burned."

They slapped the cuffs on Lane and heaved him into the back of a patrol car like yesterday's trash. Outside, a parade of squad cars lit up the morning, their red lights painting the scene in shades of trouble. Half the uniforms played keep-away with the rubberneckers, while the plainclothes guys pumped the locals for the skinny. In that cramped car, time turned sluggish, dragging its feet; though his watch, stubbornly honest, ticked off a measly forty-three minutes.

Two clearly irritated detectives in cheap brown suits hauled him out of the backseat. One of them pointed to the handcuffs, and the cop who'd warned him earlier grudgingly took them off. Lane rubbed his wrists before firing up a smoke.

"You boys don't look so happy," he said.

"I'm Detective Morris, my partner is Detective Kensington. Let's hear what happened."

Lane gave them the bare facts, leaving out his speculations, or anything to alert Silver Dollar Sam Carollo that he was onto them.

"What'd the dead man tell you before he died?" Morris said.

"He called me a few choice names, that's about it."

"Any idea who might want you dead?"

"Other than a few jealous husbands, no."

Kensington took over the questioning. "What are you working on?"

"Pottery. I'm taking a class."

"Drop it, Walsh," the cop whispered, his stale breath filling Walsh's nostrils. "You don't wanna know how deep this rabbit hole goes."

"Sounds like I've got something to look forward to," Lane quipped, as he rubbed his wrist where the cuffs had bitten into his skin moments earlier.

"Funny guy, huh? You know what's wrong with goons like you, Walsh? You don't have the guts to either be a crook, or a cop, so you hang out in the middle with the other crumbs and greaseballs."

"What about a crooked cop, Kensington? What kind of guts does that take?"

"How 'bout I run you in for impeding a police investigation?"

They were taunting him, daring Lane to take a swing so they could throw him in the slammer. Lane felt his temper cooking up a storm. He'd been strung along, shot at twice, drugged, and topped it off with a heavy dose of Voodoo straight out of a cheap horror flick. He was wise enough to know better, but the words spilled out anyway, biting like an alligator. "How about I squawk to the brass about you playing policeman," he said. "Taking money under false pretenses."

Kensington drew back his fist and took a step forward. Lane put up his hands the way they'd taught back in boot camp. Before either could strike, Morris wrapped his arms around Kensington.

"Cool off, John." Nodding with his head, he told Lane to beat.

"You'd better listen to him, Walsh," Kensington said, nearly shouting. "If you know what's good for you. Word is you're sticking your nose where it doesn't belong."

"Thanks for the warning, boys," Lane said, using every ounce of restraint not to retaliate. "But I've got a job to do. So tell whoever's chasing me to strap in, it's going to be a bumpy ride."

"Get out of here," Morris said, casting a disdainful glance at the dead man on the ground. "And count yourself lucky... this time."

"Much obliged," Lane said, tipping an imaginary hat as he turned to leave. He knew he was walking a razor's edge, but he couldn't afford to back down. In his racket, a private eye who got the shakes about a case might as well hang up his hat and take up knitting. You stuck to a case like bubble gum on the sole of your shoe, because if word got out you were yellow, you were as good as washed up. The only cases you'd get were finding lost cats.

Lane found his fedora in the gutter. As he walked away

from the grisly scene, the weight of his predicament roiled Lane's mind. He'd had always been one to dance with danger, but this time, he was waltzing with the devil himself.

Maybe it was time to meet his dance partner.

The answering service had a dozen calls from newspaper reporters when Lane got to the office. Tommy guns spitting lead into quiet homes wasn't the kind of story that let a reporter snooze. But of the eager pack, Lane only threw a bone to Clayton Comeaux of the New Orleans Item-Tribune, a man who'd made it his life's work to shine a light on the city's darker corners. Over the years, they'd shared more than a few drinks and off-the-record whispers.

Comeaux's voice crackled through the phone, sharp as a tack.

"Word on the street says you're playing with fire, Lane. Last I checked, we're still miles away from Chicago's chill. You getting your wool from there now? Chicago overcoats aren't known for keeping you warm."

"Not if I can help it, Clay. Listen, if I give you something, can you sit on it until I tell you otherwise?"

"If you're squeezing me for bread..."

"Nothing like that. I've stumbled into something *big*. Nothing I can prove yet, and if you take it public they'll hunt me down no Jacker how long it takes."

"You said 'into.' Most people would have said 'onto.'"

Lane smiled at the phone; Comeaux didn't miss anything.

"I'm up to my neck."

Comeaux paused a few seconds. "Who is *they*?"

"Nice try, Pally."

"If I agree not to print it, you'll tell me?"

"Everything I know, everything I think I know, and everything I'm not sure about."

"Deal me in."

"It started when this blonde walked into my office—"

"It always does."

Lane chain-smoked four cigarettes telling the story of missing people, missing bodies, Voodoo rituals, phantoms roaming the French Quarter, threats, the multiple murder attempts and the Carollo Crime Family. He intentionally left out the names of Rebecca Davis, Vivian Moore and Arthur Greaves. When it was over, Comeaux didn't respond for half a minute. Lane assumed he was finishing writing up his notes.

"That's a wild story even for New Orleans," the reporter finally said.

"Let's hope it doesn't end with yours truly vanishing like all the others."

"What do you think happened to them?"

"There's some giant catfish at the bottom of the river, and they're always hungry."

"Torpedoes for hire?"

It was Lane's turn not to answer. He'd thought the missing people were more about robbery gone wrong, or money owed to Papa Ghana, but maybe Comeaux was right. Clara Redwood seemed more anxious to find her husband's body than to find Claude himself. While that would explain the Redwoods, it wouldn't explain the missing mobster. He said so.

"I've got a buddy who writes for *The New York Herald Tribune*. We talk every now and then. The D.A. up there is a man named Dewey. He's making his name investigating the rackets, the mob, cleaning up the city, he's a real crusader, that one. My friend is pretty connected, and he keeps hearing the term 'Murder, Incorporated.' Apparently there's some sort of enforcement group within the mobs, that kills anybody who gets out of line."

"You said 'mobs?'"

"Yeah, it seems this is like some sort of company you hire to do cleanup work, get rid of malcontents, that sort of thing."

"Mobsters killing mobsters."

"Yes."

"Huh."

"Sounds like Carollo might not have wanted to get his hands dirty killing one of his own."

"So you think this Murder, Inc., sent somebody down here?"

"Could be. Or maybe these Haitians have started their own version of Murder, Incorporated."

Despite his throat being raw from too many cigarettes in a row, Lane lit another one. The puzzle was coming together.

After hanging up with Comeaux, Lane phoned Rebecca Davis.

Sometimes winter in New Orleans felt like winter. Sometimes it didn't. That day, winter had forgotten its teeth; the warm air spoke more of May than February. Sweat ran down Lane's temples as he cut through the narrow streets to meet Rebecca Davis. Lane wished for Jack's steady presence by his side, but the guy was tangled up in another mess. The sun was dipping low, painting the streets in long, bony shadows, while somewhere in the distance, a blues guitar cried its heart out, the notes sinking into Lane's soul. This city, it clung to you, like the memory of a good woman or a bad debt.

He found Rebecca in Louie's Bar, cradling a cola like it was fine champagne. Her eyes sparkled like chips of emerald when she spotted him, and damn, if she didn't look like something out of a dream.

"How did I beat you here?" she said, not bothering to hide her irritation. "I don't have time to waste, Lane, I've got a job, cases of my own, this had better not be a trip for biscuits."

Louie's was buzzing, but the crowd kept their distance from the most striking dame in the room. It wasn't a place for the silver spoon set; it was a haunt for small-time hustlers and guys with too many pages in their rap sheets. Even a cop in lipstick and a plain dress like Rebecca could be sniffed out faster than fresh bourbon at a wake.

"Sorry I'm late, I'm being more careful these days," he said. "I've got things to tell you."

"Lucky me," she said. "So, why am I here?"

"First I need a drink."

He waved over a waitress. Once a head-turner, the chubby woman now moved wearily, her faded floral dress clinging to a frame softened by time, her tired smile hinting at lost youth and forgotten dreams. She brought his Daiquiri without interest, until he handed her four quarters and told her to keep the change.

"Merci, mon cher," she said with a thick Cajun accent. The smile broadened into something genuine. "My name is Yvonne, what is yours?"

"Beat it," Rebecca said, using her thumb as a pointer.

Yvonne ignored her, still speaking to Lane. "Your jealous girlfriend, she is not who should be wit' you."

"I said, *beat it!*" Rebecca repeated, in her best cop voice.

"Let Yvonne know if you need anyt'ing else, Sugar." Turning her nose up at Rebecca, Yvonne went to check on her other tables.

"So you're my jealous girlfriend, huh?" Lane said, barely able to keep from laughing.

Rebecca grabbed her purse. "I'm leaving."

"Please stay, Angel."

"That's *Lieutenant* Angel to you."

Lane let out a laugh, a deep, throaty sound that cut through the tension and deceit he'd been dragging around like a second shadow for days. Several patrons glanced over, but quickly look away. Sipping the Daiquiri, Lane's eyes opened wide; it was the best he'd ever tasted. Even the cigarette he lit tasted good.

"Get ready, Lieutenant Angel, I'm giving you all of it."

After making sure nobody could overhear, Lane repeated the story he'd told Clairborne Comeaux, only with the names included. Watching Rebecca Davis react, he saw both interest and dread. Lane knew how she felt.

"Why do you and Jack always get cases with dirty politicians and mobsters?" she said after he'd finished. "Big cases you drag me into. Why me, Lane? There's plenty of other cops, call them next time, will ya?"

"Can't," he said, "you're the only honest one in the bunch."

Rebecca opened her mouth to argue, closed it, and finally responded with a weak, "that's not true."

"Yeah, it is, but we don't have time for that now. I need you to find something on Ghana and Carollo," he said, glancing around the room warily. "Something to use as leverage, just in case."

"In case of what?"

"This might be a one-way street for me. If it is, I wanna know you'll crucify those Brunos."

Rebecca suddenly leaned forward, face showing genuine concern. "What do you mean? Are you about to do something stupid?"

"Probably," he admitted, meeting her gaze. "But so is crossing the street these days."

"Fair enough," she conceded, finishing her drink. "I'm off the clock for today, so let's get to it. The last thing this town needs is more chaos."

As they left the bar, the sounds of laughter and clinking glasses fading behind them, Rebecca said, "Vivian Moore, huh? I didn't know you knew her."

Lane smiled. "*There* she is!"

"Who?"

"My jealous girlfriend."

"In your dreams, Cowboy. Listen, that Voodoo stuff... I've been thinking about it, that's a twist."

"Don't tell me you take hoodoo seriously?"

After a pause so long he wasn't sure Rebecca would speak again, she said, "if you tell anybody I said this, especially Jack, I'll deny it. But I've seen things, Lane, things I can't explain. Things I'd rather forget, only I can't."

"Getting caught between worlds," he replied, his voice barely above a whisper. "The tangible and the supernatural."

"I didn't know you were such a philosopher," she mused.

"All us PIs are, it's the only way to stomach the things you see."

"Tell me about it," he said, a bitter edge to his voice.

9

Lane Walsh leaned back in his worn leather chair, a burning cigarette forgotten between his fingers. His body ached from the close calls and near misses that had plagued him ever since Clara Redwood first walked into his office. The outer door to the office creaked open, and Jack Callahan sauntered in, soaked to the bone.

"Look who's up with the farmers, Jack said, hanging up his overcoat.

"I couldn't sleep," Lane said. "It's hard with one eye open."

"So I've heard," Jack said, dropping into the chair behind his own desk.

"Davis?"

"Yeah, she filled me in last night. I got the whole story."

Lane nodded, wondering about the circumstances of that conversation. Pillow talk, or something more professional? It was none of his business, but part of him wanted to know. Rebecca Davis was put together in all the right ways.

"Good, now I don't have to repeat it again."

"So you think Clara Redwood is hinky, huh?"

"She's a looker, we both agree on that. But her beauty is the kind that's sharp and deadly, we've both seen it before, with a smile hinting at cold calculations, the kind that wouldn't flinch at trading a husband's life for insurance gold."

"What have you found out about the husband?"

"Claude wore a mask of respectability, we've seen dozens like him over the years, all toothy grins and gladhands, smooth and deceptive. But under the veneer, he was a slave to the dice's rattle, the bottle's call, and the siren songs of forbidden dames."

"Without guys like him we'd be out of business. So this is

another insurance murder?"

"I think so, but there's more to it I don't know yet. That's where the Haitians and the Mob come in. It's all connected in some kind of racket. I know a lot of it, but I'm still missing something."

"Those Haitians, I heard there was a... supernatural flair."

"Supernatural?" Lane said. "Davis tell you that?"

"Yeah."

"Maybe not quite supernatural, but definitely strange," Jack said. The forgotten cigarette burned his finger. He stubbed it out and lit another one.

"Not hoodoo?"

"Hoodoo? Come on, Jack. It's not Hoodoo or Voodoo. We're dealing with mobsters and crooked politicians, not some Hoodoo hokem." The force behind his words was meant to be convincing, but Lane didn't know who he was trying to convince, Jack or himself. He knew it was ridiculous, but he couldn't help wondering at some of the things he'd seen lately.

"We've always disagreed on the possibility of this kind of thing."

"Vivian Moore would agree with you."

"Hoodoo or no Hoodoo, I think you're on the right track, Lane," Jack said, leaning forward. "Haitian thugs, mobsters, shady politicians – all playing together in our very own backyard."

"The Mayor Hale thing?"

"Yeah. It's gotta be more than a coincidence."

"Coincidence or not, we need to stay sharp," Lane said, crushing out his cigarette. "These people don't play by the rules, and they sure as hell aren't afraid to kill. They've nearly got me more than once."

"Damn right," Jack agreed, his eyes narrowing. "We gotta watch our backs, Lane. And if there's even a chance that this voodoo crap is real, you need to be prepared for anything."

"Voodoo or not, I'm sick of being shot at," Lane said.

"I don't mind people shooting *at* me nearly as much as I do their bullets *hitting* me."

"Are you done with the brother thing? I'm paying our client Mister Carollo a visit. You wanna tag along?"

"Can't. You're not the only one trying to keep a lid on this city. Let's meet up at Rick's when this is over."

"Naw, everybody comes to Rick's. Make it The Blue Parrot."

"The Blue Parrot it is. Drinks are on you."

Lane paused at the door of his building, halting as Stoney Joe and his shoeshine rig came into view, squatting on the sidewalk like a vulture at a feast. The rain had taken a break, scrubbing the grime off the city's face, giving it a kind of raw, cleansed look. But the aftermath left shoes splattered and murky, lining up victims for Joe's eager rag.

"Be wit' 'chu in a minute, Mistuh," he said to Lane. It wasn't the words that made Lane wait, though, it was the wink that went along with them.

Lane scanned the faces of each passerby with a hawk's vigilance, poised to dive into action or bark lead if trouble stirred. When his moment turn finally came around, he fixed a hard stare on a fella who entertained being close enough to listen in. The guy caught the look and thought better of it, disappearing into the street's anonymous flow.

"You're the last person I expected to see down here. What d'ya got, kid?" he said, low enough not to be overheard.

When Stoney Joe answered, his drawl was toned down, like he'd left half of it behind. Tourists expected the locals to all sound like Cajuns from the bayou.

"Mister Adrien sent me down here. We all been listenin' the way you asked, and I gots to tell you, you the talk o' the Quarter, Mister Lane, sir."

"And not just the ladies, I'm guessing."

The kid grinned. "Them too, yeah, 'specially Ruby Lane."

Lane was acquainted with Ruby and her sleazy pimp, Lionel. Ruby might've been a looker before the world went to war, but twenty years of hard living hadn't done her or Lionel any favors. As far as Lane was concerned, they held no beef with him.

"Ruby's been talking about me?"

"She's a Hoodoo lady, like that Miss Moore over on Burgundy Street–"

"Miss Moore practices Voodoo, not Hoodoo. She is a

Manbo, kind of a Voodoo priestess."

The boy spread his hands in a 'who cares' gesture. "She, Miss Ruby that is, she said you must have powerful magic protecting you not to be dead now. Said Papa Ghana put a Death Curse on you, somethin' only a powerful Hoodoo man can do."

Lane's hand instinctively went to the gris-gris tucked in his trench coat pocket. The apparitions he'd seen in France he wrote off the battle delirium, and in general he scoffed at superstitions, but considering the string of murder attempts he'd dodged, he wasn't tossing Vivian Moore's protective token aside anytime soon.

"What else have you heard, Joe?"

"Not just me, boss, all the boys hearin' people want you dead."

"What kind of people?"

"The men in the black suits."

That surprised him. If the shoeshine boys heard that, it meant Carollo's crew was in the Quarter spreading the word that Lane Walsh was fair game.

"Silver Dollar Sam's crew."

"That's them."

"Killing me is a popular game right now." Lane handed him a fiver. "Share that around, Stoney, it's not all for you. Tell the boys to keep their ears to the ground."

Lane lifted his shoe off the stand and turned away.

"Mister Lane?"

"Yeah?"

"You gonna be alright, sir? Lotsa men talkin' 'bout hurtin' you."

Lane caught a glimpse of something rare in the kid's eyes – real worry.

"Ease up, pal. I ducked the whole Kraut army. A handful of greaseballs aren't going to give me the shivers."

Lane walked to his car on full alert. The Colt he held under the fold of his coat, ready to use. Any of the passersby crowding the sidewalk could be one of Carollo's gunsels, and if somebody tried to get frisky, he wanted to make the first move.

"Hey mister, got a cigarette?" A ragged voice asked from the shadows beside the corner grocery.

Lane looked over to see an old man huddled against the wall, bent and shivering in threadbare clothes. His gut had kept him from taking a dirt nap in the war, and for too many close shaves afterward, and it was hollering now that this character wasn't on the level... yet, he didn't smell like trouble either. Keep his head on a swivel, he dug out a cigarette using his left hand.

"Sure," he grumbled, handing the man a smoke. As he lit it for him, Lane's eyes were drawn to a nearby shop window filled with trinkets and charms. There were shops like it all over New Orleans. Most were junk for tourists to buy, most... but not all. Among the items displayed in the window was a small figurine carved from bone, a token of protection against evil spirits.

The sight of it sent a shiver down his spine as memories long buried clawed their way to the surface. He felt a warmth on his left leg where the gris-gris rested in his coat pocket.

"Thank you, sir," the old man said, taking a drag on the cigarette.

"Think nothing of it," Lane muttered, his thoughts elsewhere.

"You know, they say some of those charms really work," the old man continued, following Lane's gaze. "But I don't put much stock in that voodoo hoodoo."

"Neither do I," Lane replied, but his words felt hollow. He couldn't shake the memory of a night long ago when he'd first encountered the inexplicable. He'd been a kid visiting his Aunt Leticia, exploring the bayou with his cousin Tommy when they'd stumbled upon a shrine to the dark arts. They'd watched, hidden, as a woman danced around a fire, her body writhing and convulsing as if possessed by something otherworldly.

"Stay away from it, Lane," his cousin had whispered, terrified. "It ain't right."

And they had run, leaving the woman and her strange ritual behind. But the image had stayed with Lane, haunting his dreams and fueling his skepticism.

"Believe what you want, mister," the old man said, exhaling a cloud of smoke. "But this city's got secrets that'd make your skin crawl."

"Tell me about it," Lane muttered, thinking back to the war and the ghostly figures he'd imagined walking through No Man's Land at night. Were they just figments of his overactive imagination, or had he really seen something beyond the realm of reason?

"Thanks for the smoke," the old man called after him as Lane continued on his way, lost in thought. "Papa Legba, tanpri mande Gede Doub avèti bon mesye sa a sou danje. Without explanation, the shriveled man walked the other way between the grocery and the adjacent building. It was a tight squeeze even for someone small. Lane would have had to turn sideways to follow.

"Huh?" Lane recognized the language as Haitian Creole, and knew 'Papa Legba' had something to do with Voodoo, but the only other words he could make out were warn' and 'danger.' "I thought you didn't believe that stuff. Hey! Hey!"

The man dissipated into the deep shadows.

Smoke slipped out the driver's side window as Lane drove through a neighborhood of neat bungalows toward Rebecca Davis's house. Crushing the cigarette out in the car's ashtray, he searched for the correct street number, finally pulling into the driveway of a narrow two-story house with the required wrought-iron balcony. He needed someone to talk to, and she was the closest thing he had to an ally in this mess.

"Be glad you called first," Rebecca said when she opened the door. "Otherwise they might be picking lead out of your liver."

"I read that book," he said. "Jack and I met the author when we worked for Pinkerton's. Can I come in?"

"It's my day off, Lane."

"Yeah, mine too. Can I come in now?"

Rebecca stepped back to let him enter. She wore waist overalls with muddy knees, and a blouse that clung to her like a promise. Her blonde hair was pulled back into a tight bun, revealing a face that could've been chiseled from marble – all smooth lines and icy resolve. A red bandana held back all but one loose strand of hair.

"Can't say I expected a warm welcome," Lane replied, stepping into the bright living room. "Or to find you in such a cozy home."

"It belonged to my parents. How did you find me, I'm not in the book."

"I'm a detective, remember?"

"I need to know, Lane. Cops don't need their addresses to be circulating, if you know what I mean."

"The library keeps census records. You've never been married, so Davis is your maiden name. Finding your father and mother was easy, only two Davis' in this part of Louisiana had a daughter named Rebecca. Tax records showed the other one moved in 1931, which only left one."

"Damn," Rebecca said, closing the door behind him. "If you found me, so could any creeper off the street."

"Thanks."

"What do you want?"

"Let me lay it out. I'm neck deep in a swamp full of gators, and some of 'em ain't got no business walkin' on two legs."

"Careful, Lane. Day off or not, I'm still a cop."

"Maybe, but you're still from New Orleans, you can't be happy about what's going on in this city." Without being invited, Lane sank onto the couch, massaging his temples. "I need to know who's on my side, Rebecca. Who do I have in the department watchin' my back? Anybody besides you?"

"More than you think," she replied. Perching on the armrest, her green eyes fixed on his, Rebecca's voice softened. "I can't give you names, but there are people willin' to help. Carollo probably knows it too, what with all the dirty cops on his payroll."

"Great, so I'm playin' chess with an invisible army," Lane said. "No wonder I'm startin' to see ghosts."

"Or maybe you've just got a guilty conscience," Rebecca suggested, her lips curling into a sly smile.

"Ha, guilt. Sure. I tossed that out with my last pair of Sunday shoes."

"Sure you did. I know you better than that... so what's the play?"

"I'm going to meet my client, and I thought you should know."

"The not-so-distraught wife?"

"The other one, Silver Dollar Sam Carollo."

Rebecca scratched her lower lip. "Is that smart?"

"I highly doubt it, which is why I thought you should know."

"When?"

"Tonight."

"Damn you, Lane Walsh."

Other than Fort Knox, Lane figured the safest place to spend the day was back at the office. The grocery where he'd seen the old man made the best Muffaletta in New Orleans, so he grabbed two, along with cigarettes, coffee, and two colas. The store was also the only place that sold his favorite snack, Moon Pies, so he picked up two of those, too.

One Muffaletta was gone and Lane was eyeing the other when the shrill ring of the phone cut through the silence of the cramped office, jolting him out of his thoughts. He snatched up the receiver, his voice edged with annoyance.

"Delta Private Investigation, Lane Walsh speaking."

"Lane," came a sultry voice on the other end. "It's you Vivian, mon amour sa wap fè kounya. "

"I'm eating lunch, Vivian. Please speak English, my creole isn't up to par."

"I think you need come by my apartment. They's somethin' you should know."

"Can't you tell me over the phone?"

"Non, moun ap koute. "

To his surprise, Lane understood the entire phrase, *no, people are listening.*

His phone was tapped? And if it was, how did Vivian know and he didn't?

"J'y serai sous peu," he said, in the Cajun French that his relatives in Lafourche Parish spoke as their first language. *I'll be there shortly.*

"Trust me, it will be worth you time, my love," she purred,

hanging up before he could reply.

Lane stuffed the remaining food, cigarettes and colas into a sack. There was no telling how long he'd have to stake out Nonna's before Carollo showed up.

The afternoon had turned cloudy with a promise of more rain. Once at Vivian's place, he mounted the stairs and found her at the top, leaning against her open door. Stepping into her parlor, he watched as she slunk across the room to a velvet-upholstered sofa, her dark eyes smoldering beneath the flickering glow of candles.

"We having a séance?" he said.

"Take a seat, mon amour," she said, gesturing to a worn armchair across from her. "They is somethin' you should know." She paused, letting the tension build before continuing. "They's a high-level meeting between Carollo and Papa Ghana tomorrow night at this abandoned warehouse down by the river–"

"I think I know the place."

"That make sense. See, you is the reason for the meeting. You, my lover."

"Me?" Lane said, lighting a cigarette. "What do they want with a two-bit gumshoe like me?"

"This is you beloved you is talkin' to, not some cheap dame over on Bourbon Street. You investigation makin' them nervous, lover," Vivian replied, her voice low and dangerous. "They both wonderin' if they is a double-cross in play. You marked for lanmò, for death, but here you is still alive. Papa Ghana, he think Carollo not want kill you because you have police detective on you side. Carollo, he think Papa Ghana the one interfering with killin' you."

"Why would either of them want to keep me alive? Carollo owns half the cops and most of the judges."

"They is vòlè ak move moun."

"English, Vivian, please?"

"They is thieves and bad men. Who can say why they think how they think?"

Lane took a long drag, his mind racing. "How do you know all this?"

Vivian smiled enigmatically. "You wouldn't believe me even if I told you. But like I tell you many times, lover, anything in this city that involves Voodoo, involves Rèn Vivian."

Lane believed every word she'd said. He didn't want to, but he did. Which meant that he needed to find a place to hole up, since they knew where he lived.

"You stay here is where you stay," Vivian said.

"Huh?"

Her grin had the hungry edge of a wolf eyeing a lamb. "You not hide from me, lover, not even what you thinkin'."

"No, I appreciate the offer, but I can't put you in danger like that," he said, surprising himself by meaning every word.

"Rén Vivian got many friends in Vieux Carre. They not anybody get close to my home without me knowin'."

The words rang true. "Okay, thanks Vivian. I'll take you up on it."

"Natirèlman ou pral... o' course you will."

"But first, do you have a phone I can use?"

Her lascivious smile vanished. "Who you call? That lady police?"

"Lieutenant Davis, yes."

"You think she pretty?"

Lane knew enough about women to recognize the dangerous undertones of jealousy when he heard it; Rebecca Davis had sounded the same way when Vivian's name came up.

"She's a cop who doesn't want me dead," he said. "That's all I care about."

"Ou se yon move mantè, mennaj. "

"I didn't understand that. "

"Vivian says you is a bad liar."

"The phone?"

"Downstairs in my shop."

10

The first light of dawn slithered through the blinds, casting crooked shadows on the plush carpet of Vivian Moore's apartment. In a city like New Orleans, where sin lurked in every corner and the line between right and wrong was often drawn by dollar signs, it was a wonder the sun bothered to show up at all. But it did, bringing with it what might turn out to be Lane Walsh's final day.

Vivian was gone, but she left a note to make himself at home until she got back. He settled for toast and coffee. The morning paper sprawled open before him, its headlines screaming about crime and corruption, Mayor Hale, secret societies and murder... in other words, business as usual. He glanced at his watch, the hands ticking closer to that final appointment with Carollo. By the end of the day, he'd either be alive and well, on the run, or dead. It was one hell of a trifecta, and he wasn't betting man when it came to his own hide.

There were still holes in the story that needed answering, mostly surrounding the missing hoodlum, Marco Dantoni. Something itched the back of his mind about that. If Mas Nwa really killed Dantoni, as Lane speculated, and Carollo hired Lane to hide his involvement... *why?* Wouldn't Carollo want others to know what happened if they got out of line?

No, the more he thought about it, the more it didn't fit.

Unless...

Lane blinked at a sudden realization. Getting up, he went downstairs and found Vivian opening her shop.

"Lane, I"

"Sorry doll, I need the phone."

Vivian followed him in as he dialed Rebecca's number, hoping she hadn't left for work yet. As the phone rang he spoke to Vivian. "I need Adrien Gantil. Do you know anybody I could send to find him?"

"Oui," she said. The urgency in his voice cut off her usual repartee.

Rebecca Davis answered her phone. "Lane, if this is you again–"

"It's a powerplay," he said. "We're about to have a gang war on our hands."

"Are you sure?"

"Nothing else fits. Meet me at four, write down this address."

He dictated the location and hung up.

Seconds later Vivian returned. "Patrice, he gwan to find Adrien Gantil, fetch him back here. You tell me now what is happening?"

"Yeah, good idea. I need to lay it out. Listen up, Rèn Mwen, it's one helluva story."

Lane paced the apartment like a caged cat until nearly noon. He'd put the Muffaletta in Vivian's icebox the night before, and had just unwrapped it for lunch when someone knocked at her door. His hand reached for the Colt until a voice came through the door.

"Friend Lane, it is Adrien Gantil."

"I'm under the gun, Adrien," Lane said after opening the door. "I need information and I need it fast." Quickly outlining what he needed from Adrien, Lane added, "I need it no later than three-thirty."

Instead of telling him it was impossible, Adrien simply nodded. "I can tell this is important to you, my friend. It will be done."

"Just like that?"

"Oui. I learn many things in my business, secrets that certain people might wish to keep quiet. Sometimes I ask for something in return for my silence, when I feel the reason is good enough. Today you ask, that is all the reason I need. If anyone knows what you seek, Adrien will soon know it, too."

"You might be saving my life."

"As you and Jack once saved mine. I can think of no better reason. Next time do not wait to ask me."

"I only thought of it this morning... besides, I don't like putting my friends in danger, Adrien."

The Algerian wagged his finger as he might to an errant child. "These are not Germans who trouble you, friend Lane, they are only Haitians and American gangsters. *Them* I do not fear."

Adrien Gantil returned within two hours bringing the answers Lane needed. Before leaving, Lane handed him the P08 Luger.

"I've got one more favor to ask, and it's a big one. I need you to smuggle this into a warehouse over by the river..." Next, he handed over a piece of paper with a phone number scribbled on it. "Call me there at precisely three-forty-five and tell me if you managed to get it done."

"Too easy, Lane. I'll do it with no problems."

Aside from a lingering question about how Clara Redwood factored into the situation, everything had fallen into place. Vivian Moore watched as he checked the action on the Colt. He'd cleaned the weapon and reloaded the magazines before leaving the office, and for good measure brought the 9mm as backup iron.

Lane met Rebecca at a garage three blocks from the river. Owned by the same Army buddy who supplied Lane and Jack with bullets, they could safely stash their cars out of sight while Lane outlined his plan. She parked next to Lane against one wall.

"You look like hell," she said, getting out of the unmarked police car.

"Thanks for the pep talk, sweetheart," Lane snapped back. "Let's get down to what I've learned."

Rebecca arched an eyebrow.

"Spell it in straight lines."

"Listen carefully," Lane began, his voice steady despite knowing he might be permanently running out of words. "We need to work together on this one, and we can't afford any screw-ups. You'll be out there, but not directly involved. Got it? Unless somebody starts slinging lead, butt out. And remember, not a word in advance to anyone... especially other cops. There's no telling which ones are in somebody's pocket."

"So you're going through with this cockeyed plan to barge in on Carollo unannounced?"

"Not if you think announcing myself will improve my odds of not getting plugged."

"Are you out of your mind?" Rebecca asked, her voice rising in pitch. "You know how dangerous that is, right?"

"Of course I do. But it's the only way to make this work."

"Tell me, what do they call it when a man volunteers to walk straight into a lion's den?" Rebecca's eyes narrowed, her gaze penetrating Lane's soul.

"Courageous or stupid, depending on who you ask." Lane forced himself to grin. "In my case, probably both."

"Carollo won't think twice about putting a bullet between your eyes if he smells a rat," she warned.

"Which is why I'll just have to make sure I don't reek of rodent. I've got a few tricks up my sleeve. Besides, who'd ever suspect a guy with a face like this?"

"Very funny. Just remember, Lane, there are no second chances in this game. You screw up, and it's curtains." Rebecca's gaze held his, her expression unreadable. "Don't expect me to play nice with those red hots."

"Wouldn't dream of it," Lane replied, flicking ash from his cigarette onto the oil-stained concrete floor.

"What's so urgent you've got to meet Carollo himself? He's also tried to kill you how many times?"

"I'm not sure that was him." He leaned forward to punctuate the urgency in his voice. "So here's the skinny. That missing mob guy Carollo paid me to find? I found him. I think he was behind all the gunplay."

"So what's the problem? Where is he?"

"Trying to make Silver Dollar Sam think he's dead. Remember I told you that Carollo hired the Haitians to rub out somebody? His name was... is... Marco Dantoni. Sam wanted to make him disappear like all the others up north?"

"Yeah, that Murder Incorporated thing."

"Right. Somehow, somebody cut a deal. I don't know all the details, but instead of killing him, Papa Ghana's got him at a place over off Rampart. According to one of my informants in the Quarter, the Haitians are moving in to replace the Carollo Family and take over their business, with Dantoni as their partner. Whether that's true, or whether Dantoni is insurance, I don't know. But the guys who tried to kill me weren't Sicilian, so my guess is that Dantoni is starting his own crew to partner with Mas Nwa."

"So this meeting tonight is a play by Papa Ghana to get rid of Carollo?"

"You've got it. The question is whether Carollo gives me a chance to fill him in before he fills me with lead."

Rebecca frowned, her brow furrowing beneath the same loose strand of hair Lane noticed at her house.

"You really think it'll come to that?"

"Hope for the best, prepare for the worst," Lane replied. "But somebody's probably sleeping underground tonight. I just hope it's not me."

"Alright," she agreed, resignation tightening her voice. "But I'm a cop, Lane, I can't stand around and do nothing. Innocent people might get hurt?"

"I get your point. Tip 'em off the cops you can trust, but not too soon. Wait until right before the meeting starts. Last thing we need is for somebody to get trigger-happy and blow this whole thing wide open."

"Fine," Rebecca said, her eyes betraying a flicker of doubt. "But if this all goes haywire, Lane, I swear…"

"Let's just focus on making sure it doesn't, huh?" he cut her off, forcing a grin. Inside, though, his gut twisted like a snake, fear gnawing at the edges of his resolve.

"Okay," she sighed, turning to leave. "Listen, you and your partner are annoying as hell, but I'm used to you… be careful, alright?"

"Always am," Lane lied.

The phone rang as the second hand on Lane's watch reached the '12', at precisely three-forty-five. He snatched up the receiver, feeling an itch at the base of his skull that told him this call would be the deciding factor.

"Adrien?" he barked.

"Qui," came the breathless reply. "I stashed the gun in the garage like you wanted. There are two tables in the middle, it is under a case for soda bottles over to one side. Best I could do, Lane, there was nowhere else. I got in through a busted window.

"Good work," Lane said, "You didn't let anyone see you?"

"No, but there were four guards there already, two Haitians, two of Carollo's men," Gandil men. "Rèn Vivian gave me a charm to keep me from being seen."

"Thanks Adrien. For everything... and in case I don't–"

The line went dead.

His Dodge waited for him like a loyal hound. Heat inside the garage had built up in the car. He climbed in, the leather seat sticking to the back of his coat as he fired up the engine and headed for Nonna's. Tension crept into his shoulders, a serpent coiled and ready to strike. The drive took ten minutes.

The city passed by in shades of gray, a world where angels feared to tread and demons danced with glee, where men like Carollo held sway over the weak and innocent, and too many of those sworn to protect the public were on the take. Momentary panic filled his mind as he feared what would happen if Carollo wasn't at the restaurant, but it was far too late for that now. Nonna's was the unofficial headquarters of the Carollo Family, and if the Boss wasn't there, Lane had no clue where else he could be ahead of his meeting with Papa Ghana.

Mid-winter sunlight waned early in February, so when Lane pulled up a block away from the restaurant, the neon sign cast a sickly green glow over the street. He could see the familiar faces of Carollo's crew lounging in front like a pack of wolves waiting to pounce on their prey. Unsurprisingly, there was also a handful of uniformed cops milled about, and Lane knew better than to trust them. If they were there, they were dirty.

With that, he got out of his car and started walking towards Nonna's, each step bringing him closer to the heart of darkness.

The air was thick with the stench of stale cigarette smoke and damp pavement, Lane approached Nonna's through tendrils of cigarette smoke from the knot of men standing around the front entrance, a fitting perfume for this city of sin. Carollo's crew sized him up like a slab of meat in a butcher's window.

"Evening boys," Lane said, raising his hands. "I need to speak with my client for a moment. Tell him it's urgent."

"Who says we're gonna let you waltz in and talk to the boss?" one of them sneered, a scar running down the side of his face like a river of malice etched into his flesh.

"Because, my friend," Lane replied, letting his gaze drift over to six cops loitering nearby, "I'm sure Mister Carollo wouldn't want any unexpected fireworks tonight. Now, would he?"

"What's that supposed to mean?

"You the Boss now?"

The thugs exchanged wary glances before nodding towards the entrance. One went inside and returned with the man named Albert. Once again they took the Colt, then Albert led him to the same room as before. Unlike the last time, a dozen men surrounded the Boss. The well-lit room was filled with low murmurs and the clinking of glasses, the patrons blissfully unaware of the storm brewing outside.

Carollo sat at his usual table in the corner, a cigar smoldering in his hand as he surveyed his kingdom with steely eyes. Lane approached, his heart pounding like a drumbeat to hell.

"Good evening, Mister Carollo," Lane said, not bothering with pleasantries. "We've got a problem."

"Is that so?" Carollo drawled. "I was told that have information about Marco Dantoni."

"That's the problem."

Carollo twirled the cigar in his mouth, staring at Lane through slit eyes.

"Albert, clear the room," he said in a low voice. Within thirty seconds they were alone.

"Papa Ghana's planning an ambush. Tonight."

"I paid you to find Marco Dantoni."

"I did. He's part of this."

Carollo blinked, thrown. "He's still in the land of the living? Where's he holed up?"

"I've got the spot jotted down, but rest assured, he's breathing and bucking."

Lane spelled it out, mixing what he knew with what he theorized.

Carollo barked, puffing smoke into the stale air. "You expect me to believe that? Papa Ghana wouldn't dare."

"Believe it or not, that's up to you. I'm just the messenger," Lane said. "But you paid me to do a job, and I did it. I've been beat up, shot at, and Tommy-gunned. There's even been talk of Voodoo thrown around, and before you ask, yeah, I found out about your visit to Vivian Moore, too."

"So..." Carollo said, "I'll have to talk with her about that."

Lane sat and leaned on his elbows, his eyes reflecting every bit of the rage boiling up within his body.

"I've got no beef with you or your organization, Mister Carollo, but Vivian Moore is out of the picture. Got it?"

Now Carollo got angry. "You're threatening me in my own place?"

Albert stuck his head through the door to see why the Boss raised his voice.

"Get out!" Carollo fired. Then, to Lane, "you must be out of your mind."

"That's right, I'm nuts, but I meant what I said. Leave her alone and we got no problems."

Drumming his fingers on the table, Carollo finally said, "it's like that with her, huh?"

"She's just a friend, but yeah, it's like that."

"Personally I think you're a fool, Walsh, but yeah, okay, Vivian Moore is not part of this. Now back to your fairy tale, how do you know all of this?"

Lane shook his head. "Ink slingers have their sources, so do I."

"That doesn't leave me much to go on."

"That's up to you, only when the bullets start flying and the blood starts spilling, don't say I didn't warn you."

Carollo's eyes narrowed, a sinister smile tugging at the corner of his mouth as he considered Lane's words. In this treacherous game they played, trust was a rare commodity, and Lane knew he was walking a razor's edge.

"Alright, Walsh," Carollo said finally, leaning back in his

chair. "Let's say I believe you. What do you propose we do about it?"

"Simple," Lane replied, his voice a low growl. "We turn the tables on Papa Ghana and give him a taste of his own medicine."

He could feel their eyes on him, watching, waiting, weighing his words like vultures circling a dying man. And for all he knew, that's exactly what he was.

"Go on," Carollo urged, his interest piqued.

"Here's the plan..." Lane began, laying out the details with the precision of a master chess player, knowing full well that one wrong move could be his last. "First thing, I'll be your hostage."

"So far, I like this plan," Carollo said.

11

Lane rode to the meeting in the backseat of Carollo's car, with a goon on either side and Carollo in the front passenger seat. The black sedan's tires crunched over the gravel as it pulled up outside the warehouse, a decrepit structure that had seen better days. Lane Walsh glanced out the window, wondering those were his last moments. Something about an alley they passed remind him of a ruined French village.

"Remember, Walsh," Carollo said, his voice low and dangerous, "if you're lyin' about this meet, they'll never find your body."

As they stepped out of the car, the early evening darkness seemed to swallow them whole. Armed Haitians stood guard around the garage, their faces a mixture of mistrust and suspicion. Plainclothes cops lingered on the fringes, exchanging furtive glances with an advance team of Carollo's men who were ready for anything. Some Haitians lingered several blocks away in both directions. They parked near an open double-door once used by wagons.

"Only Papa Ghana's gone inside so far," Luca Moretti, a large man with a scarred face, informed Carollo as he approached. The sheer size of the man was enough to make anyone think twice before crossing him.

"Good," Carollo grunted, lighting a cigarette and letting the smoke curl lazily into the night air. "We don't need any surprises."

The smell of fish and mud came from the nearby Mississippi River. Lane could feel the tension crackling in the air like a live wire. He knew all too well the danger that came from mixing volatile elements, and here they were – a potent cocktail of criminals, cops, and egos waiting for a spark to ignite the whole mess. Worse, he knew Papa Ghana had already lit a match. He couldn't help but wonder if he'd made the right choice, bringing Carollo to this meeting. Dead gangsters was one thing, but in the moment, putting himself in the middle of a Mafia war didn't seem very smart.

Carollo stubbed out his cigarette, the butt sizzling as it met the damp pavement. "Luca, you and two others check inside for any surprises before I step foot in there."

"Got it, boss," Moretti replied, picking out a couple of tough-looking goons from Carollo's crew to accompany him. The trio moved towards the garage entrance, their wary eyes scanning every shadow for potential threats. Four big Haitians emerged as they neared the doors.

"Look at this," one of the Haitians muttered, a sneer on his ebony face. "They don't trust Papa Ghana. They think we tryin' to double-cross 'em."

"Easy, let 'em do their thing," another Haitian said, but his dark eyes burned with resentment. Spotting Lane, he said, "what you bring him for?"

"Because we *felt* like it," Moretti said. "Get out o' my way."

"Let me tell you something, my friend," the first Haitian spat, turning towards Lane. "Papa Ghana is inside that place all by himself, waiting for your boss like a man should. And now you send your dogs to sniff around? That's an insult."

"Seems to me that someone who ain't got nothin' to hide wouldn't mind a little sniffin'," Lane shot back, his voice a cold blade slicing through the thick air.

Moretti glanced at Lane, but didn't say anything.

"Is that right?" the Haitian growled, taking a threatening step forward. "Maybe man what oughta be dead keep he smart mouth shut before someone shut it for you."

Moretti stepped closer to the Haitian. Big as Moretti was, the islander was even bigger.

"He's with us. You got a problem with that?"

"Take it easy, boys," Carollo said. "We're all just tryin' to make sure everything's square, that's all. Once Moretti gives the all-clear, we'll all sit down like civilized men and talk business."

"Business," the Haitian scoffed, shaking his head. "You people not know the meaning o' the word." He spat on the ground, the venomous contempt in his eyes making it clear who he thought the real animals were. "You sell your own momma if it mean a few extra bucks in you greasy little pockets."

Moretti stepped back and drew a revolver. The Haitians raised pistols of their own. Seeing what was happening, the cops and other mobsters took out their guns.

"Enough!" Carollo barked, cutting through the mounting tension before it could erupt into something more dangerous. "We're here to do business with Papa Ghana, not kill each other. If you got a problem with our precautions, take it up with him."

The Haitians stood their ground. They'd been pushed to the edge, and it was evident that one wrong move would send this whole thing spiraling into chaos.

"Listen, we're all on edge here," Lane said, trying to diffuse the situation. "But there's no need for bloodshed. We'll get through this if we just keep our heads." He scanned the scene, his mind racing to find an escape route, should things go south.

"You come in here, disrespecting Papa Ghana, and you expect us to just stand by?"

"Take it easy, boys," Carollo warned, eyeing the growing tension between the two groups. "Put your guns down, we meant no offense to Papa Ghana."

Everybody took a breath. Lane read the shifting in their eyes, the dawning of sense over folly. The storm had skirted by, at least for now.

Then a man appeared in the warehouse doorway, behind the Haitians. He wore a black suit, a white shirt, and polished black shoes. In his fist was a .38 revolver, which he aimed at Carollo.

"Kill 'em!" the man yelled.

Lane reacted faster than anyone. Lunging forward, he pushed the biggest Haitian into the flight path of Marco Dantoni's bullet, the one meant for Carollo. The Haitian's eyes went wide. He reeled as three shots hit him in the back. Lane grabbed the pistol from the man's dying fingers.

In that split second, the twilight erupted into gunfire. Bullets tore through the darkness, sending both sides running for cover. The sound of shots rang in Lane's ears like a twisted symphony, drowning out the panicked shouts and cries of pain.

Lane's mind remained sharp; memories of shellfire and mustard gas lingered from the trenches of World War One, making him all too familiar with the sounds of death. For him, the swirl of people shooting, screaming, falling and dying, seemed to happen in slow motion.

Rapid-fire shots echoed down the narrow street, a staccato symphony of death and destruction. Lane's eyes narrowed as he squeezed the trigger at a figure inside the warehouse, but his aim was off, deliberately so. He had no interest in adding to the body count, only in keeping Carollo alive long enough to get what he wanted, a guarantee of safety for him and his friends.

Haitians spewed out of the warehouse, verifying Lane's story of an ambush. Luca Moretti and the others near the warehouse door were down. Cops with shotguns fired back, as did the surviving mobsters, but Haitians were running at them from two directions down the street. In that chaos, Lane saw his chance.

"Carollo!" he shouted, grabbing the mafia boss's arm as he ducked behind a nearby truck for cover. "We need to get you out of here!"

"Go where?" Carollo yelled back, his voice barely audible over the roar of bullets flying past them. "There's nowhere to run!"

"Trust me!" Lane insisted, his mind whirring with potential escape routes. He'd navigated worse situations before, and he knew that to survive, they had to act fast. As another hail of bullets whizzed past, Lane spotted a narrow alley between two buildings, partially obscured by shadows.

"Follow me!" he yelled, seizing the momentary lull in gunfire to sprint towards the alley. Carollo hesitated, glancing at his crew, before nodding and following close behind.

Lane hit the gas with a twist of regret souring his gut. Right or wrong didn't weigh much against the lead storm they'd kicked up, with possible innocents chewing on a hot meal of bullets. Reflection was a luxury bought with time, and right now, they were paying in full just to keep breathing.

"Almost there," he yelled back to Carollo as they dashed through the alley, zigzagging to avoid becoming easy targets. The sound of sirens wailed in the distance, adding urgency to their flight. They were running out of time. Cops on the take were one thing, only now honest cops might roll up at any moment.

Lane shouted again, motioning towards a rusted stairway close ahead. In the old days there had been clubs on rooftops to escape the heat and stink of the nearby riverfront.

"Up there! We can lose them on the rooftops!"

"Lead the way," Carollo panted, his face a mask of determination. And so, with bullets still chasing them like vengeful ghosts, Lane Walsh and Tony Carollo climbed into the night, escaping the chaos that raged below. Once on the rooftop, both men knelt down to catch their breath.

"You're a real piece of work, Walsh," Carollo said.

Watching from above, Lane could only follow the action through muzzle flashes and car headlights. The Haitians' return fire intensified, forcing Carollo' men to duck for cover behind the hulking shadows of abandoned vehicles. But the darkness couldn't conceal the blood and the fallen, not for long.

As the gunfight dwindled to a ragged chorus of dying moans and spent shell casings, the full extent of the carnage came into focus. Most of the Haitians lay sprawled across the sidewalks and pavement, dark hulks with lifeless eyes staring up at a sea of stars in the night sky. The first flames of a conflagration came from inside the warehouse, where Lane's prized Luger lay buried under a case of soda pop. In the light of the fire, Papa Ghana's once-imposing figure was now slumped against the open doorway, his face a grotesque mask of red, white and black. Long feathers crowned a top hat still atop his bulbous head.

"You were right, Walsh. Damn, but you were right."

"You paid me a lot of money, Mister Carollo. I wanted to earn it."

"Could you see what happened to Marco Dantoni?"
"No, I was kind of busy."
"Doesn't matter. This is family business, I'll take it from here."

Still wary, the two men climbed back down to the street, ready to shoot or run.

"Mister Carollo!" A voice cut through the noise, pulling Lane back to the present. It was Sergeant John Rose, one of the city's many crooked cops. "You better scram before the cavalry arrives!"

"Right," Carollo said, his eyes narrowing as he assessed the damage. "Take care of our boys and make sure the stiff's get the blame." His gaze flicked to Lane. "What about you?"

"My car's back at Nonna's, and you've still got my gun," Lane replied.

"Then let's go," Carollo said, clapping a heavy hand on Lane's shoulder.

"I do have one favor to ask."

"Anything, Lane, anything at all."

"I need to know exactly what happened to a man named Claude Redwood."

"I don't know that name."

"No reason you should. He's a small-time gambler, pays the ladies, that sort of thing. But I was to find him."

"Yeah, I remember. You told me about him at our first meeting. Lemme see what I can find out about this Claude Redwood character."

Epilogue

The sun was a half-hearted apology for light when Lane Walsh finally cracked open an eye, like the lid of a rusty tin can. Had it been up to him, he would've slept through the dawn chorus and straight into the late morning. But a persistent throbbing at the back of his skull had other plans. His body ached from the previous night's events, a reminder that danger flirted with him as easily as a two-bit floozy in a smoke-filled blues club. But for Lane, ever the cynic, danger was his destiny, a familiar companion, one that kept him on his toes whether he liked it or not.

Dragging himself out of bed, Lane's legs felt like they were made of lead, the kind of lead that weighed you down more than it shielded you from trouble. He stumbled across the room, every inch of his six-foot frame broadcasting bone-deep weariness. Sleep had done little to erase the disheveled mess of a man that stood in front of the mirror; his once neatly combed hair now resembled a bird's nest after a storm. The shadows under his eyes were dark enough to make a raccoon envious, and his unshaven face told of a man who'd been too busy chasing shadows to bother with grooming.

"Christ," he muttered, rubbing a hand across his stubbly chin. "You look like you've been chewed up and spat out by a cheap dame."

His reflection merely stared back, unimpressed. Lane didn't blame it. After all, it wasn't the first time he'd woken up looking like he'd gone ten rounds with a heavyweight. And if experience had taught him anything, it wouldn't be the last.

Still, there was one more detail to wrap up before he could move on: Clara Redwood. He splashed some cold water on his face, the shock of it jolting him into something resembling alertness. If he was lucky, maybe he'd find some answers today, or at least a stiff drink to dull the pain.

A hot shower loosened the knots his back and neck, while the day's first cigarette got his blood pumping. As he stepped under the warm spray, he allowed himself a moment to simply exist, ignoring the aches in his body and the ever-present danger lurking just outside his door. The water sluiced away the grime from the previous night, and for a brief moment, he felt almost human again.

"Nice try, Walsh," he muttered, shaking his head as he turned off the water and grabbed a towel. "But you're still in too deep to wash your sins away."

He shaved carefully, nicking the edge of a fading bruise but otherwise managing to avoid any major damage. The steamy mirror reflected the face of a man who'd seen too much, done too much, yet somehow still clung to a shred of hope that he could make a difference in this rotten city.

Feeling alive again, he pulled on his last clean suit with practiced ease, and took extra time to get his tie knotted just right. Satisfied, he pointed at his reflection. "Let's see what this city's got in store for us today."

As Lane stepped out of his cramped apartment, the slightly sour air of the hallway greeted him with a sense of familiarity that was as comforting as it was irritating. He knew he should be more cautious, any number of leftover dangers could be lurking around every corner, waiting to pounce, but the truth was, he just didn't have it in him to care. Maybe it was the exhaustion, or maybe it was the ever-growing disillusionment that came with working the underbelly of New Orleans. Whatever the reason, Lane's usual vigilance had all but evaporated.

As he descended the creaky stairs to the lobby, Lane couldn't help but notice a large package propped up near the front door, wrapped in plain brown paper and tied with twine. His curiosity piqued, he approached cautiously, half-expecting some kind of trap. But as he read the attached note, his eyebrows shot up in surprise. The package had his name on it.

"Compliments of Silvestrio Carollo," the note read. "For services rendered."

Lane stared at the parcel for a moment before breaking into a wry grin. In all his years working this city, he'd never once received a thank you gift from the likes of Carollo, let alone a case of what appeared to be fine whiskey. Wrapped around the bottle was one sheet of paper in the same hand, detailing the fate of one Claude Redwood.

"Must've done something right last night," he chuckled, hoisting the package onto his shoulder and heading for the office.

Once there, he unlocked the office door and sat down. The unexpected gesture of gratitude left a strange taste in his mouth, like a well-aged bourbon mixed with suspicion. But as he carefully placed the case on his desk, Lane couldn't help but feel a smidgen of pride. After all, when even the head of the New Orleans Crime Family took notice of your work, you must've either been doing something right, or very, very wrong.

Lane stared at the note, flipping it over to find another message scrawled in that same tight script. It detailed Marco Dantoni's fate, explaining that he'd been kidnapped by the Haitians, had rejoined the family, but unfortunately suffered a fatal wound during the gunfight.

"Damned shame," Lane said, grunting a laugh as punctuation. Then, dialing a number he knew by memory, he called Rebecca Davis, filling her in on all the details of last night's shootout.

"What a mess, Lane," she said, "Two cops shot, one dead, bodies everywhere. You were busy."

"Not me. You won't find my fingerprints anywhere, except maybe on a certain pistol found in the warehouse."

"Which one?"

"I'll tell you over dinner."

"Dinner *and* drinks, Lane Walsh. And it won't be a date, it'll be you repaying a debt. I suggested to the Captain which cops he might want to send to the scene last night, and why. He got the message. You should be down at headquarters right now. Thanks to me, there won't be any awkward questions."

"You an Angel, Angel."

"Save the sweet talk for somebody who cares."

"I'll give you all the details when I see you."

"No you won't. What I don't know, can't get me indicted."

Lane laughed "In New Orleans? You know better."

Next he phoned Vivian Moore.

"I thought you should know, I made it in one piece."

"I know that, Lane, mon amour," she said, putting extra languid syllables into each word. "You Rèn Vivian know everything 'bout you, lover. You come see me tonight, show me how grateful you is."

"Not tonight. Tonight I'm meeting Jack. Tomorrow."

"Tomorrow *night*," she said, and hung up.

The last call went to Clara Redwood.

"I know what happened to Claude," he said when she answered. "Meet me at the diner next to my office in twenty minutes."

Clara's voice sounded almost giddy. "I'll be there!"

The morning sun cast a golden glow as Lane stepped into the diner next door, a comfortable, worn-down sanctuary from the troubles outside, where the clink of silverware against plates and hushed conversations drowned out all of his worries.

"Morning, Mister Walsh," said the waitress, a plump woman with a smile that could warm even the coldest heart. "The usual?"

"Yeah, but with a short stack instead of grits," he replied. "I'm hungry today."

"Rough night, huh?" she asked, scribbling down his order.

"Did you read this morning's Item-Tribune?"

She gave him a 'you-must-be-joking' look. "I got four kids, a deadbeat husband, and two jobs... do I look like I got time to read the Item-Tribune?"

"Sorry. Let's just say I've had better nights." He shot her a wry grin as he settled into his usual booth by the window. It was a prime spot for watching the world go by, each passing face a story waiting to be told, or untold, as the case may be.

As he sipped his coffee, the bitter brew chasing away the last cobwebs of sleep, Lane couldn't help but think about Clara Redwood's husband. Sure, the poor sap had it coming. You don't welch on a debt, particularly to a pimp connected to the Mob, so in that respect he deserved no sympathy. But if Lane had to deal with Clara Redwood, he might've gone chasing skirts, too.

The eggs, bacon, toast and grits were gone, and Lane was halfway through the plate of pancakes, when Clara slid into the chair opposite his.

"Well?" she said, foot tapping against the floor.

"Claude's not coming home," he said, "but then, you already knew that. Jack and I suspected as much right off the bat."

"What do you mean by *that*?"

"Drop the act. You found out Claude was throwin' dice and payin' the ladies, so you scraped up the money to get him rubbed out. I'm guessing there's a life insurance policy behind all this, but I don't know that for sure. Jack and I suspected your story was bunk right from the start."

She tilted her nose. "If that's true, why did you take the case?"

"I didn't take the case, I took the money, the case just came along with it. But anybody who pays two hundred smackers for a fifty dollar job is playing an angle."

"You can't prove any of that."

Lane shook his head and forked a mouthful of pancake into his mouth. "Nope, not a word of it."

"Presumably you found Claude's body?"

"If you want Claude's body, you'll need to look inside a gator, or maybe a gar down in the river."

"I don't understand."

"The people you hired to kill your husband aren't in the business of leaving behind evidence."

"But they said–" Clara stopped herself. "I don't know what you mean."

"Suit yourself. But Claude is long gone, and none of him is comin' back."

"I want a refund. I paid you to find him and you failed."

"Read your contract. Besides, if you squawk, I squawk. The insurance company will delay paying any claim until you're put out to pasture as an old lady, on suspicion of foul play."

"You are a dishonest man, Mister Walsh."

"Nope, not even a little bit. Crooked, maybe, but that's a different thing."

"I'll see you in court," Clara said, storming out of the diner.

"We'll see about that," he laughed in her wake.

"Jack here yet?" Lane asked Riley upon entering The Blue Parrot.

"Haven't seen him. Based on what I'm hearing, I'm lucking to be seein' you."

"Some weeks are like that."

Riley finished pouring three drinks before motioning the waiter to serve them.

"Between you and Jack, I'm surprised there's still a New Orleans to drink in."

"Yeah. I'll be in the back."

Lane turned to find his regular table, but stopped when a young female voice called out to him. The owner was fresh and pretty and could have been his daughter, if he had one.

"Hey Mister, buy me a drink?"

"Sorry, I'm waiting on somebody."

"You can wait here, with me."

"I can't afford to do that."

She huffed. "I'm not that kind of girl!"

"In that case, I *really* can't afford it."

The End

Coming Next

Callahan and Walsh return soon in *Crescent City Killers*.

In the shadowy alleyways of 1938 New Orleans, sin is cheap, but life is cheaper.

In the wake of the mayor's death, amid an influx of criminal gangs looking to profit on the Crescent City's lucrative trade in forbidden pleasures, a new threat lurks — can Callahan and Walsh crack the case before the city crumbles under its weight?

Dive deep into the seductive underbelly of New Orleans with Crescent City Killers, the riveting next chapter in the series that brought you the first critically acclaimed noir tale of Jack Callahan and Lane Walsh, The Jazzman's Requiem. As vibrant jazz notes fill the fetid air of the New Orleans waterfront, and the clinking of glasses echoes from dimly lit bars, our duo find themselves entangled in a web of deceit more dangerous and intricate than they've ever faced.

Raymond Chandler's sharp wit meets Dashiel Hammett's raw intensity in this tale where every corner turned might be your last. Be among the first to unravel the mysteries lurking in the French Quarter. Pre-order now and journey with Callahan and Walsh through the Crescent City's darkest secrets.

https://www.amazon.com/Crescent-Killers-Delta-Private-Investigations-ebook/dp/B0CM4T3NN4

Crescent City Killers
A Delta Private Investigations Book

William Alan Webb
Kevin Steverson

Made in United States
Orlando, FL
03 January 2024